NOT LIKE A LADY

LORDS AND UNDEFEATED LADIES BOOK 1

JUDITH LYNNE

JUDITH LYNNE

BOOKS BY JUDITH LYNNE

Lords and Undefeated Ladies

Not Like a Lady

The Countess Invention

What a Duchess Does

Crown of Hearts

He Stole the Lady (January 2022)

Cloaks and Countesses

The Caped Countess

The Clandestine Countess (July 2022)

DISCLAIMER AND CONTENT WARNING

This is a work of fiction and as such its characters, events, words, and places are the product of the author's imagination informed by history.

It contains small references to past child abuse but tries to be low on angst, high on fun, like all Judith Lynne books. It does also contain a dreadful dinner party.

CHAPTER 1

LETTY KNEW that proper young ladies did not put their heads out of carriage windows to check on the progress of their pet horse.

It would have taken a great deal more than that knowledge, however, to prevent her from doing so. Besides, it was something she had already done a dozen times before.

"Is she pulling to the side, Anthony?"

Anthony, her groomsman—her only servant, in fact, as the driver was hired, and so was the carriage—twitched the reins ever so slightly. Maggie, to Letty's eyes the most beautiful chestnut horse in the world, drifted slightly closer to the carriage, though still far enough away that the swaying body of the carriage rocking between its four wheels represented no danger.

"She is not pulling. She is not fighting, she is not tired, and she is not overheating. In general, mademoiselle, I would say she is surviving this journey better than you are."

Letty frowned at him, her pursed lips and puckered brow her only answer before she plopped back in her seat. Truth be told, Anthony was undoubtedly right. Letty was tired, and she was definitely overheating. It was like an oven in the dank little carriage.

Of course Maggie was comfortable being ridden. Letty was only worried because the horse was a pet, and less often ridden than simply walked. And she worried about the state of the horse's shoes, which might be due for upkeep. But even if she had been able to ride Maggie herself, they would have had to hire a horse for Anthony, as he would not allow her to make the trip to Roseford alone. And they both knew Letty was not equipped to ride the horse in public, certainly not all that way.

Propriety was not what concerned Letty. It was Maggie's stamina she was worried about.

She stuck her head out the window again.

Anthony and Maggie hadn't moved from their spot pacing next to the carriage. It was as though he had been waiting for her to re-emerge.

How irritating.

"She's barely two. She's built for traveling, mademoiselle."

Letty scowled at him and sank back inside the dark of the carriage again.

Anthony was not going to be any help at all. He had produced not one single idea regarding how to stop the sale of her horse. Her father had sold Maggie, and that was all Letty could say about it. The fact that she had raised that horse herself, petting her and talking to her and making her a friend almost from the moment she could stand, didn't hold any water with Anthony because it didn't hold any water with her father and that was the letter and spirit of the law.

Her father. Letty wondered, as she had many times before, if she was going to prematurely wrinkle her forehead by scowling so much, but she simply couldn't stop. She hadn't been able to stop since she'd received his note. "Sold horse to Roseford buyer. Get her ready." That had been the sum total of it, that and the direction of this cursed buyer. There was no need to specify which horse, because at this point they owned only one.

Only one horse, only one saddle, only one shovel for cleaning out her stall; inside, one table, three chairs, and two kitchen kettles, one of which was broken.

Letty was tired of counting down the things they owned, and tired of brusque orders from her father about what to give up next.

But there was only one possession she really cared about, and the only plan of action she could devise to protect against the loss of her heart, her friend, her Maggie, was simply to stick close to her and perhaps try to convince this heartless buyer to reconsider.

* * *

"She's not a doll, she's not a baby, and she's not going to rock you to sleep tonight in return," Anthony said with more than a little bite as he watched Letty, wisps of yellow hair drifting around her hot, sweaty face, sleeves rolled up to show her arms dotted with sun spots, rubbing Maggie down with a bit of twisted hay to clean off the sweat and dust of the road.

"No, she is a magnificent steed," Letty retorted with a little smile, watching the rich burnished sheen of Maggie's coat, like polished wood, emerge from the cleaning. No one would ever call *her horse* spotty or stupid or stumpy—all epithets that Letty herself had borne from time to time. "She is sleek and so strongly muscled—how could anyone appreciate this beauty more than I do?"

Anthony sighed, thumped his black-haired head against the rough planks of the wall behind him. It was emasculating enough that Letty refused to let him tend to the horse. Other groomsmen were watching, and a few of them were smirking. He'd do well if he could avoid a fight in the inn tonight over this little spectacle. "The fellow doesn't have to appreciate her. He bought her. He can do that, and he did."

Feeling her lips purse up again, Letty forced her face into a smoother expression. She could do it, she knew how; she'd had years of practice.

What she still failed at was keeping the tears from running down her cheeks and dripping off her nose, like they were doing now. She hated that.

Anthony saw her wipe her cheek. The horse was cleaner than

Letty was now. He'd have to make the innkeeper at least bring her a washing basin. She'd never ask for herself.

"Princess," he said, more softly, "I know it's cruel that your father can do this. I know it's cruel that he did. But you and I and all our friends, we can't fight that fight, not today."

It was an old joke between them and a bad one, because between the two of them, they had no other friends. The circumstances of their household had not led to friendly relations with any neighbors, not for a long, long time.

Maggie turned her head to lip at Letty's hand. Maggie's lips were soft and warm and something in her dark, sweet eyes told Letty that she knew how sad Letty was. Letty stroked the horse's nose. She was a bit small in height, was Maggie, only fourteen hands, but every inch of her was beautiful.

"Every time he's sold something of ours away you've said the same thing, Anthony. But she's all I have left. And even if we can't win... I am fighting this fight."

* * *

LETTY HAD GRITTED her teeth when counting out coins to the innkeeper, not because they weren't earned, but because she had so few left.

She'd told Anthony that she would have been perfectly fine sleeping on the floor of the carriage. She was already as dirty as it was possible to get and she knew it would be some time yet before she could truly bathe. What was the point of spending good shillings on a room when she was just going to get up and continue the journey the next day?

But Anthony had put his foot down. The hired driver would likely sleep in the coach, and no, Letty could not sleep in the straw on the floor in Maggie's stall; that was where Anthony would be himself.

Really, he was unreasonably bossy, Letty thought to herself and stopped herself before she could scowl again. Were all servants like this when they had known a person for half her life? Letty didn't know; she had not visited other households in her village since she was ten, when it became clear to everyone that her father owed money to them all and had no intention of paying anyone back.

During the years, all the other staff in the house had disappeared one by one, mostly by simply leaving in the middle of the night after many months of not being paid. Letty had gradually come to realize that for whatever reason she didn't know, Anthony had stayed. Apparently he had nowhere else to go.

Part of her brain calculated that it would have been much more efficient for the household if he *had* run off somewhere in the middle of the night: one less mouth to feed, and a bossy one, too. But another part of her brain, one slightly less practical, one that she seldom paid any heed to, reminded her that her life these past few years would have been unbearably lonely if she had not had Anthony at least as company.

Anthony, and Maggie.

"We should reach Roseford today," she said as she approached the carriage block to climb up into the cabin.

Anthony, who had a piece of golden straw sticking out of his straight black hair where it was tied at the nape of his neck, put out his hand and helped her up.

Her skirts were more than slightly dusty and had more than a touch of horse-sweat to them, but Letty, eyes pale but steely, set her plump chin in a way that people might not have expected if they had not known her. "Today we have only one job: to convince an unscrupulous man not to deprive me of my horse."

Anthony laughed at her as she settled herself in the carriage seat, a dilapidated lap robe settled over her skirts. "He's not unscrupulous, princess," he told her, with the air of repeated argument. "He's not *trying* to deprive you of your horse. He likely does not even know that you exist."

"Well, we'll fix that today," Letty said as firmly as she had set her jaw, and nodded to Anthony to tell the driver to set off.

* * *

"SARAH, I know I asked you to take up *all* the carpets!"

Sir Michael Grantley, the baronet of Roseford, knew that he sounded more like he was angry than like he was whining. He didn't want to sound angry but he couldn't afford to sound like he was whining.

Still, he knew Sarah wouldn't hold it against him and she didn't. Not just because she was a pleasant young woman who had a good job here and knew it. Because she wouldn't hold anything against him; no one would.

No one ever held a grudge against him now.

It drove him rather mad.

Sarah twisted her hands in her snowy linen apron. "I know, sir, I'm sorry, sir, it's just that that was your mother's favorite! So proud of it she was, and I remember her mentioning how much she loved the roses on it every time she had the ladies from town in for tea. Cabbage roses were the roses the village was named for, she said."

"It's not like anyone was going to argue with her, was it?" Now Michael knew he sounded snappish. Dammit, why couldn't he find the right tone? "See here, just tell Griggs to help you take it up, and store it in the attic with the rest."

"It will be awfully cold on the floors in here come winter," she said, her red curls bobbing as she looked around sadly. Most of the furniture had been removed and other than the table and chairs that rested on the proud gold and green carpet, what remained—a sideboard, a divan, and two end tables—all rested on the bare polished wood of the floor.

"That's not a problem we're going to have today, anyway," said Michael, pushing his hair back off his own forehead where he could feel the sweat gathering. Surely it was too warm for this early in the summer. "Look at it this way—it will be that much easier to sweep in here, will it not?"

"True enough, sir," and her face brightened, tossing him a smile as she bustled out the door to carry out his orders.

It was hot enough that Michael indulged himself in laziness just a little, staying put in his wide-winged upholstered chair and reading correspondence in front of the mercifully empty fireplace.

But eventually, as he always did, he grew restless sitting still in the chair, and reached for the wheeled contraption next to him that was quite singularly his own.

He had acquired it from the brilliant Mr. Cullen in London who had specifically designed and built it just for him. A second was under construction now, just in case of damage to this one, as Michael had found it sufficiently indispensable that he did not want to do without. And money was not a barrier to Sir Michael.

Mr. Cullen had been concerned with the strength and sturdiness of wheeled cart's axle design. Michael swung himself up out of the chair, balancing on one foot using a hand against the wing of the chair to brace himself. The small wooden cart wheeled smoothly up under his knee, which he rested comfortably in the shaped leather cradle suspended from the frame of the little cart. His knee was unencumbered by any further extension because the rest of the leg was gone.

Extending upward from the front of the cart was a bar handle high enough for Michael to use it to steady himself as he rolled himself along in the cart. He'd used the handle when he'd first got the thing but he seldom needed it now, using it only when turning sharp corners. He did tend to get rather up to speed, using his full leg to push himself quite quickly and without any bumps or snarls now that most of the house had most of the carpets removed.

Perhaps he should put the extra wheeler upstairs when it came so that he wouldn't have to carry the thing up and down, Michael contemplated as he rolled toward the library, a pile of letters clutched in his hand that he intended to answer. The faded color of the back of his hand betrayed his preference, which would have been to be outside in the sunlight. But since he had inherited this house and this title—and been forced by events to be discharged from the Navy—he'd had to spend far too much time writing letters and far too little time outside.

That, and the newly presented difficulties of riding horseback.

Michael had reason to hope a solution was near at hand to those problems, at least. It was only a hope. Several of the merchants in the village, including the innkeeper, baker, and grocer had all complained to him of an indigent scoundrel who had passed himself off as gentry and then run them up bills, all of them serious bills, in the course of living off the village for nearly two months. Michael had had little to do with the case, but when Griggs had returned from court to inform him that the thief had no money but claimed to have a biddable horse, Michael had paid those debts in exchange for the horse unseen. The debts were small enough to him and he would have had to pay them anyway; as patron of the village he felt it was his duty to balance the villagers' books when strangers took advantage of them. Fortunately there were few strangers in Roseford; undoubtedly why the scoundrel had been hiding here.

But Michael entertained the hope that it had at least been true that the fellow's horse was as biddable as he said. He needed a horse big enough to carry him. At six feet tall himself, he was not small and not a light burden, though his build since reaching manhood had remained more rangy than sturdy. He'd ridden horses all his life as anyone of his station would, but they had been more of a necessary convenience than an interest, and it frustrated Michael to have to spend so much time thinking about his equestrian needs now.

The estimable Mr. Cullen, whose usual work leaned more toward useful furnishings, had sent a letter advising him regarding building a clever device for mounting, but the dangling ropes had made his horses shy. Then it had also spooked the daintyish mare that Griggs had brought back for him from the county fair. He couldn't do any worse with this fellow's sight-unseen horse, and calmness and ability to be controlled was what he needed most in a horse.

Till then he could crutch around the property if he liked, or even pull out the appalling cane and the even more appalling wooden leg he'd brought home from the war instead of the flesh and blood leg he'd started with. He hated the thing—it hurt his knee and he detested the way it looked, a thick hewn fake foot of wood sticking out below the hem of his trousers. He much preferred Cullen's little wagon thing, and for smoothness and speed, at least on floors, it couldn't be beat. Cullen had promised to consider some sort of outdoor version but the unevenness of even the most cultivated terrain proved quite a challenge.

No, Michael needed a horse.

A good horse. A cooperative gelding would be best. Or even a calm, pretty mare, just like—

The one walking up his drive.

Michael startled himself and looked out the window again. Passing the portico, he was close enough to catch a glimpse of rich dark chestnut color out of the corner of his eye, multiplied by the cut glass panes of the window, and he rolled over to swing open the door and look.

She was a beauty, the color of the bottom of a cold clear stream, the color of the rich earth on which Roseford was built, in fact. Thick in the withers and a bit short, she would never win any races. But something about the square set of her shoulders and the soft look in her eyes struck Michael as very pretty indeed. She was the prettiest thing that Michael had seen all day, in fact.

He felt himself start to crack a grin.

And then the carriage door swung open, and the horse's rider swung down and stepped to the carriage block to help out a delectable little doll of a woman. A woman with a froth of pale gold hair and dimples and an adorable little bounce to her step, a woman who just came up to the shoulder of the man handing her down.

And Michael admitted to himself that in a prettiness contest, the horse was a far second.

* * *

LETTY HAD HOPED to find a way to refresh herself after the travel. She hadn't been quite clear on just how she would sneak into a house that wasn't expecting her and wash both herself and her clothing, since the day dress she wore was the only frock she had.

But she absolutely had *not* expected to see a man standing in the door as if to greet them as soon as she looked at the house.

A tall man, with caramel-brown hair waving in the heat and slightly sticking to his skin. Skin that looked golden with health, matching the square shoulders and narrow hips of the man, which she could see disconcertingly well as he was entirely without coat. His linen shirt clung to him a bit, as did his trousers, and unconsciously she licked her lips. They tasted of dust and salty sweat.

Letty wondered what *his* lips tasted like. After all, they were right *there*, a startlingly full lower lip for a man and shadowed a bit with whiskers all along his dark jawline, as though he had forgotten to shave.

He clutched a sheaf of papers in his hand and stood in the open doorway just staring at her. Well, partly standing, partly leaning on some sort of wheeled contraption he had next to him, casually slung below one knee.

And now she was staring at *him*. Oh dear.

She spoke softly, trying to get Anthony's attention without turning all the way around and losing sight of the man in the doorway, as though he might disappear.

"*Anthony,*" she hissed urgently.

"I had to finish paying the driver, and—oh good Lord."

Apparently made of sterner stuff than she, or simply more aware of what protocol required, Anthony made his way up the stairs and bowed. "Miss Letitia Stapleton for Sir Michael Grantley, of Roseford," he said.

"Yes," said the man standing in the doorway.

Anthony just raised his eyebrows.

"Oh yes," and the man seemed to shake himself. "I am Sir Michael."

"Indeed." Anthony's eyebrows did not come down. "Miss Stapleton apologizes for disturbing you, sir, but she has come at the request of her father to deliver your horse."

That stirred Letty into motion. "Actually, I've come—"

"Miss Stapleton." The fellow seemed to wake up somehow. Was he really a baronet? He looked like a blacksmith who had just fallen out of bed. A ridiculously beautiful blacksmith, with that regal nose and strong jawline, but still. He moved backwards with a bit of an odd hitching gait and motioned them inside. "And—"

"Miss Stapleton's groomsman Anthony," that fellow supplied smoothly. "I'll take the horse to your stable and see she's settled in, shall I, sir?"

"There's no need—perhaps if you could just walk round that way and alert the stable boy—"

"I will return immediately, sir."

And Anthony stepped out, leaving the space in front of the gentleman empty, and there was nothing Letty could do but step in.

"Your lordship—"

"It's Sir Michael, though I haven't begun getting used to it myself. At least it has the benefit of being shorter than Lieutenant Grantley, which is what they called me in the Navy," the shockingly under-dressed man told Letty absently, his eyes still taking her in.

"Thank you, Sir Michael, I've—"

"Have you no governess accompanying you, Miss Stapleton?"

At that she bristled, and was glad for it, for she knew it made her taller. "Governess? I'm twenty-one years old, your lordship."

"You don't say." His lordship's manners were lacking along with his grooming, Letty decided, but unfortunately not so lacking that he failed to notice her unconventional traveling companion. "You have no lady's maid, no chaperone?"

"I'm afraid not." Letty didn't bother to blush; what was the point of being embarrassed by things she could do nothing about? She was embarrassed enough by her filthy dress and filthy hair and the situation anyway. "Sir Michael, about my horse—"

"What?" That seemed to startle him. "Don't tell me that miscreant tried to sell me something that wasn't his to sell."

He grasped a handle at the top of the odd wheeled thing, and moved back another step, gallantly gesturing for her to accompany him. "Will you walk into the library, Miss Stapleton? I do apologize for preceding you however slightly but perhaps you will forgive me if I show you the way, as my butler is currently elsewhere employed."

Letty stepped to his side, and glanced down with curiosity. Now that she could see him from the side, she could see that he was not just leaning on the odd little wheeled cart; at least not by choice, because where a lower leg ought to be sticking out behind him, there was nothing at all.

Mean neighborhood boys might have called Letty slow, but slow to think she was not. She immediately knew why the mysterious Roseford fellow had wanted to buy her horse.

And why by any moral compass Letty would have to let her go.

CHAPTER 2

MICHAEL WAS USED to the moment when people caught sight of where his leg was missing and he was used to different reactions. This delectable young miss went rather paler than he thought she would—rather paler than he thought anyone could—and he wondered if she were, in fact, going to faint as she took a step back.

Yes, that was a reaction he'd better get used to seeing in young ladies, one corner of his brain told him bitterly, but he had little time for bitterness and stepped—well, rolled—closer anyway, in case she did in fact start to topple.

"I'm sorry," she said so faintly that he had to bend closer to hear her. "I've made a silly mistake, and—and that doesn't matter at all now anyway. Please excuse me. It is so nice to have made your acquaintance."

And just like that, as suddenly as she had appeared, she was gone, silently closing the front door of the house behind her.

Michael was sufficiently stupefied by her disappearance, let alone her appearance, that he had to consider for several moments what he should do, before following to the door and drawing it open again.

She was right there, that round delicious armful of a woman, sitting right on the step and, if the shaking of her shoulders was anything to go by, sobbing her heart out.

Silently Michael cursed the situation. This was why he didn't dress and didn't go out. Just these sorts of awkward encounters where by all rights any reasonable fellow would walk around front of her and try to politely catch her attention, or if determined to be more friendly, perhaps sit down on the step next to her.

Both of which would be extraordinarily awkward for him to accomplish.

He could at least roll himself behind her and clear his throat in an attempt to catch her attention.

So he did.

Immediately there was a flash of her hands and she leapt up and whirled, her face showing signs of tears only in the streaks of dirt that unfortunately smudged her rosy cheeks.

Remarkable. "Were you not weeping, Miss Stapleton?"

Her jaw set and suddenly the candy doll girl struck him as having something of a steel backbone. "If I had been, surely it would be rude of you to call attention to it, Sir Michael."

"Quite right. My sincere apologies." Surely she hadn't been sobbing that way just because he was missing a leg. "You were trying to tell me something about your horse. My horse."

"I'm not sure I…" The girl had been trying to make a speech since she'd crossed the threshold, and now all the air had gone out of her. Michael had no way of knowing if this sort of thing was usual in females her age; his experience in school and in the Navy were all of young men and he was finding that background less than useful here.

He decided that perhaps both of them would be willing to forego the speech for now in view of more pressing matters.

"I realize that you must have business elsewhere, but you have traveled a long way to bring me a valuable horse and I of course invite you to dine with me here this evening and enjoy the hospitality of the house." He quirked a half-smile at her. "I assure you the rest of the house is more comfortable than the entryway."

"Thank you, no, I..." The set to her jaw disappeared. She cast those blue eyes about as if looking for something. "I must not trouble you..."

"I don't mean to delay you long, I know you must surely be anxious to return home."

Her eyes met his. Hers came to a fetching point in the corners, and were as clear as the sky.

She said, "Why on earth would I want to return home?"

Michael reared back.

With another one of those quick changes of aspect her face went from absolutely certain to lost again. "I beg your pardon, I'm sure that's not an appropriate thing to say. I'm just—"

Someone had to get this conversation back on track and Michael felt certain it would have to be him. "Miss Stapleton. You have been traveling for a long while, and you have brought me a very valuable property for which I am grateful. Please accept Roseford's hospitality."

Afraid she would begin to argue again if he gave her the opportunity, Michael turned his head back over his shoulder. "Sarah!" he bellowed at the top of his voice.

"Oh my!" Letty started as if someone had fired a pistol.

"My apologies," said Michael again. "I have not—I have only been returned from war a short time and my household is still adjusting to my circumstances. My father never retained many staff and now, you see, the family consists only of myself. My mother passed away some fifteen years ago and the staff are perhaps too used to a bachelor household."

"Yes, Sir Michael?" Sarah said breathlessly, trying to disguise the fact that she had clearly come on the run.

"Please show Miss Stapleton to a comfortable room and settle her in, would you please, Sarah?"

* * *

LETTY DIDN'T REMEMBER AGREEING to anything, but it did not matter. What she had realized, standing before his lordship's front door, was that she had nowhere to go at all.

"I can have your luggage brought up here, Miss Stapleton," the red-haired maid was saying as she smoothed the coverlet on the high spindled bed.

"I only have a—" Her reticule, which she was carrying. A bundle that had been in Anthony's pack with a change of linens and her only other pair of shoes, small slippers she could wear when she changed out of these boots. "There's no luggage, thank you. My groomsman will have a small bundle that you can bring up, miss …?"

"I'm Sarah, miss."

"Thank you, Sarah."

Letty could see that Sarah was struggling to come to grips with the situation herself. Given his lordship's claims about the state of the household, perhaps Sarah was unfamiliar with house visits, but a guest with no luggage, and therefore no belongings, seemed not just peculiar but a whole new set of difficulties.

The easiest way out was through, Letty decided.

"I can see what you're thinking and you're quite right, Sarah," Letty said with a little self-deprecating smile. "I have nothing to change into, and as you can no doubt smell the aura of horse about me, I am in dire need of a bath. I don't want to put you to any difficulty but I would be grateful if you could help me find a temporary solution."

Sarah nodded with a bright enough smile, but then bit her lip. A solution might not be easy to come by.

Letty went on. "At home I wash my dress and then iron it immediately, so that it is ready to wear again—perhaps you could show me the washroom so that I might do the same here?"

Sarah's brown eyes met Letty's pale blue ones, and Sarah made a decision. This girl could have been a grifter up to no good, but she truly seemed to be as surprised by her own logistical difficulties as Sarah was. It was up to Sarah to help her out. That she could do.

"If you wouldn't mind a loan, miss, I know where there are a couple of her ladyship's things that you could make temporary use of, and never you worry about washing your dress, I can wash and iron it for you in a jiffy myself."

Sarah hadn't been in service long, and she had some idea that loaning things out to visitors wasn't a maid's place. But since Roseford only had a handful of servants, and those sharing the work really however they could, and Sir Michael wasn't a formal sort, Sarah decided to take the matter in hand and solve it for herself.

Letty looked doubtful. "I'm quite accustomed to—"

But Sarah had made another decision, based this time on the circles under Letty's eyes. "If you don't mind my saying so, miss, you look like you've marched all the way here on your own two feet. Let's get a bath up here for you and get you feeling more like yourself again, and we'll go from there, won't we."

She left Letty no choice but to stand by the window, unwilling to sit on the embroidered chair seats in her dirt- and horse-stained dress, while Sarah flew about, arranging the small copper bathtub behind a screen in the room and then zipping away, to be followed by two young men, all three of them carrying buckets on bars across their shoulders full of water.

"I'll tell Sir Michael that you were too tired to dine, miss, which I suspect to be only the truth, and I'll bring you up something to eat. You can sleep yourself out and by morning you'll be right as rain."

Sarah laid out a thick smooth bar of rose-scented soap and drying linens. Next to it she placed a folded square of a snowy white bundle with some lace peeping out. "I'll be back in just a moment, miss, just you enjoy that bath while it's warm and we'll sort you right out."

Letty didn't wait. As soon as the door closed she unbuttoned the buttons on her dress, located on the side so she could reach them herself, and wrapped the thing inside-out, leaving it on the floor. One benefit of living in the country with no one to impress and no social requirements was that she also had no corset. In moments she was in the tub, bending herself to duck her hair under the water and already feeling how heavenly it would be to be clean.

She *did* have a work dress at home, the one she used to muck out Maggie's stall. She hadn't packed it because it irretrievably smelled of the stable, but she realized now that she hadn't been thinking at all. She had been so fixed on convincing this gentleman not to take her horse. That was foolish, she now saw. Undoubtedly money had already changed hands and that meant her father had simply disappeared somewhere new. She hadn't thought that the buyer would truly need her horse, but it was clear that he did, as well as that he had in fact bought her.

Some small part of her had been hoping that it wasn't true, as most of the things her father said weren't true.

She *didn't* want to go back to that house, the house that had gotten lonelier and emptier year by year. Letty didn't dream about the future; she figured out how to get through each day and each week, one by one as they came. She now realized that she might have come to the end of the line. She had no idea how she would manage tomorrow. She had little idea how to manage tonight.

It was an oddly freeing thought. Whatever happened, she would not be at home trying to convince the grocer to trade her one more dozen eggs for her last hair ribbon or asking Anthony to patch the baker's roof to keep them in bread for another few weeks.

She let the suds run out of her hair, pried the last dirt from around her fingernails. She could not deny that this Sir Michael needed her beloved Maggie. He must have been used to being out of doors; the loss of his leg must be relatively recent. Clearly he meant to ride again, and he would need a gentle, cooperative horse to let him do it. Perhaps he needed someone to help him and Maggie figure out how to proceed.

Letty smiled to herself. Yes, this was an excellent plan. She could earn her keep. She was the best horse trainer she knew, and not at all daunted by the fact that she was the only horse trainer she knew. She would not be bored staying in this room this evening waiting for her clothes to dry. She would make plans on how to teach what she and Maggie had learned together. She would not go back to that village or that house. She would stay right here and help Michael Grantley ride a horse again.

CHAPTER 3

MICHAEL HATED SITTING at a desk but that was nevertheless where he found himself that night, still answering the letters that had never been attended to that afternoon, when a knock came on the library door. "Come."

He pushed back his chair to see the fellow who had come with Miss Stapleton. "Anthony, is it?"

"Indeed, Sir Michael. I apologize for disturbing you, I only wished to ascertain—"

"You're French?"

He hadn't noticed the accent before but it surprised him, how much he felt a visceral reaction to it. Michael felt his shoulders tense and his lip start to curl. It was so faintly there but it was there—the language of Britain's enemy, and the cannon that had taken so many of his friends, and his leg.

"I do apologize for that as well, sir." Anthony's bow was deep and his expression carefully neutral. "I have lived here for half my life but your lordship obviously has a discerning ear."

"Are you a spy?" Michael had not before had such a longing to stand firmly on his own two feet and face someone. He settled for narrowing his eyes. He had a pistol in the drawer of the desk but of course it would take too long to load it for it to be useful. But then, he could be very dangerous with his fists when necessary.

"Sir! I have been employed in the Stapletons' stables for a decade. I left my country long before the current conflict began and I assure you, that I love my new home dearly and no more wish to see it invaded by imperial forces than do you."

Michael's hackles were still up. "No insult intended."

Anthony stood his ground. "I am not a gentleman, sir, and cannot afford to take insult."

Point taken. "What do you want?"

The groomsman had stood straight as an arrow, slender but unbending, but at that he seemed to falter. "I had a rather delicate discussion to undertake, sir, and now I fear we have begun it badly. Yet I cannot abandon it, so I must beg your leave to speak without fear of your anger at least until we have talked."

The man spoke like a peer for all he slept in the stables, and the talk among the sailors had painted the French as a duplicitous people. Michael disliked generalizations but was not inclined to relax his guard, especially here in his own home. "Speak."

Anthony didn't waste more time. "Sir, I know how unusual it must seem for a young lady like Miss Stapleton to arrive on your doorstep without chaperone, and I wanted to explain. Miss Stapleton is young but she is determined, and she has raised that horse herself from the time that it was weaned as a dear pet more than a mount. She should perhaps not have undertaken the travel but it was my fault that I could not dissuade her."

Michael digested that for a second. A young woman absolutely should not have undertaken the travel with only a groomsman for protection and chaperonage, but if Anthony were in the position of servant his ability to object might have been limited—and there seemed to be no one else to monitor the girl at all. "She must be very distraught at the idea of giving up such a dear pet."

Anthony's face relaxed minutely and suddenly Michael realized the fellow had to be several years younger than himself. Dammit, what were two near children doing gallivanting around the countryside?

But then, how old had he and his men been, when they had originally set sail?

"She is nearly beside herself," Anthony admitted. "She had placed all her hopes on the possibility of persuading you to change your mind about the transaction."

Had she? Then why hadn't she said so?

"I will not," Michael said slowly, "as I have need of a horse of this one's description, and she looks to be exactly what I need. I merely extended the hospitality of the house to Miss Stapleton in thanks for her completion of the transaction."

Anthony nodded, but he looked troubled. "My lord—I will undertake to arrange transportation for Miss Stapleton home tomorrow. I know that you would not wish to damage her reputation by extending her stay here with you beyond what could reasonably be understood as an unavoidable emergency."

Oh. Aha. An only child, Michael had nonetheless spent enough time at society functions in town to understand that a young woman unchaperoned in a man's home was not only bad *ton*, it was bad news for the lady's reputation in general. "I see. Should I expect a visit from any angry fiancés?"

"Miss Stapleton is not affianced."

"Sweethearts?"

"Miss Stapleton is quite out of society, my lord. Perhaps you may have noticed that she is out of practice in the rules of polite society."

Meaning most likely that she never knew them. No, that was not what Michael had noticed about her. And the young man was right, this *was* a problem. Letitia Stapleton was an appealing armful of delicious womanhood and it would not do to have it get out that she had spent the night in a man's home unchaperoned. It would not do at all.

"All right, Anthony, I see your point. I will arrange for Miss Stapleton to have a chaperone immediately, and I will take it upon myself to arrange for safe and comfortable travel for her as soon as she is ready to leave."

* * *

"I'M NOT LEAVING."

"I beg your pardon?"

Sir Michael Grantley of Roseford was having a great deal of difficulty with his repast. And none of it was presented by the food, which was perfectly fine, or the weather, or his leg, or anything else except the presence of Miss Letitia Stapleton.

She had appeared just after he had seated himself, which meant that he had avoided her seeing his shifting of his body into the chair from his rolling cart, which still felt awkward to him, but meant that he was required to lever himself up again to acknowledge her arrival.

She had acknowledged his gallantry with the sweetest little dimpled smile he had ever seen, which had so dazzled him that he failed to follow the conversation for some time, until he found both it and himself in a deep morass with no way out to be seen.

"Maggie is the dearest thing and I think she will want to cooperate with you. With me to introduce you and help her learn what you need you two will get along famously."

Michael sat back and watched Letty butter a scone. "This isn't a dance at a ball. She's a horse." Then remembering himself, "Miss Stapleton."

Letty smiled again. The most adorable dimple appeared and disappeared on her right cheek, hiding among the faint sprinkle of freckles he could see there. Her hair, clean and simply pinned back, gleamed like a sunbeam and Michael was having a tough time following the conversation among all the sparkling details. Yesterday she'd looked delectable but apparently there were still new horizons to discover.

Yesterday his manners had also been appalling and Michael had berated himself last night after Anthony's departure. He was not so far removed from good society that he had forgotten good behavior completely, as different as it was from the Navy and from the front.

"I will arrange transportation back to your home for you," he added. "It is the least I can do after your long trip here."

"No, that is not the most efficient plan," Letty said, shaking her head and ignoring that wisps of hair worked themselves free from the pins. "I'm here now, as is Maggie, as are you. It's the ideal combination. We can begin work today."

"Horrible."

Letty looked up at the interruption.

An older woman, back bent and feet shuffling under the hem of her gray skirts, had managed to make her way into the breakfast room, in fact all the way over to the small table, where she was pulling out a chair right next to Letty, without Letty noticing her till now.

She was small, shorter even than Letty though some of that might be due to the bend in her back. Her face was grooved with deep wrinkles and her eyes looked as though a veil had fallen on them.

She was by far the oldest person Letty had ever seen. But her gnarled hands pulled out the chair quite firmly, she wore a gorgeously woven scarf Chinoise over her shoulders even though it was not yet noon, and over her gray twist of still-thick hair was perched a beautiful cap, composed of lace like spiderweb silk over a jacquard lining.

Michael started to stand again but the new arrival just waved him back. "Sit down, Michael."

"Miss Stapleton, may I introduce Mrs. Peterborough, my housekeeper."

"Retired. Extremely retired. What on earth has possessed you to drag me up here in the morning, Michael. Morning, of all things."

Eyes wide, Letty passed Mrs. Peterborough the scones, then the butter, then the jam.

"As you can see I have a guest, Mary, and Miss Stapleton requires a chaperone."

"I don't, not really," Letty said, causing Michael to nearly choke on his own scone.

"Do tell," said Mrs. Peterborough, buttering her scone while still somehow watching Letty closely.

"So then have you decided to return home?" Michael didn't like the idea though of course it was the simplest answer.

Letty shrugged one shoulder. "No one would care if I work here. No one ever does."

"Mm hmm. And what work is this that you'll be beginning?" Mrs. Peterborough asked before filling her mouth with buttered scone.

"Sir Michael has acquired my—an extraordinary horse." Michael didn't fail to notice how Letty's face fell for a second, but the girl pushed on gamely. "And I suspect he intends to ride her despite missing part of a leg."

The silence that fell over the room felt thick and brittle. Mrs. Peterborough just looked at Michael.

Whatever feelings rolled through his chest at that moment, for whatever reason, they passed just as quickly. It was unforgivably rude of her to mention his injury, but Michael found he preferred it to dancing around the topic. He'd seen few acquaintances since his return to Roseford and all of them had scrupulously made no mention of the missing bottom half of his leg, yet he felt somehow that it was all they were thinking about. He'd been desperate to end every conversation.

For Letty it was pertinent to the topic, so she'd said it, and apparently pressed right on. Whatever qualms she had felt about his injury upon seeing it for the first time yesterday, they didn't extend to discussing it.

"I've raised Maggie from a foal. She's a very special horse, my lord, you have no idea yet really, but you'll see."

"You should refer to the baronet as Sir Michael in public," Mrs. Peterborough interrupted as though she didn't care that much, continuing to chew scone.

"Oh I'm sorry." Letty dipped her eyes sincerely in Michael's direction but then continued on straightaway. "She's not a pony, she doesn't do tricks. She can do what you want, and she can do it any time you want, once she understands what you need. You have to be consistent about telling her."

"Like any good horse, I imagine," Michael agreed.

"But so much more! You'll see. She's very smart and very sweet."

"I know you might find this difficult to believe, Miss Stapleton, but I have ridden horses before. Many, many horses."

"Really?" She opened her eyes wide. "You don't look that old."

Mrs. Peterborough coughed. Michael glared at her. In truth he had not been much for horses at any point in his life. He simply wanted to be able to get about outside.

"Military horses have been trained for centuries to ignore distraction." There had been no horses aboard his ship. But Michael had some vague idea that the Army trained horses. Really, conversing with the girl was more challenging than he remembered conversations with girls usually were.

"Oh," Letty waved a hand as though battle was mere amateur work. "I've no doubt Maggie might have made an excellent war horse but that's not what's wanted now."

"Not too far off, I think. I need her to stand upon command, even if she doesn't like the ropes or anything else waving above her, and I will need her to learn a rider who cannot direct her with two legs. I suspect it will ruin her for others to ride, once she becomes used to my needs."

"Oh, she..." Letty trailed off again, that sad expression coming and going like a cloud as she no doubt realized what Michael meant. Maggie would no longer be suitable for *her* to ride. "She'll do so well," Letty said but the animation had gone out of her.

Which Michael hated.

"Let's go visit her," Michael said even though his food was still largely untouched.

Letty brightened immediately. "Let's! But may we finish breakfast first? I will admit I am famished."

Which somehow struck Mrs. Peterborough as hilarious, as she started to laugh.

* * *

MICHAEL LEFT his wheeled cart by the door and took the crutches Griggs handed him.

He didn't like them, they hurt under his arms and they made him feel more crippled than the actual loss of the leg, but they were much the easiest way to get around outside and they were going to be the fastest way Michael could accompany Letty to the stable.

She paid the crutches no mind at all; her short stride only moved at about the same speed as Michael on crutches, after all.

She ran ahead of him as they got close, though, and by the time he caught up with her, she was in Maggie's stall, rubbing noses with the horse and stroking a hand down her neck.

Michael felt something like a pang, watching Letty's happy reunion with her pet. No one was ever that glad to see him.

"Come over and be introduced," said Letty, holding out her hand to Michael.

She looked so certain and so alive, that sweet little smile coming and going as she waited for him to accede to her demand. Order, really.

"It's a horse," Michael said abruptly. One didn't need introductions to a horse.

"It's Maggie and if you want her to carry you about you're going to have to get to know her." Letty flexed her fingers impatiently. Even the horse shifted from foot to foot, as though it agreed.

Knowing she was right, Michael swung himself forward. It made him feel like a child again, approaching the horse. It made him feel a bit small, and he couldn't afford to feel small, not now that he was shy part of a leg.

He balanced using one crutch and left the other against the wall of the stall so he could give Letty his hand.

He thought he'd braced himself.

Her touch on his hand was soft, as he'd known it would be, and warm. Even in gloves, her fingertips danced over the surface of his hand, touching his knuckles, the pad of his thumb, and the palm where his skin was worn a bit raw.

"Oh dear," said Letty, scowling fiercely at the reddened skin of his hand and making Michael want to laugh.

"It will toughen up," he said with a shrug.

"How long have you been using these crutches?"

"My injury is almost a year old, Miss Stapleton, but I spent the first part of that bedridden. I've been using the crutches often only about six months."

"But you're using them less now that you have your rolling whatsit in the house," she observed, not technically but quite correctly. He'd used her formal name hoping that she would stop her very personal inspection of his hand; she didn't. Instead she drew it up closer, examining it, and Michael suddenly had the idea that she would kiss it.

Which of course she did not.

Where had that thought come from? He berated himself, as she finally dropped his hand and looked at the crutch itself, giving its grip just as close an examination.

"We can do better," was all she said before turning back to him and taking his hand once more.

"Maggie, this is Sir Michael. He's going to be your... owner now." Letty kept her face down, moving Michael's hand so Maggie could sniff it.

It felt ridiculous, letting a horse sniff his hand when he wanted the hand to stay in Letty's possession, but Maggie's nose was soft and Michael remembered what Anthony had told him about Letty's feelings toward her pet. He knew Letty was right, of course. And if he had never cared much about horses, he still very much needed this one.

It was not like this was his first horse. "I should have brought her some carrot or another treat."

Letty shrugged. "There's no need. Maggie will do what you want because she likes you."

Well, that was a novel approach to horse thought. "How else am I to reward her good behavior?"

Letty kept her face close to the horse's. "Maggie is always very understanding if there are no treats to be had."

Ah. Aha. Letty hadn't just lacked tutelage and chaperonage.

She and the horse seemed to have a brief whispered conversation, during which Michael repossessed his hand.

Letty finally turned back to him and though her face wasn't sunny, it wasn't cloudy either. "Let us look at the rest of your riding equipment," she said.

* * *

"The challenge is that I can't both stand on the step and simultaneously put my foot in the stirrup."

Letty nodded, taking in the arrangement of handrails that had been deeply sunk into the ground next to the mounting block, and the ropes looped from the tree-branches over it.

"Yes, I see." She tested the strength of the handrail. "Once you are up the stairs, you don't feel you can simply pull yourself into the saddle?"

Michael didn't want to explain the debacle of the black horse currently eating him out of house and home and accomplishing nothing, or the timid little roan that was also gracing his stable for no reason. Neither had been good at standing. The problem was that Michael lacked staff able to purchase the right horses for him, and even if he claimed to himself that he would have been able to pick a good one, he had not had the time to leave the house. His own business interests were growing rapidly, and he still had work remaining that had fallen to him when he inherited his father's estate.

He looked up at the arrangement through what he imagined were Letty's eyes. Overly complex, now that he thought about it. But he'd been so worried about taking a fall. He couldn't afford to break the one whole leg he had.

Mr. Cullen had sent him advice, but then Mr. Cullen primarily manufactured items for inside the home, he now remembered.

Michael crutched up to the mounting steps, swung his foot up to the first one. "And I'm going to need a place to put my crutches," he muttered to himself as he did it.

"Quite," she said, and extended her hand for him to give them to her.

Surprised, Michael gave them. He also stripped off his fawn-colored coat. If he was going to be immodest, he might as well be immodest. She had already seen him in his shirtsleeves.

Free, his hands could take hold of the handrails and he easily swung himself up to the top step.

"So now how can I get my foot into the stirrup? Especially if the horse moves? So I've arranged these—"

Reaching up Michael grasped a low-hanging loop of rope. The tree branch it hung on swayed and lowered slightly, but Michael held on and pulled himself up, swinging the other hand out to grasp a second loop and then he was holding himself suspended in midair.

Letty found herself closing her jaw before he noticed it was hanging open. She had never seen raw masculine power in action and Michael looked mesmerizing, carelessly holding himself up by the power of his arms, a boyish grin on his face as a lock of his hair fell across his forehead.

His hair was very similar in color to Maggie's, Letty thought.

Michael swung himself back to just the first loop, then down the handrails to stand next to her again. She hoped she wasn't pink in the face. She felt pink.

She handed him his coat, then his crutches.

"I see the problem," she said. "Horses wouldn't like those tree branches bobbing about over their heads, nor the rustling sound. And while you're up there, how would they know that you are trying to mount?"

"I'm assuming a groom would have to bring her."

"Perhaps. I think all will be well with a well-behaved horse, that's all. If you saddled her in the stable, Maggie will follow you here and stand for you. We can get her used to you mounting however you prefer."

Michael's heart thumped in his chest. He realized at that moment how very, very much he wanted this to work. He wasn't one of the men who had come back embittered by what he'd done, or what had been done to him. Michael was truly grateful that he was alive, and while he would rather have come back with both his legs, he was also quite conscious of how close he had come to not coming back at all.

But they grated on him, all the little difficulties of the day, of just getting up out of a chair or going outside. It would be heaven to be on horseback again, heaven to be able to move around the countryside again, or even only around his own property.

Letty was surveying his arrangement of rails and ropes, her head tipped back. "I think we can do better, though."

She pointed back toward the house, several dozen yards away. "You can build a mounting block there, and nearly wheel straight up to it. If you like ironwork, you can have a hook made at the base of the handrail that will hold your crutches. I think that is more necessary than the ropes, perhaps."

"And smoother," Michael said jokingly, but it only caused Letty to grab one of his hands between hers.

"Oh dear!" She ran those small fingertips over the abrasions on his palms, and Michael wondered for a moment if one crutch under his arm might completely support him if he grabbed the delicious Miss Stapleton around the waist with the other.

Ungallant of him, he immediately told himself, and yet the question persisted in the back of his mind.

She looked up and was scowling fiercely at him, that scowl that he thought was the most hilarious thing he'd ever seen. He felt the chuckle bubbling up inside him.

"Certainly something much smoother! This is a simply unacceptable level of damage."

He burst out laughing.

"You find injury comic? I assure you, sir, that you need these hands and this sort of abrasion can be deep enough to become septic. You will not be laughing then."

"Of course, you're quite right," he said, absolutely unable to completely stifle the laughter that seemed to come up from somewhere inside him. She looked like an angry kitten, half a cup of anger ready to fight, and he had never seen anything so funny.

He was laughing at her, but Letty could not imagine why. Shaking it off, she went on, "Let's work this afternoon on you calling Maggie to you. I think we can get her to a state where, once she's saddled, she will follow you to the mounting block, and you can even ride without the attentions of a groomsman, should you prefer."

His heart thumped again. What she'd just described was pure freedom. "That would be beyond my hopes, Miss Stapleton."

"She can do it. And you can do it. I can show you how."

And, diminutive though she was, Letty marched back toward the stable with as much determination in her spine and her stride as any naval commander Michael had ever known.

* * *

BY DINNERTIME, Michael was feeling rather less impressed by Letty's determination, and more exhausted.

She had drilled him in the art of attracting Maggie's attention until even Maggie had started to look exasperated. She had already taught Maggie hand signals to get the horse to come to her, to stand still, and even to lay down.

"I don't want her to do that," Michael had objected. "That is dangerous for her knees, and a horse always looks like things are going badly in that position."

"You should know that she can do it," Letty had sniffed disapprovingly before returning to drilling Michael in the hand signals.

Maggie had not seemed thrilled with the idea of following the man's commands instead of Letty's. It seemed to Michael that the horse's attention was just as attracted by the sun gleaming on Letty's hair as Michael's was. Maggie seemed far more inclined to go to her old friend than the strange new man waving his hands in the air nearby.

But Letty persisted, and by the end of the afternoon the mare was strolling up to Michael and letting him stroke her nose when he gave the signal for "come", and Michael was not just exhilarated, he was relieved. He had started to think this plan would not work at all.

"I told you it would," was all Letty said when she parted from him to retire upstairs upon returning to the house.

Michael had retired to his chamber, which he kept on the first floor for sheer convenience's sake, to wash and even change before dinner. He ran a hand along his jaw and decided to shave, too. There must have been a very hairy Viking in his ancestry, he mused, because left to its own devices his beard would extend out past his shoulders, he was sure of it.

Now following his ablutions, he looked polished as any ship's bell, and stood when Letty joined them, one of his hands lightly balanced on the table to keep him gracefully upright. Griggs pulled out Letty's chair for her and she smiled at him as she seated herself opposite Mrs. Peterborough.

"The kitchen is a disgrace and I've been at Mrs. Dunphy all day about it," that woman began the dinnertime conversation immediately, as Griggs served the soup.

Mrs. Dunphy, Michael remembered abruptly, was as staid as any middle-aged Scotswoman could be, and was likely up in arms about Mrs. Peterborough dining at the baronet's table. Of course. Nothing so untoward had ever happened in his parents' day. It truly was a shocking breach of household etiquette.

But Michael had other more pressing concerns, one being that Miss Stapleton needed chaperonage of *some* sort, and his options were limited. He was grateful to Mrs. Peterborough for leaving her comfortable cottage and returning to the manor house when he knew that she had all the discomforts of extreme old age. She'd said as much when he'd first returned, and urged him to find a new housekeeper. She had retired, she reminded him repeatedly, because she could no longer do the work that his house needed.

He didn't want a new housekeeper; he wanted the one he remembered.

She kept up a running commentary about the state of the kettles, the knives, the floor and the pantry while Letty ate and snuck glances at Michael that she very much hoped Mrs. Peterborough was too near-sighted to see.

"What about you, you have any opinion about how to scour a burnt kettle?" Mrs. Peterborough suddenly directed at Letty, making Letty jump a little and wonder if the retired housekeeper was all that near-sighted after all.

But if she thought to catch Letty out she was mistaken on that one. "I don't like using sand, I think it just makes the pot burn again," said Letty without a pause. "A little salt on a rag works wonders, I find."

"Salt! Well I like that. If you have salt to waste."

"I find it far cheaper than a new kettle. And of course, it is preferable not to burn the kettles at all."

"True." As if by that answer she had passed some sort of a conversational gate with Mrs. Peterborough, Letty found herself addressed again. "You seem to have experience with keeping house."

"I suppose it was mine to keep." If only it had been, Letty mused.

"Helped your mother quite a bit, did you?"

"I've never met my mother."

Michael paused in the act of raising a spoon, and Mrs. Peterborough's face softened. Which was very interesting; Letty had wondered if it could do that. "I am sorry, child," Mrs. Peterborough said, a little gruffly but sincerely.

Letty smiled. "It's not a painful topic, Mrs. Peterborough; do not feel a moment's alarm, I assure you. I simply never met her. I wish I had. I am sure she would have saved me a great deal of trial and error in finding solutions to many things around the house."

"Perhaps not," Michael put in, and Letty felt herself getting a little pink again. How awkward, must she blush just at the sound of his voice? He was so large, and so masculine, and *right there*. Why on earth was it so different from dining with Anthony, which she had done nearly every day for years?

His eyes were green, she decided, though outside in the afternoon sun next to Maggie's gleaming coat, they had seemed to contain shards of golden brown.

"You seem to have a talent for trial and error, Miss Stapleton. Discovering solutions is perhaps a talent that you would have made use of in any event."

Definitely too pink, Letty thought to herself, putting a hand to her cheek hoping to cool it. Had she ever received a compliment from a handsome man?

Had she ever received a compliment at all?

How in one day had she gone from hating this man who was

taking her beloved horse away to sitting here eating dinner with him and blushing because he had said something nice?

Well, she'd met him, she thought to herself. It was hard to hate people you'd actually met.

Letty found herself grateful, too, for Mrs. Peterborough's presence. It was clear to her now just what a chaperone was *for*. Without her there the dinner would have been far too intimate. She was already sitting so close to Michael that she could have leaned over and touched the back of that golden, strong hand. She could have taken one step and been close enough to sink her fingers in that thick glossy hair, slide her fingers down the back of his neck and—

Oh *my*.

Yes, it was very clear now what the purpose of a chaperone was.

"Are you well, Miss Stapleton?" The baronet looked rather alarmed and Letty realized she must have turned not just pink but bright red.

"Of course," she said as though surprised by the question, and immediately looked at Mrs. Peterborough instead of the large glossy man seated next to her. And Mrs. Peterborough helpfully began to lecture on the topic of storing onions.

* * *

"ANTHONY! Where have you been all day?"

He looked up from where he lay in the straw against the wall of Maggie's stall. "Right here."

"Oh you have not." Letty stomped a foot. "Michael and I were down here working with Maggie all afternoon and I didn't see you."

"You didn't call him Michael, I hope."

"Of course not! I am not stupid." But she had gone a bit pink in the cheeks; Anthony could see it even in the faint glow of the one lantern still lit in the stable.

He sighed.

She drifted over to stand next to Maggie's neck as if drawn by simple magnetism, laid her hand against the horse's flexing, gleaming neck.

"Letty my princess, let me ask you: what do you think a baronet looks for in a lady to marry?"

She scowled at him. "What a question. I'm not silly enough to think that he might want to marry me. Don't be making up stories, you know me far too well for that. I am not giddy that way."

He nodded, sitting up in the straw. "And how might you describe the women a baronet likes but does not marry?"

Face flaming, Letty turned to lean her shoulders back against Maggie's side, looking down at Anthony's earnest, familiar face in the shadows cast by the lantern. "Oh dear."

He nodded again. "Please be careful."

She fell to her knees in the straw before him, causing Maggie to shift a step or two away.

"Anthony, did you really think we would ever go home?"

He sat silently for a moment, shredding a golden husk of straw in his hands. When he looked at her again, shadowed as he was by the lantern behind him, he looked older.

She nodded. "I think you are cleverer than I am, and you must have had the same thought I had."

"I doubt it."

"Then I'll say it. There was nothing left in that house for him to sell but me."

Anthony's lip curled and he threw the piece of straw away from himself with more vigor than it could withstand.

"I would not have let that happen."

"Legally you could not have stopped it. And... how long has it been since he's stayed there for more than a day? Since there was food in the pantry? Since we had more than a coin or two? He was using that house up from a distance, with us in it. How long could that go on?"

He had picked up more straw to shred. He seemed anxious, or angry, or both. "I had been thinking that I would find work this summer in the fields. A tenant who was willing to let me help."

"A tenant farmer. When none of the farmers has a penny to spare and all too many mouths to feed. Anthony. Does that sound like a plausible plan to you?"

"A plan, Letty? At this late date, you are lecturing me about plans?" Anthony jumped to his feet and left the stall, startling the horse into shuffling her feet sideways again.

Outside, he looked up at the stars.

Letty followed him slowly. She said quietly at his elbow, "It has not been a great strength of mine, making plans. I'm sorry. I have been too focused on one day and one week at a time... but perhaps it was because I did not want to wonder, knowing that the answer could only be, submit to my father's will or defy it. And if I had given myself time to think about it, I would have known there was only one answer."

She reached out to pat his forearm, feeling his fists clench. "But I didn't want to cause more trouble for you."

"For *me?*" He turned to her in the dark, sounding astonished.

"I know you worry about me," she said, even more softly. "I don't fear to make decisions for myself. Wherever, however I found work to do, I believe I can provide for myself. But I knew you would worry."

"Exactly what kind of work do you think you can do? You have had no education, I taught you to read; you are terrible with needle-work, you cannot make lace, you have never provided care for small children and you have no skill in the arts at all."

"Nor do I have the looks to work in a bawdy house. I mean! If you're going to list my faults, list all of them!" Letty's voice rung much more sharply now.

"Unfortunately," Anthony said and sounded as if his jaw was clenched just as tightly as his fists, "I think you have far more capability to become a lady of ill repute than you give yourself credit for."

Letty gasped and pulled away.

He made an exasperated sound and put out his hand in the dark, but Letty avoided it. "Princess. My apologies, I am too crude. I am taking my anger out on you that I am a failure of a man, that I cannot see a way to take you safely home and I fear for your safety here as well and I am just a servant sleeping in the stables and you..."

His hand found hers in the dark and she finally let him take it.

He muttered as if he didn't want to be caught saying it, "You are my only friend."

She squeezed his hand.

He squeezed back. She hoped he was smiling; she couldn't see out here in the dark.

He said, "Let's just say this. We are in someone else's home and you are too trusting. Also too small and too frail."

"I learned how to kick! You made me learn it!"

"But you never let me teach you to box. Please, mademoiselle. Let us devote ourselves to figuring out what we can do, where we can go. But let us not pretend that we can stay here indefinitely."

She patted his hand, let it go. "The situation is not so dire yet. I do have a job to do, Anthony; I am training Maggie to be his lordship's horse. She will do splendidly, she always does. I feel in good conscience that it is appropriate to accept Sir Michael's shelter and food during the time that the training goes on. You have worked so hard all these years. Remember when you learned to thatch roofs so that the baker would have a reason to owe you favors? And how to butcher so that you could earn a ham for us every fall? You've become a jack of all trades while I have done nothing. I can do this work, and I have a thought that if it goes well he will recommend me to others. I need your companionship, old friend; when it is time to move along, I will not go without you."

"And if we stay in one place it will make it too easy for your father to find us," Anthony put in.

Letty didn't answer that.

"Very well, horse tamer to the peerage, you and Maggie do your jobs and then we will find more work for you and me. Look at that! A plan. For more than a day."

"Or even a week," she said, and hugged him with one arm around his waist before starting up the hill toward the manor house.

CHAPTER 4

MICHAEL HAD NOT EXPECTED at this hour to catch a whiff through his open library door of evening air, and ... horses?

By the time he had levered himself up and rolled himself into the hallway, he found his houseguest had mounted nearly all the stairs. He could just see her in the dim light, her pale gold hair glinting below her bonnet. "Miss Stapleton?"

"Oh!" She ran swiftly right back down again. "I did not mean to disturb you!"

"Not at all. Have you been visiting Maggie?"

She nodded with that sunny, dimpled smile. "And Anthony."

Michael suppressed that returning urge to curl his lip with disdain. A lady would not want her only companion criticized, and there-fore... "Are they both comfortable?"

"Quite. Please inform me, sir, if we all present too much of a diffi-culty as your guests—I mean Anthony and myself, of course, Maggie isn't a guest—"

She looked like she had flustered herself, and Michael felt a need to rescue her somehow from the topic of Maggie staying right here when she herself had to leave.

"A guest she is not; I've never had a guest work me so hard. Or perhaps I should blame you instead of Maggie."

"Not too hard, I hope?"

Descending the last two steps Letty reached out and took Michael's left hand in her own, holding up to the dim lantern light to inspect the palm, no doubt to make sure that it met her standards for lack of injury despite the day's toll.

Still in her gloves and bonnet, she nonetheless wore no wrap, only that same blessed green dress she had been wearing when she'd arrived, and as one of her palms curled underneath Michael's much larger hand and the soft fingertips of the other traced patterns along the heel of his hand and the pad of his thumb, it occurred to Michael again how easy it would be, all too easy, to wrap her waist in his other arm and pull her very, very close.

He had to clear his throat and still his voice came out more rough and deep than he would like.

"I would say that you worked me just hard enough, Miss Stapleton, but I fear that at this time, in this place, and without a chaperone, you might take my words to mean more than is appropriate."

He heard her take in a sharp breath, and he could see the curve of her cheek and the top of one ear turning that bright shade of pink that even in one day he had already learned to associate with a very, very flustered Letty.

She didn't look up, but in a voice far steadier than the deep shade of pink might indicate said only, "The house has a chaperone, surely for well behaved adults that is enough."

Michael could feel his heart beating, his own blood ringing in his ears. What had he been doing with himself in the weeks, the months since he had returned home, when it felt as though the sensation of his heartbeat was unfamiliar and strange?

As if on its own, her thumb stroked the back of his hand.

The touch jolted through him, startling other parts of his body awake that he had ignored for some time.

He leaned his head down even closer to hers, and wondered about his own upbringing, but still he said, "Mrs. Peterborough is not sufficient chaperone, not even if she were armed with pistols and a much better shot than she is, if you are going to touch me like that, Letitia."

Michael heard her sharp intake of breath again, but instead of jumping or moving away, she stayed where she was, and instead of releasing his hand she merely curled it in her own, as if his were the smaller.

Still looking down at where their hands were joined she said, "Don't say such things to me, Mr. Grantley. I am not accustomed to compliments. Surely the touch of only hands is innocent. In gloves yet!"

She was so perfectly sized for him to pull into his arms, onto his lap.

"The correct address is Sir Michael," he said very quietly, his eyes, like hers, on their joined hands.

He slid his hand out of hers and turned it so that his palm could feel the softness, the warmth, of hers. It required only that he flex his hand slightly and he was sliding the sides of his fingers between hers, just his fingers between her fingers, and the slide of his skin against the barrier of her glove was like tinder lighting. Just that, and he had her hand captured in his, her fingers in his, and he could tell by the way she was breathing, faster now, that he could capture the rest of her so very easily.

"There is a line in a play by Mr. Shakespeare, have you seen it?, where his lovers talk to one another of a touch just like this."

He brought up his other hand, placing an elbow on the steering bar to keep his cart from rolling, and used both his hands to slowly, carefully peel the glove from her captured hand; and once he had it bare, he ran his thumbnail along the center of her palm. "Even if you have not seen or read the play, Letitia, I think you know that a touch like this is not innocent at all."

She finally looked up, and he realized that she did know. Because he had expected her expression to be shocked, or at least surprised. Instead she was flushed and her lips were parted and she was—

She was just as affected as he was.

Whatever she saw in his face finally made her move. Back.

She took a step backward, toward the staircase. Then another.

"It occurs to me, Sir Michael," she said, and her voice was also rough and she was breathing fast and God above, he wanted to follow her and make her breathe that way in his ear, "that you have found at least one solution yourself; gloves would greatly protect you against both the crutches and the ropes."

And then she took a third step back and, before he could move, turned and ran back up the staircase, just as fast as she had the first time—or perhaps a trifle faster.

As if she had just realized that gloves might protect his hands but there was nothing to protect her if they continued to look at each other that way in the dark.

* * *

In the room Letty could not find a candle, but she opened the drapes and managed to undress by moonlight. It was later than she had realized.

How inappropriate. She hadn't planned to meet Michael in the hallway so late at night, and just what had she been doing, when she'd just promised Anthony she'd be careful?

She could tell Anthony that she had wanted to be kind to the tall glossy man who had suffered such an injury, a loss she couldn't imagine. The loss of her beloved Maggie seemed petty and small beside what he had gone through, and perhaps some sympathy had made her cradle his hand the way she had.

But she would be lying, and she knew it.

He was so warm, his hands so strong; it had been delicious to hold his hand in her hand, it had made something similarly warm curl in her veins and made her heart beat faster.

She had a feeling this would not qualify as what Anthony had meant by being careful.

"SHE'S GOING to appear in that same dress, you know," Mrs. Peterborough told Michael over her tea the next morning.

"Hmm? What?"

Michael had been so busy watching the door for Letty's appearance that he had failed to pay attention to the food, or his tea, or Mrs. Peterborough at all.

"The dress. She's clearly only got the one. What are you going to do about it?"

"What do you *suggest?*"

"I'm asking you," his ex-housekeeper said calmly as she broke off a piece of scone and popped it into her nearly toothless mouth.

Michael narrowed his eyes at the woman. She'd known him his entire life and was at least as familiar with his shortcomings as he was. "You are perfectly aware that I am not a man who has ever involved himself in a lady's wardrobe."

"Are you going to start?"

"Mary," he almost hissed, keeping one eye on the door lest Letty interrupt this conversation which he expected would embarrass her more than he was being embarrassed already. "Dammit, suggest something or don't. I have no clever thoughts about how to improve a lady's wardrobe without making a most improper suggestion. A man buys dresses for his mistress, not for a houseguest."

"Does he." Mrs. Peterborough looked extremely interested in this information, her grooved forehead raised in positive astonishment.

"I have always liked you. Please do not disprove my estimation of you now."

She chewed and regarded him thoughtfully. He sat back in his chair, waving a hand toward her as if to indicate that if she wished to pronounce further, the time was now.

"Yes, I can do something," Mrs. Peterborough said just as Letty finally appeared, clean as the morning with her hair pinned back— God, Michael wanted to see that hair flying free and *that* was not a helpful thought when he had to stand to acknowledge her presence.

"Good morning," Letty told the room in general, her ears pinkening a bit. Perfect, now she could not look at him either. He definitely should stop looking at her. Or sit down. Sitting down would solve at least one of his immediate problems.

"Good morning, Miss Stapleton," he said as he settled himself.

"I'm so glad you're here," said Mrs. Peterborough, pouring Letty a cup of tea. "I was just boring Sir Michael with the story of how my great-granddaughter has outgrown a few of her day dresses before they've had time to wear out, and I don't know what to do with them. I don't suppose you're handy with a needle, Miss Stapleton. Even though she's a few years younger, I think the dresses might have to be taken in a bit to be your size."

"What a lovely thought, Mrs. Peterborough! But I'm afraid I'm terrible with a needle and thread. I'm sure she can find a good home for them." Letty looked by turns excited, then regretful, then resigned. What a terrible liar she would be, Michael thought.

"No, I think I've already found the home I like for them—we'll send back down to my house for them after breakfast and see if one or two of them might not suit you."

"Won't she miss them, your granddaughter?" Letty looked simultaneously excited and a bit worried over depriving someone else of a needed dress.

"Not at all," Mrs. Peterborough raised an insouciant, bony shoulder. "She is making a bit of a new wardrobe with some money that a rich relative left her as a wedding trousseau. Right, Sir Michael?"

"Is that right?" And then when Mrs Peterborough's eyes bored into him and he realized he was the rich "relative" who would be funding the trousseau and thereby gaining a second-hand wardrobe via proxy, "Oh yes, that's right, that's what you said."

"That's what I thought I said," said Mrs. Peterborough, stirring her tea.

* * *

"You are not trying at all."

Michael looked over to where Letty stood on the other side of the small paddock, her dirty boots clearly visible under the short hem of

43

that damn dress, her face with a few more freckles today, he thought, even given the brim of the bonnet she wore.

Maggie stood opposite both of them, nosing at what was left of the grass on the ground among hoof gouges and, here and there, the evidence of a horse's occupation in the paddock all. Day. Long.

"Well then we are at opposites, because I find you very trying indeed," Michael bit out.

"I must have shown you ten times the difference between stand and walk. It's not as though they are the same thing."

"Miss Stapleton, how many weeks did it take you to teach Maggie to understand your hand signals in the first place?"

Letty clamped her jaw shut to keep back a sharp answer about Maggie learning more quickly than Sir Michael.

"And why the devil didn't you just teach her to follow spoken commands?"

"Why on earth would I want to speak to her out loud where anyone could hear me?"

He seemed stumped by that one, Letty thought.

Michael did not like these glimpses of her life at home that Letty betrayed when speaking about her horse. He didn't know what sort of a house trained a person to be silent. He couldn't imagine Letty staying very silent, but he found himself hating the idea when he did try to imagine it.

Balancing on his one foot using his crutches, Michael looked sweaty and tired.

She must have lost track of the passage of time, Letty realized.

Or perhaps she just wasn't used to passing the day with human beings, she thought wryly to herself.

"My apologies, Miss Stapleton. I did not mean to swear in the company of a lady."

"Don't be silly. We both know I'm not a lady."

This, *this* was why Letty didn't trust herself to speak out loud. She was terrible at it. Now she'd embarrassed them both and thrown his apology back in his face; plus she now needed to make an apology of her own. People were terrible. She much preferred her horse.

His horse.

"I apologize again," he said more softly, so softly she could barely hear him across the paddock, "if I have given you the impression that I think of you as anything other than a lady."

She picked her way toward him through the clods of upturned grassy earth, and piles of horse manure.

"Sir Michael," Letty said heavily, "I did not mean to cast aspersions on your manners. I have no way of measuring anyone's manners when my own are so sorely lacking."

He smiled down at her. When he stood next to her like this, it was clear how much taller than her he was. She should try to make a point of standing farther away. Plus up close she could see the curve of the corner of his mouth, where farther away she might not have even noticed such a bare beginning of a smile. And she could see his earlobe. It seemed to call out to her, that earlobe.

He said, "If the title is oppressive for you, you can always call me Lieutenant Grantley instead. I suspect I will still answer to it."

Letty just shook her head. "You see, this is exactly what I mean. I should call you Sir Michael in public, which also includes over breakfast with Mrs. Peterborough. You ask me to call you Lieutenant Grantley when we are alone, but we should not even *be* alone."

Maggie snorted, and tossed her head.

Which made Letty laugh. "Sorry, you're right, we are not completely alone," she called to the horse.

When she looked back at Michael she had to look up yet farther, as he was a step closer. How had he moved so silently on crutches?

He was looking intently down at her. "When we are this alone, I would enjoy it if you called me simply Michael."

She just shook her head, hoping he couldn't see how his nearness made her breathing speed up. What an inconvenient side-effect. "I will not be so forward as to call you Michael."

"I called you Letitia last night."

Desperately Letty hoped that the shiver she felt in her spine at the tone of his voice didn't show.

"No one calls me Letitia," she said, giving him what she hoped was a quelling look as she craned her head up to see past the brim of her bonnet.

Instead of being quelled, he just looked pleased. "I very much like the idea of being the only person to be so privileged."

She wanted to stomp her boots, but it didn't feel like the ladylike image she was *trying* to project. For however much good it was doing her. "I'm not trying to give you special privileges."

Michael looked at her thoughtfully, the dark green of his eyes very clearly running over every inch of her. She felt that look shivering through her in the tops of her shoulders, in her elbows for heaven's sake, and down to her wrists where her hands twitched as though if she didn't stop them they would do... something.

Michael's tone shifted a bit, as if he were telling her something privately in a drawing room rather than standing in a horse paddock. He said quite calmly, "Some men like the idea of taking special privileges rather than waiting for them to be given."

Letty felt her mouth open. She clicked it shut. But she couldn't take her eyes away from his, fixed on her.

"I have always thought of myself as a gentleman. Indeed I would like to go on thinking of myself as a gentleman. But I've just discovered the appeal of the thought that, for instance, if I snagged the side of your skirt, or the corner of your sleeve, and backed up enough to lean against this fence here, I could comfortably pull you into my arms and you would—well, there would be nothing you could do about it at all."

Letty felt the flush in her face but this time she felt it was called for. "That is... a despicable thought."

"Isn't it." Michael nodded, and tore his eyes away from hers to look out over the rolling greens that sloped downward from Roseford to the stable and beyond to the edge of the small wood that was the rest of his property. Hardly primitive, his woods, but a good deal more wild and less civilized than the house. Both had come with the title. He had not thought about the contrast before. "I would shoot in an instant any man who would so take advantage of a woman without her willingness, so it is an uncomfortable feeling to have, and an even more uncomfortable feeling to admit. And yet, since you are the person about whom I had the feeling, I seem compelled to share it with you. Which is also odd, don't you think?"

"Is it a—do you mean to warn me?"

When he looked down again at her his face looked much older. "Letitia, I barely know what I'm saying at all."

It seemed to Letty that the appropriate tactic here was to take a step back, both physically—which she did—and mentally. "When you say things like that, it seems to me that you must have spent little time among ladies your own age."

That seemed to amuse him. "What makes you say that?"

"If you had, this wouldn't be the first time you had such thoughts, that's all."

That made him laugh outright. He swung himself over to the gate and let himself through. "You are determined to give yourself no credit for inspiring such thoughts at all?"

She followed him out. "We've agreed that it was a despicable thought. Why would I want to give myself credit for inspiring that?"

He inclined his head in agreement, and they smiled at each other, as if arriving at a shared joke, and that seemed peculiar to her as well. It was as though his sharing the thought was more intimate than if he had actually done it.

Letty wasn't sure that explanation would be clear but she went on, "I am not trying to be rude by refusing to use your given name alone. It is a lovely name, Michael. It would be too much of a liberty to use it with someone that I barely know."

He nodded, looking down at her boots. "And how do you feel about Letitia?"

"I feel I barely know her either."

Chuckling, Michael raised one hand and gave the signal for Come to where Maggie still stood shifting her feet slightly in the paddock.

And on cue, the horse stepped her way through to where the two of them stood in the open gate.

Maggie's demonstration of trust made it that much more difficult for Letty to keep her distance, Letty mused as they strolled back to the stable, man swinging on his crutches, she keeping up with him, horse following placidly behind. If Maggie trusted the man, Letty felt like she ought to trust him herself. But he'd just explained why she should not.

Why was she so determined to keep ignoring such good advice, she wondered.

CHAPTER 5

HE WAS A SCOUNDREL, Michael told himself as he swung himself out of the bathtub that evening.

He'd attended school with young men who'd been very used to being bathed and dried by footmen and valets, but Michael hadn't liked it then and he still didn't. He'd placed a few of Mr. Cullen's handrails near the tub, drilled into his great-grandfather's oaken floors so that he could lean his weight against their wrought iron strength and dry himself, then swing himself into the chair where he could shave, in front of the washstand mirror.

He couldn't seem to stop himself from accosting the poor girl, day in and day out. This was really beyond the pale. What was wrong with him that he had so forgotten his manners? Or had it been so long since he had enjoyed female companionship that his brain along with the rest of him just threw civilization to the winds and behaved like a bull in heat every time that woman stood next to him?

He knew exactly what the situation was. She was essentially an orphan foundling, with no protector, landing on his doorstep through the inauspicious offices of delivering to him her last possession in the world—of which he'd cheerfully deprived her. He frowned at his image in the silvered glass.

And whenever he was alone with her he ended up—what would he call it? Propositioning her? Nothing so crude—yet—but if he kept on this way he was going to be called out to fight a duel at dawn with that groomsman of hers, not to mention despising himself. If he was honest, even Mrs. Peterborough would undoubtedly find a way to make him pay should she discover how he was behaving. And if anyone had given him his lack of respect for precedent, it wasn't his parents, it was Mrs. Peterborough.

Mrs. Peterborough had not just kept this house, she had raised him as much as any woman had since his mother died. And if his mother were here...

Sighing, Michael closed his eyes and pictured her. Tall and willowy and elegant, physically anyone would have said she was the opposite of Letty Stapleton, but in his dimming boyish memories Michael found some similarities between the two of them. He remembered her being practical. She'd found a kettle in which he could keep his tiny frogs when he insisted on bringing them into the house. He remembered her disguising with jam and sugar where he'd taken a handful out of a cake she had baked for his sixth birthday celebration, carefully cutting the slice herself at the table so that he himself would get the part he'd already desecrated. He remembered her calmly telling him to put on his jacket, which disguised how he had destroyed his shirt wrestling with the boys in the neighborhood over some random thing. His father had not seen.

What had they been fighting about? Michael wondered to himself as he scraped away the stabbing bristles along his jaw. He didn't even remember now. Something that had seemed violently urgent to his twelve-year-old self, something that had sent him into a white-hot rage that he had never felt before. He hadn't been able to explain it to her, either, when she'd asked him about it. She'd just shaken her head and looked disappointed, and he'd felt ashamed that he'd let his emotions get the better of him that way.

His father had never known about that fight. Michael wondered what she had done with the torn shirt.

The previous baronet of Roseford had been so much older when he had met his lady, as he had always described it to Michael, that he had already learned to take life calmly by the time Michael came along. Michael couldn't ever remember his father losing his temper. He wondered if he ever had.

He wished he could ask him.

He turned to the task of dressing himself. He had a system for his linens, for lying on the bed to get himself into his breeches, for balancing against the bar to tuck in his shirt. Looking at the rumpled knot of fabric bunched up in a knot at the bottom of his right leg, he wondered if he should ask Mrs. Peterborough to have the seamstress take up his trousers while she was in residence.

It was not as though his leg would be growing back.

It occurred to Michael again that he could barely understand what he had been doing in the last year since he had been injured. He remembered the war, vividly. He remembered his anger watching the death of one friend after another, he remembered the heat and the insects crawling on his bread and he remembered waking up on a makeshift table belowdecks and seeing his foot, shredded till the bones showed through what was left of the skin, in a bucket on the floor, and he knew what he would see when he looked down his leg. He remembered the shell blast exploding next to him. He had not expected to wake up. So waking up at all, even missing part of a leg, had been a pleasant surprise.

He couldn't explain his peculiar calm about his leg to the nurses who were in charge of chivvying the wounded back to the transport ships for passage home. And it wasn't as though the pain hadn't been excruciating. He could never have imagined the fiery pains his foot gave him even when it was no longer there, the furious frustration of simply trying to go to the privy in the middle of the night when he no longer had two feet to carry him there. But it had not changed his fundamental happiness to have survived.

Michael didn't blame his fellow sailors their confusion, their hope-lessness, or their rage. Few of them would be returning to a home with the money he had to outfit himself with the new types of comforts he required. Few of them were as lucky as he was. Because that was still how he felt. Lucky.

He was lucky that he had this estate, though he wished his father had not died while he himself was still on campaign. His father had never questioned his desire to set sail even though he was his father's only heir. His father had been proud of him. Michael didn't know what his father would have said about his injury.

Michael looked down at the stump, a bit uneven where they had cut through the muscle and severed the tendons, leaving it a bit lumpy around the shin bones, front and side. It was not pretty. He was grateful that he had been unconscious during the surgery from the shell concussion; many of the men he knew had not been. And he was grateful that the latest methods of surgery, letting the stump heal in bandages rather than sewing it up in a flap of skin, had been employed by the physician whose face he couldn't even remember. Though that had been partly responsible for the ungodly amount of pain he'd had for months after he'd awoken, it was also undoubtedly responsible for the fact that he had not died of infection as many others had whose amputations had taken place at the hands of less capable surgeons.

Lucky. He was lucky.

He *felt* lucky.

So why could he not behave like the Michael Grantley of old, the fellow of his youth who could be pleasant enough to young ladies but mostly left them alone, as he had nothing pretty to say to them and found that they had nothing of substance to say to him. Why could he not focus on how to ride that mare, and leave alone—

Leave alone Letty, who was certainly not his to ride.

He wiped away the last of the foam on his chin, cleaned the straight edge of the razor. Perhaps he had simply reached the age where he needed a woman. His father had not married his mother till he was nearly fifty. Michael had expected, for some reason, that he would follow in those footsteps. But maybe he was not that much like his father before him. Maybe now, at the tender age of twenty-seven, he was more in need of feminine companionship than his father had been.

Or maybe he just needed physical relief.

His last encounter with a woman had been before his deployment, a charming young actress who was well versed in the use of the French letters he brought to the encounter and no more interested in unwanted children, or diseases, than he had been. He supposed he should also count the French courtesan who had brought him to completion using only her hands—twice, in fact, talented lady that she was, though he couldn't bring himself to visit her again. His ship had moved on, and he simply could not bear the sound of the French language while naked and vulnerable; it made him feel as though bombshells were about to fall.

That was likely what was making him so badly behaved around Letty. She was pretty and sweet and there, and that damned French groomsman of hers had put his nerves on edge, and he needed female companionship. That was all.

He could still be the old Michael Grantley, not particularly interested in women, while still keeping an eye open for an available one. One for the moment, perhaps. It would be unconscionably immoral to so take advantage of Letty. The one for the rest of his life could wait. His lady, as his father had put it. He was his father's son, and he was baronet of Roseford, after all. He would get married and get an heir as his forebears had done. Letty, the daughter of a neighborhood thief, wouldn't do for that role either. Basically he needed to leave Letty alone.

He liked the idea of looking for a lady for Roseford. Someone to run the household and civilize the place, as his mother had done. His father would have approved. Perhaps it was time after all. At least to start the search.

His eye caught again on the ridge of reddened and smooth scars that twisted along the edge of the stump of his leg.

If the right woman for him was out there, he hoped he was lucky enough to find her.

"Don't bring any flowers to trim it, Sarah. I will look like a cake."

Letty twisted to see herself in gilt-edged mirror. She had never lived with a mirror before, and she wasn't sure she liked it. It showed her exactly what she knew were all of her faults: her shortness, her roundness, her flyaway hair and pale freckled skin and the way she scowled at herself.

The pink linen dress was a bit rumpled, especially around the bottom where Sarah had simply shortened it with pins. There had not been time yet to engage a seamstress but Sarah had had the dress washed and pressed by the time Letty was ready for a bath, and Letty had to admit it fit her better than Mrs. Peterborough had led her to think. She must not be that much smaller than the ex-housekeeper's great-granddaughter, at least in no way other than height.

It fit and it was fresh. It only had one shortcoming.

"It's pink. And so am I. It blends into me so that I look like one large iced cake. A pink one."

Sarah's fingertip tapped on her lip as though she found this observation tough to deny.

"It's true that I might just be that glad to see you out of that green dress, miss."

This was also tough to gainsay. Letty sighed. "No more than I, Sarah, surely."

Sarah's dark eyes lit up. "All right, trust me then. I've a thought."

While Sarah was gone, Letty applied herself to more brushstrokes to her hair. Occasionally, on sunny days, it could be made to lie down as others' did; but brushstrokes would help to smooth it out. She simply seldom had the patience for it.

She wasn't trying to look particularly nice for the fellow who had said such shocking things to her in the paddock that afternoon, she was not. She was only glad to have a new dress. Letty repeated that to herself with each stroke of the brush.

She had to keep repeating it… because she knew it was not true.

Sarah reappeared and tiptoed up behind Letty's reflection, smiling as though she had a wonderful secret.

And she held out her hand.

There, winking in her palm, was a brooch, a jeweled brooch—Letty had never seen anything like it.

"Those are rubies making up the kernels of corn, miss, with diamonds on the leaves. I remember once Mrs. Peterborough saying when she was cleaning them that her ladyship had liked to have one single thing that wasn't covered in blasted roses."

Startled, Letty laughed out loud. Sarah covered her own mouth, as though her curse had surprised her. Then Sarah laughed too.

"I suppose if one were the lady of Roseford one would get a right lot of rose-covered things, wouldn't you."

Letty looked at the brooch. The edges of the jewels sparkled when Sarah turned it in the light, the color of the rubies just the same as a fat cherry in jam, or a fresh apple.

"I would need Sir Michael's permission to wear that," Letty said firmly, taking the brooch in hand. "But you're right, Sarah, you have the eye. Color and contrast, that's what I needed."

She ran down the stairs only to find Michael was just rolling himself out of his own rooms toward the dining room.

Letty pulled herself up short.

He grinned.

Flustered by the grin, Letty just stuck her hand out. "Sarah thought I should borrow this."

Michael's grin faded as he regarded the glittering jewel in Letty's palm.

She faltered. It had seemed an acceptable idea, but the look on Michael's face seemed anything but pleased, or even acceptable.

He rolled up to her and took the pin from her hand.

"It's not tarnished," he observed, more to himself than her.

"Apparently Mrs. Peterborough has been taking care of it."

"Indeed. Mrs. Peterborough is earning her pension."

"Or as I call it, working," said that woman as she joined them in the hall, supporting herself on a thick cane as her feet shuffled painfully along the bare floors. "Put the carpet back in my room, Michael."

"Of course," he said, but he didn't look at her. He was looking at Letty, and not smiling.

Mrs. Peterborough drew close enough to see what was in his hand. "Oh, good idea. That should get some use."

A small V drew his brows together as Michael leaned forward and slid the pin of the brooch through the fabric of Letty's gown, arranging the jewels so they just edged the neckline of her gown on one side. She forgot to breathe as the back of his fingertips slid under the edge of the fabric, then back out.

Mrs. Peterborough apparently had nothing further to say, only continuing her slow shuffle toward the dining room. Michael's brow remained furrowed, and Letty wished that she had not followed on with Sarah's idea after all.

* * *

DINNER WAS STRAINED, with most of the conversation consisting of Mrs. Peterborough's complaints about the food, the drafts on the floor, her aching joints, the poor quality of meat these days, the fact that Mrs. Dunphy refused to take her advice about sugaring the strawberries, and her own inability to sleep through the night.

"When I can't sleep I get up and see what else I can find to do," Letty observed in between bites of her dinner.

"I wonder what work you think I should be doing," Mrs. Peterborough asked her, a bit acidly though also with her face down so only Michael could see her hide a smile.

"Oh dear! My sincere apologies! Of course I did not mean to suggest that you should," Letty immediately spluttered, her face turning bright pink. "I only meant—"

"What kind of work do you do in the middle of the night, then?" said Mrs. Peterborough, by way of, perhaps, rescuing Letty from herself.

"Anything. In the kitchen, in the garden, in the laundry. I feel like I should be working more here," she said, turning to face Michael, who was still looking somewhat bemused in his chair.

"Do you?" he asked, his eyes still focused on something else.

"Yes. I'll start tomorrow."

"We did quite a lot of work with the horse today," Michael observed.

"With Maggie."

"What horse did you think I meant?"

"As with people, Sir Michael, unless you refer to them by name your reference is not always clear. Have you no other horses?"

His brow furrowed again. "That completely unworkable stallion that Griggs bought for me, and the mare that turned out to be disappointingly stupid—have you not, as you say, made their introduction, Miss Stapleton?"

"Not at all! We should visit them this evening when I say goodnight to Maggie."

"Or tomorrow." Michael still seemed distracted. "Tomorrow is soon enough."

Letty was about to query his lordship regarding whether he now also objected to her saying goodnight to her horse, when Griggs appeared in the doorway unexpectedly.

"Sir, the vicar is here."

Letty looked to Michael to see how she should greet this news. He looked faintly horrified and moreover he was looking at *her*.

"Invite him in and see if you can find another place for him, Griggs," Michael said, sounding strained.

The vicar, when he appeared in the doorway, was roundish and reddish and seemed assured of a welcome until he caught sight of his host's face.

Michael stood to greet him, even as Griggs placed another chair between Michael and Mrs. Peterborough at the small round table around which they were seated.

"Do come in and share our meal, Mr. Herrings," said Michael, gesturing to the chair.

"My deepest apologies, Sir Michael. I had no idea you were dining, and with company."

"All the more reason to share your presence with us all."

But his face didn't match the words.

"Please be seated," said Mr. Herrings, waving his host back but

Michael was already settling himself. "I should not have disturbed you at this hour. I am returning from a bedside in Pattesham this evening; I'm happy to say I left everyone there alive and well, by the graces of God. I thought you were maintaining a bachelor lifestyle and thought I would pay a visit on my way back into the village; I missed you at services this morning."

"Of course," said Michael, nodding toward where Letty was trying to become invisible in her seat. "This is Miss Stapleton, a distant relative who has delivered me a horse her father was kind enough to sell me. It is my oversight that I have been enjoying her fortuitous visit and failed to bring both of us to the services this morning. Miss Stapleton, Mr. Herrings."

"I am pleased to make your acquaintance," Letty said with a smile, and left it at that, not sure how to proceed with conversation since she had suddenly become a distant cousin and her father suddenly a doer of good deeds.

Also since apparently she had kept his lordship working through the day of rest. What an appalling lack of good sense.

"And I yours. What an unexpected pleasure. It in no way excuses my interruption of your meal, but hopefully you will forgive my exploitation of my luck."

"We are glad for the company, of course," Letty thought it seemed safe to observe.

"You're in, Herrings, settle yourself. You're just in time for the lamb stew." Mrs. Peterborough seemed no more inclined to extend herself than ever.

The vicar exclaimed so profusely over the lamb stew that Letty readily believed that, as he said several times, it was his favorite dish. She believed it so readily that she began to wonder if some servant had been bribed to tell Mr. Herrings when it was to be served, or that perhaps the smell of it had simply brought him in as he was passing by on the road. Which was fairly distant from the house.

"And I would have been that much less inclined to impose had I known that you were already dining with your company here in the breakfast room."

"Is this not the dining room?" Letty asked Michael, who was looking less and less pleased.

"No," said the baronet, still distracted but with enough presence of mind to explain, "The formal dining room is quite long and I have not had need of it."

Mr. Herrings scraped his bowl. "I do not wish to crowd you."

At this Michael turned his expression toward the vicar. "If you feel that you are crowding us, Mr. Herrings, feel free to give up the space you have taken."

This caused Mrs. Peterborough to give Michael a sharp look, but the vicar only smiled. "Quite right you are, sir, and quite right to say it! You have been too kind to share your dinner with me—" Letty noticed the generous portion of lamb stew was already gone, "—allow me to return the favor. Please come and take dinner with me Saturday evening, there will be a small group, and they will be so pleased to know that you have returned to society since your recovery."

"Thank you," said Michael with the same distracted air.

"Thank *you*," said Mr. Herrings, standing and bowing all around, indiscriminately in every direction as though he wanted to be sure to catch even people he might not immediately see. "All of you are welcome, I would be most disappointed if you could not join us, Miss Stapleton, Mrs. Peterborough, my apologies for the interruption again, and Griggs I'll have my hat."

After he had left a silence fell around the table. Letty had no idea what sort of aftermath to expect.

When Griggs returned from showing the gentleman out, his regret was written on his face. "I am clearly out of practice, Sir Michael. I should have intercepted him."

Michael just waved his hand, leaving Griggs to disappear with a sheepish expression on his face.

Michael and Mrs. Peterborough exchanged looks over the dishware.

"If something tragic has occurred, I missed it," Letty finally said. "What could it possibly be?"

Michael didn't meet her eyes. "Mr. Herrings is the biggest gossip in the county. He carries news from village to village like the plague."

"And he found us dining quite appropriately, with myself chaperoning Miss Stapleton," Mrs. Peterborough said stoutly.

"He knows perfectly well you were my housekeeper. Hardly an appropriate chaperone for a young lady. Hardly appropriate even to dine with me. Therefore he also knows that Miss Stapleton is not a lady of the *ton*, and as well is residing under my roof."

"All of which is true," said Letty, spearing another bite of excellent potato. Surely the truth could not be the problem. She had done nothing wrong.

Michael finally met her eyes, and what his expression meant she could not fathom.

He said, "...Miss Stapleton, it was not my intention to compromise you."

"Nor have you!" Letty nearly dropped her fork with shock. Wasn't that the whole point of this chaperone business?

Michael still looked bleak. "There is providing you with company so that you and I remain... appropriately segregated. Then there is the sort of company a young lady requires while visiting a bachelor's home."

Mrs. Peterborough sighed. Which was the first sign that really alarmed Letty; she had yet to see anything, at all, that moved Mrs. Peterborough in any way, beyond really important matters such as the storage of onions.

Mrs. Peterborough said, "A young lady should not *be* visiting the home of a bachelor."

"Ah." Letty put both her hands in her lap, as her appetite faded.

"But don't be angry, Michael," said Mrs. Peterborough, and somehow in the moment of crisis her use of his personal name marked the space including the three of them as even more intimate. "It was smart of you to label Miss Stapleton a distant family member, and I *am* here, and that should be the end of that. Of course you must attend his dinner party."

"I have no intention of attending his dinner party."

"You have no choice at all. If you and Miss Stapleton don't attend, that gossipy old goose will have it from here to kingdom come that you had some mysterious girl hidden away in your house and goodness knows why. And of course they will guess why, goodness or no goodness."

Michael sighed. Letty murmured, "Oh dear."

"How do you like dinner parties, my dear?" said Mrs. Peterborough, and reached across the table to pat Letty's hand reassuringly.

It was the first time the older woman had touched her, and the touch was dry and brief but somehow bracing.

"I've never attended one. This does not sound like a pleasant way to start."

At that Mrs. Peterborough laughed out loud, showing a regrettable lack of teeth but a genuine sense of humor, and even Michael cracked a smile.

CHAPTER 6

THE NEXT MORNING Michael still felt awkward, even as he and Letty walked toward the stable.

"I feel as though I should offer you more entertaining conversation than Mrs. Peterborough tends to provide with her dissertations on potato stacking," he offered a little sheepishly.

She laughed out loud.

"I will disappoint you if I admit that I am interested in her potato stacking insights," Letty told him with a slightly confidential air.

"Not really!"

"Really. I hate when the potatoes rot at the bottom of the bin before they are used. It is not efficient."

"I can be grateful at least that one of us is able to stay alert through her lectures, then."

Letty laughed again. He liked the sound, it reminded him of running water.

She responded, "I thought there might be some rules I should learn about how to provide entertaining conversation for you. You are a baronet, after all."

Michael shook his head. "If there are baronet's conversation rules,

I never learned them. And the type of conversation provided by the Navy would not be appropriate for a lady to learn."

She smiled. "I am not a lady, my lord. Perhaps that is also why I enjoy Mrs. Peterborough's thoughts on housekeeping. I think that is work that would suit me."

"Housekeepers are always married women. It would not be appropriate for an unmarried woman to keep house for a bachelor, for instance. That much I do know."

"Oh." She sounded genuinely disappointed. "Why are there always these awkward barriers to simply doing work?"

Michael felt he could explain at length why she should not keep house for a bachelor like himself without a husband in the picture. "Is getting married such an insuperable obstacle?"

"I don't know anyone I could marry. It's not like picking up a cow at the market, is it? I want one with good breath and good character, please." She shook her head. "Difficult. Awkward."

Against his will Michael barked a laugh. He had known young ladies who enjoyed introducing the topic of marriage when he had been younger, before he had gone into the Navy; they had seemed to think that bringing the topic up might induce him to spontaneously propose. But Letty truly didn't seem to think she was having a suggestive conversation.

In fact, that was rather lowering, Michael thought.

"Have you never met a suitable prospective husband?" he asked gruffly while unlatching the stable door.

"The only unmarried men in the village where I grew up were the vicar, who was at least seventy years of age, the blacksmith's son, who cut off my braids when I was ten and he was eight, and a wheelwright who was nearly my father's age and had six children left him when his wife died. The wheelwright moved away last year."

"Bad luck! In that field I would have given him good odds."

She threw him a look that said he had better be joking as she preceded him into Maggie's stall. Maggie snorted, greeting them; Letty patted her shoulder. "Fortunately my father owed him quite a bit of money and my job was to avoid him rather than court him."

"He didn't court you?"

"As I said, Sir Michael. There is the unpopularity that comes from owing people money."

Even with the title, he liked the way she said his name. "Still, I imagine men tend to do the courting."

"Really?" She grinned at him over Maggie's back. "So you are saying that at this dinner party next Saturday, there won't be many local young ladies courting the local baronet?"

Michael grunted. She had him there. There would be. It was certainly a good reason to avoid these things. Plus now they would all be ogling at Letty and angling for gossip about her.

Gossip, in Michael's experience, was seldom productive for anyone. Inefficient, in fact.

"What about Anthony?"

"What about Anthony? Oh, you mean as a marriageable young man?" She looked up at him, eyes wide as if the thought had never occurred to her. "You betray that you are an only child, sir. When two people have grown up in the same house they may irritate one another, finish each other's sentences, or depend on one another, but I can't imagine them falling in love."

"You imagine falling in love must necessarily precede marriage."

"No, I suppose not. But if I were going to do something as unimaginable as marrying Anthony it would have to be because I had fallen in love with him." She dimpled at him as she ran a comb through Maggie's mane. "Which I have not."

Michael was finding this whole conversation both interesting and dissatisfying, and he was not sure why. He liked Letty. She was a very attractive armful of a young woman. It was pleasant to contemplate that she had no suitors. But it also seemed wrong somehow. The whole idea of marriage seemed never to have occurred to her at all.

"Anthony has always been excruciatingly proper in public," Letty went on. "He makes a great deal of the fact that my mother was the daughter of an earl and that he has been entrusted with working in our stable."

"Was she?" Michael knew he looked surprised; he *was* surprised.

Her expression just made her look older. "There is lineage, my lord, and then there's being the daughter of a thief."

'I imagine that would dampen marriage prospects."

"Slightly."

"Still, I'm glad you've come away from that village, in case the blacksmith's son with the hair-hacking habits develops other plans."

That made her burst out laughing and he had to join her.

* * *

THE STABLEBOY JIM brought over the saddle and its pad, and at Michael's nod began to saddle Maggie.

"This is another one of my orders from Mr. Cullen. We need to get Maggie used to it. Tell me what you think."

Letty expected the lone left stirrup. On the right there had been fitted a leather cup on an extension that led downward from the seat, all the leather beautifully broken in and weathered.

"Have you tried it yet?" She ran her fingers over the addition.

"No."

"Have you ever ridden bareback?"

"Yes. I have the same thought as you. I'm not sure how useful the one stirrup will be and she might just find it too off-putting if I can post on one side but not the other. On the right, posting in that will not feel like posting to her."

Letty nodded. "This will help you hold your right knee against her body but there will still be an absence of the lower leg on that side."

"Which will also be my problem," Michael admitted.

"Well, sir, if you ever aspired to perfect your balance, you may get your chance," she grinned at him and went to take Maggie's reins. "Let's try this first."

"I can lead the horse," he said gruffly, twining the reins through his fingers before gripping his crutch.

"As you wish." She followed them out, rather sad that Maggie was not saddled for her... might never be saddled for her again.

"Do you think," she said as she followed man and horse around to the mounting block, "that a woman would have to be married to work in a household as a horse trainer?"

Michael stopped, giving her an odd look. He said, "I'm trying to think of a polite way to explain all the ways in which any woman with any work to do who isn't married is in a precarious position at best, a compromising position at worst."

"How irritating," muttered Letty, scowling.

"Or maybe Mrs. Peterborough could explain it better. Amongst the potato-stacking instructions."

That made her laugh. Fortunately, Michael mused, it was easy to flip her from irritated to laughing.

"Now you are teasing me. But you know I have a serious problem. I clearly don't have a husband, and I clearly do need to find suitable work."

Most young ladies would focus on the husband, he should point out, but Michael kept that thought to himself.

Letty went on, "I need you and Maggie to be brilliant at this so that I can convince others to take me on as a horse trainer in just such circumstances."

The country was full of one-legged ex-sailors, Michael had to admit to himself, and plenty of them could afford horses; there ought to be a market.

The husband problem still looming, Michael chose to avoid it for the moment and instead said slowly, "There is a marquess who owns very large stables, not too far from here; we are not intimate but we know one another. He is known, I believe, for raising horses for ladies to ride that are as gentle as any pony, but are quite rare thoroughbreds. He also breeds racehorses, but his stables occur to me because of the other."

Michael walked Maggie into position in front of the block, tossed the reins across her neck. She stood.

He crutched around to the steps. "Let me write to him and see what he says when I tell him I have discovered a talented horse trainer in our neighborhood."

"Oh! That would be—" Bouncing on her toes, Letty seemed to do a little dance around his crutches as he handed them to her, even the one that was draped with his coat.

"If that's amenable to you," Michael teased as he swung himself up.

Letty held her breath as Michael leaned over the saddle, one fist holding on to Maggie's mane, and swung his right leg over, pulling himself on to her back.

Maggie didn't move as he shifted about. She huffed out a breath, as if to say that she knew perfectly well he was doing something, but she did not even shift her feet.

Michael slipped his left foot naturally into the stirrup. Thus situated he could pull himself up a bit and settle the stump in the leather cuff, held quite comfortably against the horse's side almost as if he had a full leg to settle against her girth.

"Oh, *perfect!*" And at this Letty had to dart around to Maggie's nose and tell her what a good girl she was, what a perfect horse, and so well behaved.

And Michael, feeling the stretch in his thighs after so many months away from the saddle but looking at the world from a much accustomed position that he had worried that he had lost forever, could not but agree with her.

* * *

"It's hopeless."

Michael swung himself down from the ropes using the handrails, and had only taken one crutch from Letty's waiting hands to swing only a step or two away and then collapse on the cool grass.

Letty dropped his coat on his stomach quite unceremoniously, then plopped herself down on the grass next to him.

"Hopeless might be too strong a word," she said but her dubious tone said that on the other hand, it might not.

Maggie had spent at least two hours walking in circles.

Michael's thighs were aching and his frustrations had peaked at least twenty minutes ago. "Hopeless."

"No, no. Do you think when you learned to walk you perfected it in a day? Maggie is only doing what she knows to do, yielding to the pressure of the leg she can feel in the correct position. Of course she would, why wouldn't she?"

Various curses were ringing in Michael's head and he did not intend to share them. But he was tired of learning things over and over again that other men had mastered while still babes. The damned leg was forever going to be throwing up barriers, he could see that now. One problem after another, and for what?

It was not *efficient*, he snarled at himself in his head.

Letty was watching Maggie crop placidly at the grass. Of all of them, she had to admit, Maggie looked the least exhausted. She had an infinite supply of patience, that horse. If the human wanted to walk around in circles forever, then by all that was holy, she would walk around in circles forever.

"I think we have to take off the stirrup."

"Oh, do you?"

Letty looked down at Michael's sweating, angry face. "I have not seen you sarcastic before, sir."

"Does it not increase my lordly appeal?"

"I don't know what that might be, but I daresay even without knowing what a lordly appeal should look like, I think that it does not."

Michael sighed and closed his eyes.

She let him lie there for a moment, then one of her hands covered his and she said softly, "Don't be discouraged, Michael, truly. It is only the first day."

He opened his eyes and looked up at her where she sat by his side. Even the sky was gray to match his mood, but she still had her sunny hair and sunny smile, and they eased something in his chest.

He said, "If you are using my given name to appease my bad mood, it is working."

She gave him that dimpled smile and said, "I think a teacher may be allowed to so address a pupil, and on this I am the teacher."

He nodded. She was right. He knew how to ride a horse. But it was reassuring to have her there while he found the way to ride again, knowing that she knew Maggie and would translate between the two of them. It was only one day. And they had made progress. He ached in places he had forgotten he *could* ache. He was disappointed, but it had not been a bad first day.

Slowly he smiled. "I mounted a horse."

Letty smiled back. "You did."

And for today, that was enough.

* * *

THE HOUSE WAS EMPTY.

Even from the road it was clear the house was uninhabited, clover growing in the cracks of a walk where no one had passed for several days, and the windows dark and shuttered.

But the little shadow of a man did not enter from the road, because it was not his habit.

He circled around to the back, unlocking the servant's door with the key from his pocket and checking behind the door before closing it again.

Charles F. Stapleton had a habit of checking behind doors because he had accumulated a list of people who might well want to spring at him from behind those doors, and his life to date had persisted in being a free and easy one because he had made a habit of checking behind the doors before people sprung at him, not after.

The sun was going down and it was dark inside the shuttered house, but he felt around for a candle in the kitchen without opening the shutters. There was no fire, though, and no coals, so he had no way to light it.

Inconvenient.

He wondered where Letty was. Usually she at least had a small fire banked in the kitchen, even when there was nothing in the pantry to eat, waiting for her father to come home.

Though it was summer. And he had not been home for a long, long time.

He hung his coat across one of the remaining chairs, and took his time examining all the rooms upstairs, which looked quite bare without furniture—only two beds remaining, he noted, one in each of the rooms at the ends of the upper hall—and all the rooms downstairs.

He would have to go out to the stable to be sure—Anthony might be out there—but it very much seemed that Letty was entirely gone.

This was not something that Charles F. Stapleton had expected. He was a flexible man, understanding that, in a world where there were so many people angry with him, to say the least, he had to take things as he found them or he would soon be even more disappointed with the world than he often was. Silver coins rather than gold, bread rather than mutton, whores rather than ladies; he had given in to slightly declining standards as the years had progressed, knowing that he would not like where the progression ended but having from time to time not as many choices as he would like.

But not finding his daughter at home, that he had not expected. It wasn't simply a lowered standard; it was a massive loss and one that would have to be dealt with.

First there were more prosaic questions of drink and food and sleep. He knew better than to go out looking for any of those things at the local village inn; the least of his problems there would be the lack of welcome. No, he needed to stay indoors and preferably unseen, and to that end he would stay in the house, which was some distance from the village proper, and take care where and when he lit a fire.

But finding Letty was necessary, and Charles rearranged his nearest goals somewhat as he slipped out back again to find himself some water.

CHAPTER 7

MICHAEL WHEELED into the drawing room.

Letty, seated on the sofa, was stabbing something in her hands with a needle over and over. She had that scowl on her face, the one that made him want to laugh.

"Murdering needlework, Miss Stapleton?"

She turned the scowl on him. "Mrs. Peterborough pointed out that if I spent as much time practicing embroidery as I spent practicing maneuvers with my horse, I would be an expert needlewoman by now."

"Undoubtedly accurate," said Michael, wheeling up to the large wing chair with ornate feet in which he usually sat.

"Impolitic. Possibly even uncivil."

"But accurate," Michael said before reaching over to the chair's back and swinging himself into it. It was a heavy piece, one of a set fortuitously acquired by some ancestor, a set that was now scattered through the main rooms; it did not move when he shifted his weight to it.

He had avoided having Letty see him climb in and out of chairs; it was ungainly work, and he felt awkward at it. But she ignored it, including not asking if she could help, which relaxed him tremendously.

He waved the letters he had clutched in his hand, now a bit rumpled after his maneuvers but still there. "Forgive my rudeness if I leave you to your needlework. I had planned to finish reading these, so I can more quickly compose responses tomorrow."

"Why don't you engage a secretary for all this correspondence?" Letty stabbed the embroidery piece again. "You seem to find it tiresome."

"My father did not have a secretary." Nor, Michael admitted to himself, had he thought of it, probably precisely because his father had not already done it.

"Your father was a much older man with different interests, was he not?"

"Yes, but... he always handled his correspondence himself."

Letty nodded toward Michael's hand. "This many letters?"

"No, there is a flurry at present, I will admit, owing to some business I am conducting with a friend. We served together. When he was discharged, he went on to the Ottoman lands, and arranged with me by correspondence to enter into an importing business with him."

Letty looked up. "That sounds quite interesting."

"It is more interesting than I expected." And quite a good business for a fellow who had lost a leg and couldn't do the foreign end anyway, but could perfectly well hire warehouses and contact merchants here. "But it requires a great deal of letter-writing. My father managed Roseford well but that was all here. He did not conduct so much correspondence."

"So then a secretary might well be needed." She dimpled at him. "It would be efficient."

Michael had entirely lost interest in his letters. Letty looked more shadowed and mysterious in the lamplight, and he wanted to hear her laugh again. He could not figure out why the dimple appearing and disappearing in her cheek was so confounded alluring. As though he had to chase it, and catch it, and trap it, perhaps with his lips...

He was a scoundrel. But he did want to do it.

"I thought it was more efficient to handle it myself."

Letty shook her head. "It is not efficient to pretend that you can do everything. Why don't you hire a man to manage your stable? You have three riding horses, plus carriage horses. Why don't you hire a new housekeeper and let Mrs. Peterborough really retire? Why don't you hire a few more footmen so you don't have to shout all over this enormous house when you want something?"

Because his father hadn't needed them, Michael thought to himself, and if his father hadn't needed them, Michael felt he ought not to need them.

And he had no intention of laying in more staff than he needed just because he had lost part of a leg.

But Letty was going on. "Aren't you going to get married yourself one day? Do you want a potential Lady Roseford to run herself ragged here with no staff to help?"

"We're going to discuss *my* marriage prospects now, are we?"

"My understanding is that they will be a prime topic of conversation at the dinner party on Saturday."

But Michael was not to be distracted by thoughts of the looming dreaded dinner party. He kept his eyes fixed on Letty. "Her title would be Lady Grantley. And hopefully it would be a position that she would wish to fulfill."

Letty's brow furrowed. "Taking the place of stablemen, and footmen, and secretaries?"

"No, taking the place of the lady of the manor. My mother's place."

Letty's fingers slowed. "That would be a very large task to ask any woman to take on, the place of a long-lost, beloved mother."

Michael felt his throat closing up a bit, and a muscle jumped in his jaw. He hadn't thought of it that way. But he had, he knew he had. That was how he pictured the next Lady Grantley: someone to fill the shoes of the last Lady Grantley.

His lady, as his father had always put it, looking so pleased with himself as his mother had seated herself at the table, or in the carriage; always by his side.

Michael couldn't picture any woman sitting next to him and

looking as pleased as his mother had always looked to be next to his father.

"You have a point," he said brusquely, clearing his throat. "I'll consider adding some stablemen, and footmen, at least in the short term. It goes with the horse trainer I've recently acquired."

Letty looked up as if she were going to invite him to elaborate, but he just kept his eyes on hers, his gaze warm and a little amused and somehow also rather wicked, and Letty felt herself turning very pink under that gaze.

Letty swallowed. She knew that he was playing a game with her but she did not want him to stop.

By all rights, she should be awed by Sir Michael. She had never met anyone like him in her life, someone handsome, someone rich, someone titled. She ought to be too tongue-tied to speak.

But to her, Michael looked like all of life's freedoms rolled up into one person. His household seemed to follow protocols, even in a half-hearted way, but he didn't seem to bother. He seemed to embody freedom from worry, and yes, fear. And since she had come here, she had been free of the worry and the fear that she had always felt in her father's house, and she wanted to continue to feel free, as he did. She wanted the freedom to touch him. Whatever faint voices from her past might have intimated that she should not want such things, the truth was that here and now, faced with the reality of him, those masculine shoulders and the warmth of his skin, she *did* want such things. Wanted them very badly.

Her voice was a little husky as she said, "Hopefully you are finding that the horse trainer is fulfilling her position adequately?"

Michael's grin was slow, and said that he was not fooled by her fake insouciance at all. His voice dropped lower when he said, "Are you flirting with me, Letitia?"

Letty felt that shiver go up her spine when he said her name. She knew that she should drop her eyes, and change the topic. But she didn't *want* to. Only a few days of freedom and she had lost her head. But she did not want to pretend right now.

"I've never flirted before, Michael, but I must be doing poorly if you are not sure," she said softly, but kept her eyes on his. "Perhaps if you showed me how."

Her words hit him in the belly, fanning what felt like glowing coals inside him. "It's more traditionally done up close."

"I'm sure people flirt in drawing rooms sitting just like this," she said a little teasingly, but still holding his gaze.

"But the best parts require much closer contact," Michael told her.

Letty felt her heart pounding in her chest. He was encouraging her. And she wanted very much to be encouraged.

With just the hint of a smile she rose, leaving the hated embroidery behind her, and moved closer. She moved slowly. Here is the Letty who is putting down her embroidery; here is the Letty who is very brazenly walking to the end of the settee, within arm's reach of the baronet, and here is the Letty who looks like she is reaching for the settee but instead places her bare hand on the cool linen of his shirt-sleeve, feeling the shifting muscles of his forearm within, where it lay against the edge of the chair.

Did the man never wear a coat?

Feeling just a moment's pang for what was unforgivably ungallant behavior, Michael nonetheless reached up to take her bare hand in his, and drew her into his lap. He did it slowly too, giving her time to resist or change her mind.

But she didn't. Her eyes widened but she came willingly, so perfectly willingly, until she was seated in his lap, his arms around her and pulling her close.

He had been right since the second he saw her. She *was* a delectable armful of a woman.

"I should not do this," Michael couldn't help himself muttering into her hair as he inhaled. She must have bathed; she had shed almost all of her aura of horse, which he found he almost missed. But she smelled warm and sweet; entirely apart from the rose soap he smelled, he could smell *her*.

"But I want you to," Letty whispered back and her arms came up to encircle his neck, her bare fingertips stroking his skin just behind his earlobes.

He felt as though he had caught *fire*.

Michael's hands felt big and warm to Letty and they wandered everywhere, along her arms, her back, even into her hair with a complete lack of shyness. But it was his body that had her transfixed; all that muscle surrounding her on every side. She could feel the way the muscles of his thighs flexed under her thighs, and her cheek pressed against the wall of his chest, where she could hear his heartbeat racing just as fast as hers was.

Thank goodness this wasn't happening to her *alone*, Letty thought a little wildly.

His arms pulled her closer and it felt heavenly, being surrounded by all that warm, hard muscle. Letty had never felt held before; she had never felt so safe.

"This is heavenly," she murmured into the skin at the hollow of his throat.

She could feel him swallow, which was also fascinating.

"What exactly is heavenly, Letitia?" Michael rasped.

"You holding me like this. I am surrounded," she told him, feeling the last of her shyness disappear. After all, he was so close and he smelled so good and this was exactly what she had not known she wanted.

She burrowed closer.

Michael closed his eyes. "Letitia," he said, so softly that the sound would never have traveled but so close to her ear that she could feel every word, "there is a part of me that wants to be the man I was raised to be. And there is a part of me that wants to make you feel heavenly. They are quite opposed. I can't pretend that this isn't exactly what I wanted. But if you don't want me to kiss you, please go back to the divan."

Letty backed up so that they could look each other in the eyes once again. "Why on earth wouldn't I want you to kiss me?"

Groaning, Michael gave up his last battle for the gentlemanly side of behavior and crushed her close.

His mouth teased hers, just as plush and warm as she had expected, but his lips, his teeth, his tongue kept nipping at her lips until, astonished, she opened her mouth and they could taste each other.

Letitia whispered rather triumphantly and mostly to herself, "I knew you would taste good."

Her smug words made Michael stifle a groan against her mouth and he pulled her even closer. She must know now how she is affecting me, he thought a little wildly as she settled, soft and sweet, against the hardest part of him, aching and pressured in his trousers. And then he didn't think at all, because he could feel how he was affecting her.

Letty squirmed a little in his arms, not trying to escape, only trying to burrow closer. Michael could feel the soft heat of her breasts through his clothes and hers, could feel her arms locked surprisingly strongly around his neck and pulling him down so that she could continue to reciprocate as he explored her mouth with his own. She seemed so small in a way, the side of her body curling into his chest, his stomach; she fit perfectly there, but there was still room for his hands to wander. One of her thumbs stroked down the outer curve of his ear and her fingernail scraped his earlobe. Michael knew with certainty that they were both wearing far too many clothes.

"Letitia," he murmured as he slid one hand up the nape of her neck, his fingers sinking into her hair to tilt her head just slightly and fit her against him even more perfectly. He opened his eyes to see her with her eyes closed, flushed with color, lips bright from his kisses and open just a little, waiting for him to take possession of them again with his own.

"Sweet," he said hoarsely and then he kissed her again.

Letty wasn't paying attention to what he said; her attention was held by the way she could *feel* his voice in his chest. And by the way one of his hands seemed to cradle her from head to shoulder, palm against the back of her neck; while the other was spread across the small of her back, pulling her closer, in a way she was just learning was exactly the way she wanted to be pulled closer. She was paying attention to the way his kiss tasted of the jam they'd had for dinner, and wine. And how the heat that poured from him seemed to be doing something to *her*; she felt so hot in her skin, shivery and as though she would not fit in its confines for much longer.

She wiggled closer and the groan Michael made then sounded as if he were close to real pain.

"Letitia, you are going to cause me to lose myself right now if you don't hold still," he breathed raggedly against one of her ears.

That sounded extremely interesting, and the way his breath caressed her ear was also absorbing and something she definitely wanted to experience more, but it sounded like he meant this was a *bad* thing, so Letty stopped wiggling.

Michael sighed with relief and leaned his forehead against hers.

"I feel obligated to tell you that this is *not* flirting," he admitted, his tone much more gentle than his usual gruff pronouncements, and the tip of his nose slowly stroking along hers.

"Indeed," and to her own ears Letty sounded breathless. "Then how would you describe it, Sir Michael?"

His hands pulled her tight against him, and again Letty had that overwhelming, flooding sensation of being surrounded and being *safe*.

He didn't answer her, but he pulled back enough to look her in the eyes rather than clutching her tightly against him, which he still very much wanted to do.

Her eyes looked sky blue in the lamplight and Michael did not want to admit anything to them, they were so pretty and so direct.

But Michael forced himself to say, "That was very poorly done of me."

Letty stiffened against him. "That is surely something for me to judge."

Michael felt a throb in his groin. She had so many ways to kill him. Apparently honesty also now moved him almost as much as her derriere, sized just for his lap, grinding against him.

"If I think of what my parents would expect of me were they here, I think they would expect better of me than to take advantage of a young lady who happened to be under my protection."

Letty felt her spine straighten more. Protected was just how she had felt in his arms—protected, in fact, for the first time in her life. It had been like flying, feeling for the moment as if she were steering her own life, straight into his arms that had sheltered as much as melted her, rather than waiting for an axe to fall and deal her whatever damage was coming from the last thing her father had done.

But Michael hadn't asked her opinion about whether or not she had felt protected. So easy to forget all in a moment that her opinion could as easily be ignored by one man as by another.

Well, she was enjoying sharing her opinions even when they weren't wanted these days.

A small furrow formed between her brows but she didn't drop her eyes. "You seem to feel we have gone too far."

Michael nodded.

Letty went on, "You didn't ask, but I would be happy to go further."

Michael let out a small *whoosh* of air as though someone had gut-punched him. "Please don't say that, Letitia. You are delicious and I doubt you know what you are suggesting."

Well, she didn't know exactly, though she had a pretty good idea; she had raised horses and other animals from time to time, when they had had them. And she had to admit that she wasn't suggesting that they... she supposed mate was the most appropriate word. But she certainly didn't want to stop.

Letty sighed. Someone was always telling her what to do.

"I should return to my seat," she said unconvincingly.

And neither of them moved.

But Michael finally said, "Yes, you should."

Unfortunately he sounded as though he meant it. Letty sighed again and let her arms drop.

"Please excuse me, Sir Michael, for importuning you so."

Michael wanted to object—surely he had importuned her just as much—but even at his most chivalrous, he had to admit that she had done a fair bit of the importuning.

He wished she would importune him some more.

Letty shimmied lightly off his lap and returned to her seat. She took up the embroidery frame but left the needle alone.

"It is I who must apologize, Letitia."

She looked at him and Michael didn't like how flat her eyes, her expression were when they met his gaze. "At least you didn't call me Miss Stapleton," Letty muttered.

"I really do apologize," Michael leaned forward in his earnestness. "It is the gentleman's part to restrain himself in the presence of a lady."

She just looked at him, wisps of fluffy curls escaping around her neck where her hair had fallen from her hairpins due to the encroachment of his fingers.

She said, "I have never been so glad not to be a lady."

Still clutching the embroidery frame, she rose and said, "Good evening, Sir Michael, sleep well."

And she moved so quickly she was out of the drawing room and disappeared from the doorway before Michael could rise.

Leaving him aching and as angry with himself as he could ever remember being.

CHAPTER 8

SHE HAD RUSHED out of the drawing room before she could light a lamp, but Letty was used to her room now and could easily slip out of the dress and put herself to rights by moonlight.

Just a few days, she mused, and already this room seemed very homey to her. She was used to the little copper tub behind the dressing screen, the chair by the window where she had left a book that looked interesting from the library, the bed that was so high that there was a little stair there so she could climb into it and, once there, sink into the featherbed mattress.

It was a far more luxurious room than she could have imagined living in, back in her father's house, even before the furniture started disappearing. This room had plush cushions and lovely patterned fabrics on the furniture and the walls.

But she hadn't imagined living in a room like this. She hadn't imagined any of this. She hadn't imagined having to give up her beloved Maggie, which was awful, and she hadn't imagined a square-shouldered baronet like Michael, which was a different kind of awful.

If she *had* imagined any of it, she would have thought that it would be delightful, living in a baronet's house and being kissed like that by the lamplight late in the evening.

But it wasn't delightful. It had been terrifyingly exciting, as if she had pushed herself off a cliff. It had been an unexpected rush of sensations she was still trying to pull apart and categorize. It had been an unexpected rush of power, too, to think that she was doing what she wanted, touching the way she wanted and being touched the way she wanted.

And then to have Michael remind her that she was powerless after all... that had been as far from delightful as she could imagine now.

Letty could see now the drawbacks of being a lightskirt, or even a mistress. How frustrating it must be to feel that kind of power and then have it constantly snatched away, to be reminded that one was never, after all, the proprietor of one's own body.

As she legally was not.

But the reminder was... heartbreaking.

It took this distance from the house in which she had grown up for Letty to realize that though she thought of herself as a person who simply did whatever work there was to do, solving today's problems and preparing as best as she could for tomorrow's, there was a part of her that resented that she had never had any *choices*. She solved today's problems because there was no alternative. And tackled tomorrow's the same way.

If she could at least pick her own problems, Letty thought, that might be its own type of heaven.

Letty pulled the nightgown Sarah had loaned her over her head and climbed up into the bed. It was an odd sensation, feeling oneself surrounded and supported by the featherbed on all sides. She had thought she would not be able to sleep that way, but she had in fact slept wonderfully well the nights she had used this bed.

She had not thought it would be so spine-meltingly relaxing and simultaneously exhilarating to be surrounded by Michael's arms, Michael's body. But it had.

She would sleep wonderfully well in his arms too, Letty thought, if she ever had the chance. Pity she would not.

* * *

ANTHONY HAD SPOTTED the magistrate as soon as he had come in. But the groomsman sat at the table near the door and drank a pint of ale before even thinking he had the guts to accost the official directly.

Remembering Michael's disdain at his French accent, Anthony made an effort to match his voice to Letty's. He could hear those lilting English vowels, he thought to himself, imagining the speech he had come here to make in her voice.

When he finally approached the magistrate, he even felt himself smiling the way she would, foreign as it felt on his face. He needed this man's help and he would do whatever it took to get it.

"Good evening, sir," Anthony said, bobbing his head in greeting. "The barman, he told me you were the magistrate in this town."

William Leighton looked at Anthony. The magistrate was thick in the body, heavy about the shoulders, but his hair, grey and dark, was cropped short as were the whiskers outlining his jaw muttonchop style.

He didn't seem inclined to help with the conversation.

Anthony bobbed his head again, still schooling his face, his voice to be as English as possible. "I'm Anthony, sir, I accompanied my mistress to make a delivery to Sir Michael's estate."

Leighton grunted. "Your mistress? Where's your master?"

Anthony silently thanked the man for taking the conversational bait. "My master, sir, that's a different story. A story I think you know?"

Leighton gripped his mug. He'd come in for ale, not problems. "What are you on about, man?"

"My master seems to have spent some time in this town. He had some debts that I believe came before you, and Sir Michael settled them in exchange for a horse."

The magistrate nodded shortly. "Yes, Watsford case, I remember, it was only a few weeks ago."

Anthony felt the hair on his arms prickle. "Stapleton, sir."

"What? Don't correct me, boy, I remember the case quite well, Charles Watsford. What, do you think I'm senile? Don't let the gray hair fool you."

"Not at all, sir, it's only that... well, my master's name is Charles Stapleton."

Leighton's sharp eyes narrowed. "Is it indeed."

"And the reason I was bringing it up, sir," Anthony added quickly, "was that I wanted you to know—well, someone to know—I'm hoping not to see him here. I mean—" It was no acting job now to share this worry with someone else, "My mistress didn't give me a choice about accompanying her here, but I wouldn't want my master to think I'd ignored my duty."

The magistrate's thick hand laid flat on the table next to his ale. "What I'm understanding is that Charles Watsford is actually Charles Stapleton, and that his daughter Miss Stapleton is currently visiting Sir Michael having delivered the horse Mr. Watsford slash Stapleton promised to him in exchange for settling his debts. And you're worried that you'll get in trouble for accompanying her here."

"Well, yes sir, that is it in a nutshell."

"Seems to me you'd be in a lot more trouble if you had let her come alone, hey? You're not going to let a young lady travel alone across the countryside to settle her father's debts, right?"

"No sir, I did not want to do that."

"But you're still worried."

"Well..."

"Because this Watsford slash Stapleton fellow is a bounder and a scalawag, is that right?"

Anthony looked the magistrate in the eyes. Here was where his gambit failed or won; it depended on whether the fellow did his job as little as possible, or actually gave a damn.

Anthony told him, "I fear Mr. Stapleton has been in trouble with the law before, and I don't want any trouble myself. Or any trouble for Miss Stapleton."

Leighton scratched his chin, his blunt fingernail loud against his beard stubble even in the busy room. He had no use for gossip but he did not like career criminals and he felt some concern, even, stirring in his chest for this apparently guardianless Miss Stapleton.

He said, "Sit down, boy, and tell me more about your master."

* * *

LETTY HAD SNUCK down to the kitchen and decided to simply stay there rather than attend breakfast. She did not feel up to a lecture on potato-stacking today, and she did not want to see Michael, not until she felt less hurt. Or less attracted, whichever came first.

Mrs. Dunphy, the cook, had greeted her with some suspicion but had allowed her to stay.

Letty also had a subversive plan regarding yeast-raised bread and was trying to find the right moment to introduce it. Mrs. Dunphy's scones and soda bread were delightful, but Letty was dying for a chewy, fragrant loaf of bread, sliced thick and spread with butter.

She'd asked if she could help, and Mrs. Dunphy, apparently unused to help in her kitchen, had set her to cleaning some peas.

It was quiet in here, the pots banging against the hearth no more than necessary, and the place smelled of sugar and flour and dried herbs hanging from the ceiling. Letty liked it.

She watched Mrs. Dunphy cleaning up after the cooking and baking for breakfast, and noted that the stout woman had to bend rather a lot to use the dishtub. They could do better, Letty thought. At one point she could swear she heard Mrs. Dunphy's back actually creaking as she straightened.

"Shall I take these eggs up to the breakfast room?" Letty asked, sliding off the stool and leaving a bowl of picked peas.

Mrs. Dunphy looked appalled. "Absolutely not. Sarah will bring them. Guests don't need to work in Sir Michael's house."

Inwardly Letty sighed. She didn't want to be a guest and she would be happy to work. The only other work she had was training Michael to use her horse. And how could she do that, and still stay away from Sir Michael?

But then she remembered the smile on his face yesterday when she'd reminded him that he'd been up on a horse. An actual horse.

It was still a good idea, what she was doing.

She was just going to have to ignore the man while she was doing it.

* * *

MICHAEL WAS CRANKY. He'd breakfasted alone with Mrs. Peterborough, who did not miss the opportunity to point out that if her services were not required for chaperonage, she much preferred to be allowed to stay in her bed until a reasonable hour, and that such a privilege was not at all unreasonable given her age.

He felt simultaneously annoyed by the lack of Letty's company and relieved that he didn't have to figure out what to say to her after last night's fiasco. He was appalled at himself and had no idea what to do about his shocking behavior. He had treated a guest in his house as though she were a lightskirt at a bawdy house, and sadly there was no one to call him out for his behavior. If he told Anthony he had the feeling that he'd get his throat slit in the night instead of a duel at dawn, and it didn't make him feel better to know that he probably deserved it.

Michael hated the thought that his father would be massively disappointed in him. And even if his mother could have understood, this was far from a ripped shirt. He was already irretrievably staining the young woman's reputation by letting her stay here so long that her presence had become known to the populace at large. Every day he was continuing to let her stay only made it worse.

Yet he could not bear the thought of sending her away; he well knew she had no real home to return to. He should be putting his mind to some other solution, not attacking the girl in his drawing room!

She was too old for school or for a formal debut, however ridiculously young she seemed to him. She clearly had no extended family interested in her circumstances or she would not be in this situation. He must ask her more about her mother's family. And he must seriously find a better solution.

Michael knew perfectly well that he hadn't done it yet simply because he didn't want to. He *liked* having her here. He enjoyed seeing her at meals, working with her, talking with her. He liked knowing she was in his house. His house now, not his father's. Or his mother's for that matter.

Michael still felt the nagging sensation of unease he'd felt upon seeing Letty wear one of his mother's jewels. Why shouldn't she have the use of it? Everyone else had treated it as a simple matter of expediency, no more distressing than the need for Letty to pin up the hems on the dresses she had inherited from Mrs. Peterborough's great-granddaughter. But it had seemed to Michael like a puzzle-piece out of place. Not that he begrudged her the use of it or that it hadn't looked well on her, it had. But it just had seemed... off-kilter.

The way he felt about Letty, he was sure, was not the way a baronet felt about his lady. He spent too much time talking to her as if she were his stableman and the rest of the time thinking about tumbling her in bed—or on the divan, or if necessary on the floor. Those were not the type of thoughts one entertained about a wife, Michael felt sure of that. Sailors didn't have wives, for the most part; officers did, and they certainly did not go about bragging of tumbling their wives.

If he closed his eyes he could still picture his parents: his father, broad-chested and serious, taking his mother's fingertips to help her down the stairs, or up into a carriage. His mother, quiet and kind, nodding to his father as she passed.

Like the Navy sailor he had been, he could cheerfully imagine tumbling Letty just about anywhere. But his parents had raised him to treat a lady under his protection *as* a lady, and ladies weren't tumbled. And his parents were dead, and in his position, if he married, his lady would need to shoulder the responsibilities of *her* position. He didn't have siblings to help shoulder the load. All he had was himself.

He needed to stop importuning that poor girl and stick to work.

* * *

IT WASN'T until he saw her at the horse paddock gate that Michael remembered that Letty had done a great deal of the importuning.

She was wearing her bonnet and gloves both, and her boots, which apparently she intended to put to good use.

"I will walk to the village today and attend to some errands," she told him, staying outside the fence.

He had already brought Maggie within the enclosure; he missed Letty's presence there, as though he and the horse required her to be the third in their discussions.

"It's a warm day for such a walk; why not wait till later, and Mrs. Peterborough and I can drive you in to town," Michael offered.

She looked at him, his coat and waistcoat already tossed carelessly over the top rail of the paddock, the white of his sleeves billowing in the breeze. He had been appalled by the way she'd thrown herself at him, she was sure of it, and it stung. The best way to let the wound heal was for her to stay farther away from him.

And she needed something else to do. Looking at Maggie now, something felt more final, as though she was just beginning to realize that she would soon have to leave, and leave her beloved horse here.

Michael seemed to sense that Letty wanted to spend her time away from him. It pinched him a little but as there was no reason for it to hurt, he ignored it. "Have you introduced yourself to Strawberry yet?"

That brought out Letty's smile. Michael felt it like relief, like sunshine. "Did Griggs really think such a flighty little filly would carry you?" asked Letty, her dimple coming and going.

"Griggs is no judge of a horse's personality, Miss Stapleton, and Strawberry is about the size I asked for, especially given what a massive disappointment Odysseus turned out to be."

Letty nodded grudgingly. Massive was quite literal, in Odysseus' case; the horse was seventeen hands high, near-black as the night and just as dangerous, in her admittedly limited opinion. If Strawberry lacked the fortitude to stand at Michael's mounting-block system, Odysseus could certainly not be trusted to behave once Michael was astride.

"But just because I cannot ride Strawberry there is no reason why you should not."

Letty hesitated. Every day she seemed to fall farther and farther into the hole of impropriety with Sir Michael Grantley and she was trying to climb out. "I would not want to be further indebted to you, Sir Michael."

Indebted to *him*? He was the one who deserved horsewhipping. Michael regarded Letty thoughtfully for a moment, then turned to look at where Maggie was cropping grass across the paddock. He made the small whistling noise Letty had taught him to catch her attention, and then when she was looking at him, made the hand signal for *come*.

Maggie looked as though she were enjoying the fresh morning air and considering ignoring him altogether; but Letty was right there and Maggie clearly felt it was incumbent upon her to do her job. She ambled over to Michael's side, let him rest his hand upon the side of her neck, combing his fingers through her mane.

Michael hid his pleased smile in the horse's mane, too, for a second. Then he looked back at Letty. "As you see, you have accomplished some work here. If you want to be a horse-trainer you need to be able to teach more than Maggie. Why don't you see what you can do with Strawberry, and then when you need a break I will accompany you to the village."

Letty smiled but shook her head. "No one is willing to let me be a horse-trainer, Sir Michael."

Michael squinched an eye shut, as if he were somehow losing sight of her and needed to focus. "That's funny," he said, "I had the impression that you were going to be a horse-trainer no matter what anyone else thought."

Letty snorted in a very unladylike way, then ducked her head. "That may have been the impression that I tried to give," she said under her breath.

"I hope so," said Michael, "because I wrote to the marquess this morning about the talented horse-trainer I had discovered and invited him to come and see for himself."

"Really? Do you think he will?" Letty looked ready to jump into the paddock, and given her shining eyes and open-mouthed expression of excitement, Michael quite wished she would.

But then in the next moment she remembered herself and seemed to draw back. Still she couldn't hide all her excitement. "Will he come, do you think?"

"We'll have to see. If he keeps his stables for something other than a hobby, and I am given to understand that he does, he ought to come."

For a moment Letty looked agog, then her jaw snapped shut, she nodded to him, and without another word she turned and marched off to the stables.

Strawberry was in for an edifying time, Michael was sure of that.

* * *

WHEN HE FOUND himself some time later lying on his back in the dirt, staring up into the wide blue sky, he decided that Strawberry might have gotten the better end of the deal.

Maggie's long head hove into view and she stared down at him where he lay. She snorted.

"I hate you," he said without heat, but reached up to pat her nose. He couldn't quite reach.

Maggie leaned down a bit to close the distance.

Despite the stones digging into his back, his sore pride and bruised hip and scraped elbow, Michael had to smile a bit as his fingertips patted the bristly velvet of the tip of Maggie's nose. She really was a remarkable horse.

"*Michael!*"

Michael rolled over just in time to see Letty emerging from the barn. She had gripped her skirts in both hands and hiked them up and was running hell for leather towards him.

"I'm all right, don't worry yourself," he called and waved a hand but it didn't slow her down.

Indeed she seemed to arrive at his side in an instant, dropping to her knees in the dust and running her hands over him, examining the torn and bloody sleeve of his shirt before flattening her hands against his cheeks then the back of his head.

Perhaps the fall hadn't been such a horrible thing after all.

"Are you hurt? I can run for Griggs, send for a physician—"

"No no, Letitia, truly, please be calm. I'm fine, I am not seriously hurt," he soothed, one of his hands closing over her gloved one as she felt her way across his ribs looking for damage.

"What on earth happened?" She looked accusingly up at Maggie, still leaning over Michael's supine form in the dirt as though wondering what the human was doing. Michael felt inordinately pleased that she seemed to automatically take his side and not the horse's. Had he been asked to place a bet, he would have gone the other way.

"I thought our mutual horse friend understood that I wanted her to stand while I tried out the rope loops, but she still felt it right and proper to move once the tree branches started swaying over her head. Once I was suspended above her, she moved just as I started to drop."

"Oh!" Letty looked up again, glaring daggers and scowling at her horse, and Michael felt ridiculously outright pleased with himself. She was definitely blaming Maggie. He couldn't help but smile.

"It's not funny!" Letty bounced in irritation as she knelt next to him in the dust of the drive, presumably because she was not in the right position to stomp a foot. "You could really have been hurt. She should know better. And so should you!"

Michael's smile faded. "Wait a minute, when did I come in for a share of this?"

"A grown man, a Navy lieutenant and a baronet, and you're like a little boy throwing himself off of bridges into streams when he doesn't know how deep they are! That's how idiots like you break your neck!"

Michael's brows pulled together. He noticed again that the gravel lining the drive was digging into his shoulder, pulled himself up into a sitting position. He felt some blood trickle down the back of his elbow. "Miss Stapleton, I assure you I was considered competent to order cannon fire while in the Navy, and some might even still consider me competent to mount a horse, even shy part of a leg!"

"It's got nothing to do with the numbers of legs! You think you can just leap into the saddle and get your way. You should have just pulled yourself into the saddle like you did before. How is she supposed to know how you are changing your mind?"

"I told her! I told her to stand! She's a horse, we didn't have a salon discussion on the benefits of Lyttelton's poetry, I told her to stand and she damn well spooked at the branches just like any normal horse and I was a fool to trust her!"

Letty pounded a fist on her knee. "She didn't know what was going to happen! You needed to show her first and reassure her a little! She would have done what you wanted!"

"My apologies, miss, but I am accustomed to females who do what they're told!"

As soon as he said it Michael felt it was the wrong thing to say; Letty blanched as if he'd struck her, and he wasn't sure why but he wanted to take it back. She rocked backwards, but instead of snapping back at him, she simply pushed herself up and stood there looking down at him.

Then stuck out her hand.

He didn't want to take it, but his crutches had fallen over somewhere and Michael was doubly unwilling to go crawling around on his hands and knees looking for them.

"Don't let me overbalance you," he warned, taking her hand.

"Do not worry," she said, still without a shade of a smile to be seen. "I am sturdier than I look."

Michael made an effort to get his foot well under him and push himself up, using her hand only for balance. Letty was right; she was sturdier than she looked.

Standing, Michael still felt precarious, though he wasn't sure if that was the lack of crutches or just the fact that she was still very close even as he loomed over her.

Stony-faced, Letty stepped in and looped his arm over her shoulder, almost as if she had done it a million times before.

She had not, and the feel of her shoulder underneath his arm, her gloved hand grasping his, reminded him all in an instant of her body on his lap, in his arms, under his lips, writhing for him.

"I had no idea you were so eager to get me back in a compromising position," he said huskily.

Letty froze, and for a second he thought he was about to be dumped on his arse in his drive for the second time that day.

"Sir Michael," she gritted out between her teeth and strode immediately toward where his crutches had tipped over on the other side of the mounting block, forcing him to hop awkwardly beside her and lean on her shoulder as they went in order to keep up, "you have already demonstrated that it takes more than a touch from me before you will allow yourself to be compromised. I apologize for all my shortcomings and those of my horse."

She dropped his arm as soon as the rail of the mounting block was within reach, leaving Michael to flail out and grab it to keep himself upright.

With a slit-eyed glare Letty said, "You can be rid of either or both of us at a moment's notice. That is your prerogative. Sir Michael."

And then she stomped away.

All in all, it could have gone better with both the woman and the horse, Michael felt.

CHAPTER 9

BY THE TIME Michael had given up for the day to return to the house, he was filled with nothing but frustration.

He had practiced having Maggie stand, and of course once he made his command clear, she would do so despite movement over her head. It might take some time, he realized, to get her used to audible commands as well as the hand signals Letty had previously favored. But he couldn't immediately overcome her understanding the pressure of his right knee as an instruction to turn. It might not just be training. He might have to modify the saddle, and it would take time.

He still had several letters to which he needed to compose responses, including one to a landlord with a warehouse whose answers to his letters just seemed slippery and odd to Michael and he wasn't sure what to do about it.

The blood had crusted on his elbow, his shirt was destroyed, he smelled of dirt and horse, and most of all he would like to invent some sort of device for moving backwards in time so that he could go back and erase the moment when he opened his mouth and said the exact wrong thing.

He'd made a mull of the whole thing, he berated himself, just felt a woman's body against his own and immediately spouted the stupidest remark as though he were drunk as a wheelbarrow. And a coarse remark, as if the lady had been cheap Haymarket-ware, a coin-toss prostitute he'd run across in a London street.

He didn't like being formal with Letty, but he couldn't seem to be informal without making a complete cake of himself. He ought not to try to speak to ladies at all. Dammit, this was why he didn't leave the house, and hadn't even before he'd gone off to war and got a leg shot off.

It wasn't as if the Navy had taught him to be *more* suave with women.

He was an idiot and that was why he ought to send her away but he had nowhere to send her and dammit, she wasn't his responsibility but he felt like she was.

And truth be told he didn't want her to be his responsibility. He liked it better when they could just... talk.

By God, he needed a bath.

* * *

LETTY CONVINCED Sarah that she had a headache and didn't feel up to dining downstairs, even in their little informal setting. She also convinced Sarah to bring a scone and some butter, and the maid surprised her by bringing a bowl of lamb stew, too.

Letty ate every crumb, because it was her pride that hurt, not her head, and then curled up in a chair in her room with the book she had brought up from the library and tried to read.

It would be light for some time yet, as the days would soon be as long as they were going to get.

Letty still felt determined that Sir Michael was going to learn to ride Maggie—or more accurately, that Maggie was going to learn to carry Sir Michael. But it wouldn't work if they couldn't cooperate, and they hadn't today, and look what had happened. She hoped Michael hadn't been too badly hurt.

Then her face flamed hot when she remembered what he'd said to her, and she thought maybe it would be all right if he was bruised up just a little.

What had she done to inspire such a remark? Yes, she *had* enjoyed the feeling of Michael's body next to hers, but she hadn't betrayed that, she was sure of it. She'd been so frightened when she saw him lying there on the ground, and so relieved when he wasn't badly injured; and then somehow they'd gotten into a conversation that was more humiliating than personal.

Had he just been that angry about not being able to stand on his own? That seemed petty, but she didn't know him, not really.

Letty was going to have to find a way to work with him, and with Maggie too, as quickly as possible, and she was going to have to figure out where to go once she left him. She needed names of other possible customers for horse-training of this sort, and where she could live while she made herself known to them to explain her potential services.

She racked her brain. If only she had a relative, a friend from school, anyone who might provide her a roof over her head while she figured out what to do next. Of course, those were exactly the things she didn't have, thanks to her father's dealings with, as far as she knew, everyone he had ever met.

She had Anthony. That was all.

She needed to talk with Anthony, that was what she needed.

* * *

MICHAEL HAD LEFT the door to the drawing room open, and he heard it when someone started down the stairs.

He levered himself up and on to his wheeled cart as quickly as possible, gliding down the hall fast enough to catch sight of Letty before she made it out the front door.

And just at the sight of her, without gloves or hat, slipping out of doors looking like she had undoubtedly just looked in her bedroom, no doubt also heading down to the stable to talk to Maggie and, just as likely or more so, that damn Frenchman, flipped Michael over from the self-flagellating remorse he had been soaking in for most of the afternoon into anger at her.

"Off to visit a groomsman in the stables. Isn't that a bit declassé, Miss Stapleton, even for your father's daughter?"

Letty drew in a breath as sharply as if she'd been shot.

He reached for her to comfort her before he even realized that it was he himself who was being hurtful.

Michael's hand just managed to catch her elbow. "I'm sorry, Miss Stapleton, I cannot keep a civil tongue in my head today. Please believe that if I *were* still in the Navy and if you were my commanding officer, you could order me flogged against the mast and I wouldn't raise a hand to stop you because it would be well deserved."

She turned and met his eyes, and hers looked darker than he'd ever seen them. She'd cried the day he met her, for heaven's sake, he could well have understood if she'd shed a few tears given the cruel remark he'd just made. But he didn't know her well enough to know what to make of the clouds he saw in her eyes right now, making them look more gray than blue.

Letty pulled out of his grasp, but he rolled himself closer.

"Miss Stapleton, *please*. I apologize. I cannot—It is my fault, entirely mine, that we have had such a day at odds with each other. Please forgive me. I cannot promise to simply be silent whenever we meet but I am beginning to wish that I could if only to stop these mad things from passing my lips."

"I am sure it is not entirely your fault," Letty said stiffly.

He drew closer still. "Letitia, it is *entirely* my fault. You've done nothing, said nothing to justify my patently foolish remarks and I apologize for them."

Letty's teeth caught her upper lip, and she bit at it for a second. "Really?" Then as though catching herself, "We do not know each other well, Sir Michael, and I cannot tell what is... instigating your ire."

Michael shook his head. "We know each other well enough for you to know that I am a cranky ex-sailor, ill-suited to the business of being gentry, who left half a leg and all my manners in the Greek ocean."

At that he saw half a smile come and go like a flash across the corner of one side of her mouth, and felt himself smile. There was no doubt about it, they just did better when he was honest. He couldn't be other than what he was, but he had sides to him that weren't complete mutton-headed boors.

"Truthfully, Sir Michael, I feel like I am walking on pins and needles all the time," she said in a low voice, as if confiding something. "I know I am not educated about proper manners and Roseford is, quite frankly, above my station. You are only telling the truth when you call me the daughter of a thief."

Michael felt that like a punch to the gut. What was *wrong* with him? "It is *not* true, Letitia, and I was being unkind to say anything like that." *I was angry that I was such a boor this afternoon,* he told himself, *and repaired it by continuing to be even more of a boor. And I may have felt something like jealousy, seeing you rush outdoors half-dressed to go meet another man.*

This was the problem, Michael realized; it worked best when his speech with Letty was simple and honest, but he could not tell her that.

He took one of her bare hands in his own. It was smaller than he remembered.

Bending near her he said quietly, "You grace my house, Letitia, and are far more well-mannered than I am. Perhaps you will relax if I manage to get through an entire day without making a complete— well, without behaving like a drunken sailor with his first holiday on land in a year."

Letty looked at their joined hands.

"It is odd," she said without meeting his eyes, "that we get along so famously some of the time and so badly the rest."

"Is it odd?" She looked back up and met his eyes, and he smiled at her a little sadly. "I have no younger siblings, and fought as much as played with other boys in the village, or when I was away at school. It is most probably simply my bad influence."

At that she smiled her dimpled smile, the one that reached her eyes and made the lump in Michael's belly a bit lighter. "I am sure you are... only occasionally a bad influence."

He laughed and patted her hand, flattening it against his arm. "If you like, you can take up the slack and be a bad influence on those rare occasions when I am not. But I rather like it when we get along. That is you being a *good* influence on me."

"I like that idea." She stood, poised in the open door, with the sun just thinking about beginning to set beyond it and a breeze ruffling her green dress. "Now perhaps you will tell me what is the proper way to go about my business and visit Anthony and Maggie without disturbing you."

Michael stifled a soundless sigh. "Of course the proper way is for a young lady such as yourself not to go at all, or if you go, to go in a bonnet and gloves and perhaps a wrap and with a footman, and not dash off as if planning to attend an assignation with a lover."

Letty gasped, and Michael shook his head. "I said *as if*. I know that is not where you are going, but I admit to a visceral reaction when I see you dashing off looking *as if*. Since you are going anyway, and it is quite warm enough to go without a bonnet, and since I have already seen you without your gloves, ..." here his thumb rubbed a circle on the back of her hand, "then we will pretend that you are appropriately attired and going to make an appropriate visit and be back at an appropriate hour. Indeed, my lady, I am prepared to pretend quite a bit on our shared behalf when I am not behaving like the aforementioned drunken and rude sailor."

"Aha. And we will also pretend that you are properly attired, in a coat instead of coatless as I often see you, and that you have not said several hurtful things today, and perhaps that we will go back to being friendly as we were yesterday."

At that thought, his eyes darkened, and he could see from the flush that rose on her face that she also was thinking of their time together in the drawing room, perhaps thinking of the way that far more than their bare hands had touched, and that it had been far more than friendly.

"But not... quite that friendly, right, Sir Michael?" Her smile was a tiny bit rueful and she slid her hand from his. "Let us try that. We will both be good examples for one another."

Unaccountably sad at the loss of her hand, Michael nodded. "And we will both pretend," he said, very quietly, almost into her ear.

* * *

LETTY ENTERED the barn almost at a run, and looked half surprised to find Anthony there.

"Where *were* you last night?" she hissed at him as she plopped down to sit on a hay bale next to where he reclined in the straw.

"Business," he said shortly. "And I might be gone again. At night or in the daytime. So just ignore it if I am, all right?"

"Are you in trouble?"

"Are *you?*"

At that Letty's chin crumpled and Anthony feared she might actually start to cry.

Letty was no stranger to crying, but every time it happened, Anthony hated it. It made him feel helpless and, truth be told, it frightened him. Anthony's first reaction to the apparent threat was to panic.

"What happened? What did you do?"

"Oh I like that. Blame it on me." Letty's chin came up and she scowled at Anthony and that was a reaction that he much preferred. "I did nothing!"

"What sort of nothing?"

"Oh Anthony." Her voice dropped to just above a whisper, as if she appalled even herself. "I kissed Sir Michael."

"*WHY?*"

"Don't roar at me! It wasn't something you could answer as though there were a why! You had to be there to understand."

"I wish I had been! Letty my princess, you don't seem to understand what sort of danger you're in at all."

"Oh, I know." Her mouth twisted and the type of bitterness Anthony saw there now did not suit her. "My reputation is in tatters, soon to be more so, but Anthony, what does it really matter? Who cares what I do, really? Who cares if I walk to the moon or fall through a hole to the other side of the earth or burst into flames where I sit?"

He put out his hand and squeezed her shoulder. "I do."

Letty had the grace to look sheepish. "I know you do." But she persisted, "You know what I mean. I am not introduced to society, I never will be. I have no family that will come calling Sir Michael out to a duel if I am compromised. And anyway, *I* kissed *him*."

Anthony was very familiar with that set to Letty's jaw and he didn't like it. He didn't like it one bit.

If there were any way on earth for him to avoid this conversation he would have gladly undertaken it, but Letty was wrong; she had him, and he cared, and he had to do whatever he could to make sure she did not do herself truly irreparable harm.

"Letty my princess," Anthony said quietly, folding his legs to sit across from Letty as calmly as he could. "I am afraid of far more than you losing your reputation."

She frowned. "Such as what?"

He sighed. "What is the irrefutable evidence that a woman has been compromised?"

"That she have a child, I suppose."

"Exactly. And should you be so compromised, where will you go for the nine months that it takes to produce this child, Letty? And where will you keep it after that?"

Her brows stayed furrowed as she contemplated this.

Anthony went on. "Do you suspect that Sir Michael will want to keep you around this house watching you grow big with his illegitimate child? Or that he will want to keep it? When men of his station have such children they sometimes pay to have them housed at an orphanage—"

"No!" Letty looked aghast at that idea.

"—or sometimes they don't. Mistresses of long standing and many years might expect a cottage as payment for their services. Is that what you are hoping for from Sir Michael?"

"No!" Letty said again, this time almost spitting it out. "I wouldn't—"

"But if you don't, then what *would* you do?" Anthony tried to keep his voice gentle but he wanted to make sure this problem was clear in her mind. "Women who have been only temporarily used are simply tossed away. Where would you go, how would you live once you got there, how would you even travel there? *You no longer have so much as a horse to your name.*"

"If only I could work!" Both Letty's hands were balled up into fists, twisting the fabric of her dress where it fell over her knees.

"But you can't," Anthony reminded her bluntly. "You have no skills and no place and no champion from whom to obtain one."

"Some women do go to another part of the country and claim to be widowed," Letty tossed her head. "The country is full of widows from the war. It would not be such a rare thing."

"Some do. And then what would you do?"

"I'd be the best damned housekeeper this country has ever seen," Letty muttered to herself.

Anthony heard her, but it only gripped him with the fear that she didn't get it. "What a roll of the dice, what a chance you are taking, with two lives, not just your own. You would be at least as likely ending up trading yourself for a few coins or even a few crusts of bread in any town big enough to have cold, leaking, cheap lodgings for the sort of work you'd be doing."

She looked at him, her blue eyes wide.

Anthony pressed on. "Have you ever *met* such unfortunate women?"

She shook her head.

"I have. When I was working my way across England I met them. In Calais, and in Dover, and in London, for some time, actually."

Letty stayed quiet. Anthony never talked about his journeys, how he had ended up working for her father in a village north of London at the age of thirteen and all alone.

"Some of those women were kind. Many were cruel, as they had been cruelly treated themselves. None were old, because they tended to die young of the diseases they caught in their work. And they did catch diseases, Letty. Some had small red spots on their face; some had wandering maps of red marks all over the skin that anyone could see. And that was all in addition to their constant black eyes and bruises. They did not have long or happy lives."

Impulsively Letty reached out her hands to take Anthony's. He let her.

"One of the whores in Dover saved my life," Anthony said simply. "I was starving to death and she had very little food but she gave me some. She was not old, the same age I am now, and she had had a brother my age who had died of the croup the year before. She told me not to stay there, to keep moving as far and as fast as I can and to use what I knew to get work but not at the docks. She was right. Even boys my size were being pressed onto ships and I don't think I would have survived that."

"What happened to her?" Letty whispered.

"That was nearly a dozen years ago, princess." Anthony shook his head. "I am sure she is dead."

Letty squeezed his hand.

"Because of her I didn't stay in London, and that is probably why I am alive today. I'm not saying she did not give me an enormous gift; she did. But she was quite sure that she had no way to escape what was coming to her—the pox, syphilis, prison, worse. She was most terrified of the day she got with child, as she had already seen two others die from trying to stop their babes, and another woman die in bearing her child, as well as another whose child was taken from her by—"

Anthony suddenly found himself remembering that he was sitting in a stable in a prim and proper English village with Letty, the girl he'd grown up with, the girl with freckles and pale blue eyes and, despite her father, only the dimmest idea of how badly people could actually behave. He found himself disinclined to explain the behavior of madams to Letty.

"—She didn't have any choices, Letty. I don't want any of that for you."

Letty just nodded.

After a few moments she seemed to find her voice. "I can work, Anthony, and so can you. We have been lucky so far, so very lucky to get here and to dine on Sir Michael's kindness."

"We are both working for our supper," he pointed out. "But yes, we have had good luck."

"We need to have the freedom to leave. We can't stay here forever and I am not going back to that village." Letty didn't need to explain why not. "Sir Michael has written to his neighbor the marquess regarding my skills as a possible horse trainer. I need more names of such potential customers."

"There won't be a marquess under every bush." Anthony's sarcasm rustled as dry as the hay.

"No, there won't. But we can make a list of potential names, and we will need the direction of each. Whatever your mysterious business is, take some time to find more."

"If Sir Michael is happy to be rid of you, he will help as well."

Letty felt a mixture of things all at once at that thought—sadness that he might well want to be rid of her, and a glowing little warm coal of certainty deep inside that she did not think that he wanted to be rid of her, not just yet.

"And at the party—oh heavens above, Anthony, I haven't told you the worst part, I have to go to a *party* Saturday evening!"

That made him guffaw with unexpected laughter, nearly in her face. "Never has a party been described as such a dire object."

"How awful! I don't know what's expected of me but apparently I must go, or Mrs. Peterborough says that the local vicar will know that I ought not to be here, and spread gossip about me."

That sobered him up. "Mrs. Peterborough is nobody's fool and is undoubtedly correct. But don't be so discouraged, princess. There are only a few ingredients for a successful attendance at a dinner party. Don't drink too much, wear something appropriate, dance, perhaps sing if you are asked, and nod politely at whatever bad joke or inappropriate story anyone tells. That is what all people do at parties and it cannot be that hard as I have never noticed the bar for admission to be very high."

The list made Letty want to call upon the mercy of God himself. "Where am I going to get something appropriate to wear? What *is* appropriate? I can't dance and I can't sing, as you know perfectly well!"

"Now that's not true at all. I taught you the minuet and the quadrille, and I doubt they will enjoy *les contredanses* terribly different only this far from London."

"Are you mad? That was years ago when we were children!"

"We'll practice. And I'll teach you a song or two to sing—" Anthony snapped his fingers. "Say, here's a good old trick: don't let yourself get trapped into singing alone, say you are shy and only sing if someone else will join you. It will help cover your mistakes if you get a word or note wrong here or there."

"That is brilliant!" she breathed, her eyes wide with true admiration. "However did you learn such fantastic subterfuge."

Anthony grinned, his teeth white against his sun-bronzed skin and he bounced to his feet, bowing before her. "It was survival at the time, princess," and he offered her his hand as if for a dance.

She did remember now, he had shown her some of that in the past; it would come back.

Letty could do this. She would go to this dratted party, to help protect Sir Michael as well as herself, and hopefully come away with more names of people who could use the help she really could give.

Watching them dance, over the side of her stall, Maggie snorted her approval.

CHAPTER 10

"We really must get to the village for those errands today," Letty announced over breakfast the following morning. "I have a number of things I must do."

Mrs. Peterborough sighed, looking sadly at her cup of tea. "If we must, we must. I hate shopping. My feet swell so in my slippers."

"I said errands, not shopping," Letty corrected her.

"Shopping there will be," Mrs. Peterborough went on implacably, "as you must have something to wear Saturday and an unaltered dress of my great-granddaughter's will not do."

"That is the least of my concerns," Letty waved a hand as if dismissing a fly.

Mrs. Peterborough's eyes, watery and grey as they were, narrowed. "No, child. It is not."

Michael cleared his throat. "I'll drive both you ladies in to the village, shall I?"

Both women turned and gaped at him, astonished.

He returned their stares with equanimity. "What?"

"You have not been to the village since you returned," Mrs. Peterborough stated implacably, as though he might argue with her about the facts. "You have not driven anywhere at all."

"Good time to start," he kept his answer short, sipping his tea.

"You need not go to the trouble, Sir Michael," Letty protested, smoothing the hairs that sprung up from the twist on the back of her head, perhaps wanting to control her hair if not this conversation. "Griggs or Anthony can—"

"I'm fully capable of driving the barouche, and if the weather is fine, it will be no trouble at all."

Letty just looked at Mrs. Peterborough, who shrugged.

"You can both stop looking surprised any minute now," muttered Michael into his teacup.

* * *

LETTY AND MICHAEL spent some time examining the saddle Mr. Cullen had sent him, with the cup design for the knee without a lower leg. The left and only stirrup unbuckled, so it was no great decision to leave it off, but the strap dangled and Michael was thinking of how best to have it altered, and whether to send it all the way back to London to Mr. Cullen himself or have the blacksmith do it. The first option was undoubtedly safer but the second was faster and Michael felt some urgency to be once more riding a horse on his own.

"Now that I have a suitable horse, I should send Mr. Cullen drawings and have it fit Maggie better," Michael mused. "He can likely fit her better. The prototype is a test, and it should ultimately work."

It also came out, in their inventory of the stable, that Letty had never ridden a sidesaddle.

"How is that possible?"

Anthony, who had been cleaning the stalls of the riding horses, promptly disappeared.

Letty watched him go with narrow eyes. Traitor. He was leaving her here to figure out how to describe that she had ridden her only riding habit to rags a while ago, and that since then she had occasionally stolen Anthony's trousers, or …

"A few times," she admitted, thinking this might be the easier one to start with, "I simply hitched up my skirts and rode astride."

Michael blinked. And blinked again. Hoping that the image that came to mind, of Letty bare-legged in the saddle, thighs spread wide to grip the horse, would fade before he embarrassed himself with it.

But he reminded himself that he was supposed to try to be pleasant, a good influence, at least on himself, because in his opinion Letty wasn't the one who needed the good influence. "And were there witnesses for these rides, Lady Godiva?"

Letty didn't know who Lady Godiva was but she wasn't about to ask right now. "No, I was very careful to do it only when there was no one about." That was part of why she'd had to rent a carriage to get here. She wouldn't ride that way in *public.*

Michael just shook his head, perhaps trying still to get that image to shake loose. He wondered whether she had stockings on under her boots—and then he told himself very sternly that he really did have to stop wondering. It was putting him in a condition that might show, even in these trousers.

"No need to address it today, but you should have a sidesaddle, Miss Stapleton," Michael couldn't help but sound a bit stern, "and a riding habit."

"I should probably have many things," and Letty's tone and expression were placid, "but as I do not have the means of purchasing them, I am safe from ownership of very much."

Yet another logistical problem, winced Michael. It would be nothing for him to acquire a saddle and a habit; he could even get her another horse if none of the current options appealed to her. But he could not without branding her a kept woman in the eyes of society, a society he was fast coming to realize seemed to exist as much to thwart people as to keep their feet on a straight and steady road.

* * *

LATER, Michael told himself as he dressed for the drive after their luncheon. Worrying about how to acquire her a habit and saddle would give him something else to think about on the short drive. He should engage Mrs. Peterborough's help again; she had been so helpful with the dresses.

He was sure that Mrs. Peterborough was currently struggling with her clothes and hat and gloves, and Michael would have to give her a few moments to arrive in the foyer. He wondered if she should send one of the footmen to help. He wondered if he should repair to the drawing room to wait.

Just then Letty came half-running down the stairs as was her wont, and Michael looked up.

Saints above, there was a third dress today, a magical blue dress that fit snugly to the bust and fell below it in small pleats. The sleeves clung to Letty's small, round arms and even the hem was the right length, just brushing the tips of her toes in the one pair of slippers she owned.

Her bonnet framed her face and he could see her eyes were distracted, thinking of something else, till she caught sight of him. And then the way she smiled gratified Michael immensely. She was smiling at him.

And then she caught full sight of his own outfit, and her eyes grew very wide indeed.

He had donned an actual coat, cut to fit, over a rose-embroidered waistcoat that had been his father's. His trousers were unfashionably full, because they had to fit over the wooden leg that he had buckled on his right limb.

Standing in the foyer, one gloved hand resting on a cane, Michael looked whole.

"What have you done?" Letty sounded more astonished than anything as she descended the last few stairs before him.

Was that flattering? "I've put on my peg leg, Miss Stapleton, that is all," he replied rather gruffly.

"I had no idea you had such a thing. How surprising." Letty's eyes flew down to his shoes, which were indeed matching, though one fastened around a wooden foot.

"I don't like it," Michael's words were staccato as bullets firing.

Then why wear it? Letty thought to herself, but she did not say it out loud.

For herself, after the shock of seeing Sir Michael look so odd, so *not himself*, she became accustomed to the look. It still seemed quite wrong, but it was hard to deny Sir Michael looked fine; he always looked fine, Letty admitted to herself. But aside from the fact that she had simply become accustomed to seeing him not appearing to have two whole legs, she preferred him, if she were totally honest with herself, swinging shirtless through the air like some carefree pirate about to do some dastardly deed.

Oh dear, thought Letty, and put such thoughts away.

She said, "Sarah has just left me; she will see if Mrs. Peterborough needs any help, and then she should be down directly."

"Of course. I will check on the carriage."

"And I have a few items to collect from the kitchen."

What on earth could she have to collect from the kitchen? Michael wondered as he walked out, slowly but on two feet, using the cane to keep himself steady. The ankle joint on this particular type of leg was supposed to be very carefully engineered, allowing natural movement without being too loose. It was odd, after weeks of not using it, and the casing around the top that fitted his thigh tended to dig in. He knew by the end of the day it would be throbbing with pain. But for the moment he was a man walking like other men, and that he did enjoy.

He hoped that Letty found it appealing too.

Anthony's eyes just widened a little as he saw Michael walk out to the barouche Anthony had driven to the house. The carriage horses, Major and Lily, were a plump short pair of grays well past their prime; they stood placidly while Anthony set the brake.

He jumped down, leaving the reins for Michael.

"Are you sure you do not want me to drive, Sir Michael?" Anthony asked with a diffident head-bob as he approached, a gesture quite appropriate to a groomsman but one that somehow looked odd on Anthony, one that somehow didn't match the way he held his head. "You could enjoy the ride in the carriage with the ladies."

"I'm quite sure I will be grateful for the partial isolation of the driver's seat, Anthony," Michael assured him, casting an eye over the rolled-back top of the barouche; they would all be able to speak to each other anyway. He might as well enjoy driving for a while.

"Errands?"

Michael just nodded. "Errands."

Anthony nodded back. "Word of advice," he said confidentially as the door behind them opened. "Don't lose your patience and it will all be over quickly."

"How's that—?"

But Anthony was gone, and here was Letty, helping Mrs. Peterborough with one hand and carrying a basket under the other.

"Let me help you, Mrs. Peterborough," Michael said, offering her his arm. "And Miss Stapleton—you are bringing luggage?"

"It's for the cats. The most efficient transportation option," Letty announced and that cryptic information was all Michael got as he helped Mrs. Peterborough up the mounting stair and Letty helped the older woman seat herself comfortably.

"And it has my teacup and tea towel in it," Letty added as Michael climbed up himself.

Of course it did. Better leave it at that, Michael thought.

ANTHONY HAD ONLY BEEN GIVING him good advice, Michael realized after their first stop, at the blacksmith's on this side of the village.

Letty had charmed the blacksmith, a thickly-built older fellow by the name of Culter, with a broad smile. Within minutes he'd shown her a pile of scrap leather he had, and she'd flipped through it and selected a couple of pieces and bargained his price for them down to almost nothing.

"Since they are scrap," she'd said with a smile, and the blacksmith had smiled and shrugged and agreed with her and pocketed a few of Michael's pence.

A couple of minutes more and she was back in the carriage with her leather, a thick needle and some waxed linen thread she had also wheedled out of Culter for a tiny price.

She wrapped them all carefully together, stowing them under her seat so the needle and thread would not get lost, and informed Michael that they could go on to the miller's if he liked.

The whole visit had taken less than a quarter of an hour. Much less.

The miller's visit took longer, because the miller's wife was Mrs. Peterborough's granddaughter.

There was much hugging and greeting and aside from helping Mrs. Peterborough down and inside, Michael just tried to stay out of the way.

Tilly, the granddaughter, didn't look very old to Letty, and she took both of Letty's hands between hers, clapping them together and making Letty jump.

"That dress looks pretty enough on you to make a painting of," said the woman, and Letty smiled back into kind eyes that were much younger, but made of the same stern yet secretly kind stuff, as Mrs. Peterborough herself.

Mrs. Peterborough as the honored guest had a cup of tea but Letty refused to let Tilly feed everyone else. "We've just eaten not long ago and must get on with errands. But I've come to ask, Mrs. Peterborough said that your husband Will occasionally did a bit of carpentering. The Roseford kitchen needs a new, higher dishtub. Can he help?"

Michael, who had never heard there was anything wrong with Mrs. Dunphy's dishtub, stood by bemused as Tilly fetched her husband from the milling, watched as Letty waved her arms to indicate just what she needed and what size.

Will, a red-faced man wearing a dusty apron that fell to his knees, just nodded. "Of course!"

It had been whirlwind but thorough, and even Mrs. Peterborough seemed refreshed as Michael helped her back into the carriage in what seemed like a remarkably short time.

"Perfect!" Letty dropped down into the seat next to Mrs. Peterborough as Michael touched the reins and the horses started off. "Will can come tomorrow, or the next day, and it won't take him half a day to do; that way we will get him started while the blacksmith is doing the outside work."

"What outside work?" Michael began to wonder if he was missing so much of these conversations because he was going deaf. He hadn't heard anything about the blacksmith coming to call, had he?

"The mounting block by the portico that we discussed, Sir Michael, you remember," Letty said placidly, watching the side of the road slip by with evident pleasure. "Oh, and Mrs. Peterborough, do take care not to knock over the teacup I've placed under your seat. Your granddaughter was kind enough to gift me with a bit of raising for bread."

He was not equipped, Michael decided, to decode everything happening today. Certainly not at this speed.

"We must stop at the village shop next, to order gloves," said Letty decisively, "then we will visit Mrs. Allenby for the sewing errands, and we will stop at the Hitchens farm on the way home. That is the most efficient schedule."

"The Hitchens farm?" Michael hadn't seen Mr. Hitchens since before he'd left for the Navy.

"For the cats," Letty said as if that explained everything.

Michael stuck to his driving.

* * *

WHEN LETTY ASSURED Mrs. Peterborough that she would only be a moment in the village shop, that lady elected to stay where she was, with her feet up on the seat to slow down the swelling, while Michael escorted Letty inside.

Michael had to duck to make sure his hat cleared the door frame. Letty looked around with satisfaction, and breathed deep the smell of the cool shop inside, its paper and butter and pickle brine.

Michael thought surely now he would see a flurry of shopping activity, but as with the other stops Letty already knew exactly what she wanted.

After exchanging introductions with Mr. Gunther, the shopkeeper, she announced, "Sir Michael Grantley requires a pair of heavy work gloves."

This one startled him. He looked down at her bonnet; he could not see her face. "No I don't," he said gruffly.

"Yes, you do."

"No, I don't."

"Yes." She didn't even look up at him, just kept her tone sweet and even and kept Mr. Gunther's attention on her. "You do."

Mr. Gunther, who had no trouble seeing where the sale was going to occur, bustled about showing a couple of samples to Letty.

Michael tried again. "Miss Stapleton, I already have several pairs of gloves."

She turned enough to regard him just past the edge of her bonnet. "You have evening and day gloves, Sir Michael. I asked Griggs."

Of course she had.

Michael stood stoically while Mr. Gunther and Letty discussed the virtues of several pairs he could order for her, of the type used in fieldwork, or in blacksmithing.

The only interaction required of him seemed to be when Mr. Gunther finally turned his attention to the fit.

He approached the tall silent Sir Michael rather shyly and asked if he might make some marks to measure Sir Michael's hand.

Michael just laid his hand on a sheet of coarse paper, where he was told, and let the man make his marks.

"You can call for them next week, madam," the shopkeeper said with a smile and Michael did not correct him, though the form of address assumed Letty was his wife.

"How much?" she asked, and he could hear her smile.

Mr. Gunther named his price and rushed to add, "Madam can pay when we deliver."

"Not at all; Sir Michael will pay now," she assured him firmly.

And within moments Michael found himself escorting her back out the door.

"I am glad I came along to pay," he grumped at her, but kept her hand tucked safely into the crook of his arm.

"They're your gloves," she reminded him sweetly, completely ignoring the fact that he had not wanted them.

Michael thought for a moment. "Anthony is a very wise young man, isn't he."

"Of course he is," she answered, all unconcerned with whatever he was talking about.

* * *

MICHAEL DECLARED surrender at the door of the millinery, and Mrs. Peterborough and Letty went in together.

Mrs. Peterborough ruled the discussion from a comfortable chair while Mrs. Allenby and Letty fetched drawings for her to look at.

"I still need you to come out when you have a moment, Allenby, I've done the best I could with this blue one but we've a pink and I think there's a third one that needs your hand."

Mrs. Allenby nodded her sleek dark head. "Of course. Your work on this gown is beautiful, Mrs. Peterborough."

The housekeeper just waved a dismissive hand. Letty was surprised. She'd thought Sarah had shortened this dress; Letty had looked at the stitchwork herself, and the work was fine and done with a light hand. Clearly there was nothing wrong with Mrs. Peterborough's fingers.

"But the more important question is, what can you do in a few days? Miss Stapleton requires something festive for this week-end, and we need your help."

Letty held her breath. Mrs. Peterborough had assured her that dressmakers didn't ask awkward questions, and indeed Mrs. Allenby did not disappoint.

She brought drawings and two plates from a magazine and she

and Mrs. Peterborough discussed design elements with all the intensity of generals discussing troop movements.

"The Greek waists will work well for her. They do not necessarily require a corset. But how daring with the drape? Ladies in town even dampen their skirts to show their legs."

"Ah!" Mrs. Peterborough leaned back as though she smelled something bad. "The exact opposite of what we need, Allenby. Miss Stapleton isn't even out."

"You have not had a season, Miss Stapleton?" the dressmaker asked dubiously.

"No, but I am over twenty." Letty was used to people thinking her young. Wetting down skirts to show off her legs? That sounded alarming. And damp. What was she getting into?

Mrs. Allenby tapped on her lower lip with a thoughtful finger. "I think I can do something quite quick—fitted sleeves but draped and still with an overskirt, conservative, but flattering for a young lady."

"You can do it with fabric on hand?" Mrs. Peterborough reminded her.

"Yes. Yes, absolutely." She cast an appraising eye over Letty. "Something with a bit of color but that won't make you look washed out. Or perhaps lighter? Like a presentation dress?"

Letty wanted to say that she didn't know what a presentation dress was but that light colors were not practical. Mrs. Peterborough beat her to it. "Perfect. Can you deliver it Saturday?"

"I can."

"Good."

Letty was fascinated that the details of payment were completely glossed over as Mrs. Allenby dove into taking Letty's every measurement. How different from purchasing leather scraps, or beans by the pound!

Both ladies were after her own heart, though, and in less than half an hour Letty was helping Mrs. Peterborough back over the threshold.

Sir Michael was sitting outside in the barouche. Upon seeing them emerge, he swung himself down. Letty thought she saw him wince as he walked up to them, but his expression stayed quite calm as he offered Mrs. Peterborough his arm.

What did he think of the errand of buying her a dress, Letty wondered, and was he the least bit interested in how she would look in it?

CHAPTER 11

THE THROB in Michael's right leg distracted him on the drive home, making it seem five times longer than the drive in to the village, which it was not, not even with the stop at Hitchens' farm.

Michael might otherwise have been curious enough to ask about the cats, who did not want to be in a basket and who yowled at the top of their voices all the way home to express their displeasure with their lot.

Letty must have seen some sort of strain on his face because she apologized as they disembarked. "Your stables are full of mice, Sir Michael. You need help keeping them in check."

Michael was interested—again, no one had mentioned any mice in the stable to him—and he wanted to ask about her planned process of persuading two angry young cats to adopt his stables as their new home. He also wondered about the nature of the cats—if she had mixed the sexes, he might soon be up to his ears in cats.

But the throbbing in his leg had reached a point where Michael could swear he could actually hear his pulse beating in his ears. "I'll leave you to it, Miss Stapleton," he said brusquely, leaving her to her basket of cats and her teacup of bread rising and to tell Griggs to have the horses and carriage tended to, in fact.

He managed to walk to his room even though he felt as though he were wading through broken glass, and managed to wait until his door was closed to rip off his coat, waistcoat and trousers and throw himself into a chair where he could unbuckle that cursed leg.

Michael hissed as he lowered himself into his chair. The bruising was livid this time, and some abrasions bright red—nothing actually bleeding, thankfully, but angry enough for a hold full of sailors.

He couldn't imagine strapping the thing on a few days from now to make a showing at the damn vicar's party.

But he would.

* * *

THE SUN WAS FINALLY GOING down when Letty tapped on Michael's door that evening.

She had missed him at dinner, and wondered if he had tired of her during the whole day of errands.

"Don't—"

She had already pushed the door open, as it was not latched, and found Michael struggling to rise, hands gripping the arm of his large Grantley chair, stripped to his shirttails and with bare legs showing below.

Shocked, Letty drew in a breath and backed up, about to leave, with an "I'm so sorry, Sir Michael, forgive me—" when she caught better sight of his legs.

One was very interesting because it was long and bare and *right there*,

"Oh my," Letty said under her breath,

...but the other—

"Oh *dear*."

Michael gave up the struggle to stand and just sat while Letty looked anywhere but at him, and turned bright red, but did not leave.

"You can go," he dismissed her shortly, rudely, but she did not leave.

"What *happened*?"

119

My leg got shot off, Michael wanted to say, as he felt self-conscious about his bare stump—it was certainly not something he wanted Letty to see. But he had a feeling she was talking about the bruising and red marks that showed even below the long tails of his shirt. "It's nothing."

Letty still refused to look directly at him but did not budge. "You've had no dinner, Sir Michael. All the staff have taken their evening off—I am going to fetch you something."

And then she disappeared from the door opening in which she'd been so stubbornly standing.

Michael half-sighed to himself. It wasn't as though he could run after her and stop her. And he was hungry. And...

Well, he hoped she would come back.

It was lonely just sitting in here, he told himself.

When she returned she had a scone balanced on top of something on a plate, and a bowl in the other hand. The juicy tart smell hit Michael and his mouth watered.

"Is that—did you bring me pie?"

"And a scone," Letty said, stepping into his room and offering the plate, still without meeting his eyes, still quite pink in the face.

And neck, Michael observed as she leaned down to give him the plate. He wondered how much of her skin was flushed right now.

Letty stood but did not retreat.

Michael could feel his bad mood ebbing and a desire to laugh replacing it as he watched her, steadfastly standing in his room, not looking at him, looking anywhere *but* at him, yet refusing to leave.

"Yes, Miss Stapleton?" he finally took pity on her and said, even between bites of pie. He had been so hungry.

Sure enough, she started talking, still without looking him in the face. "I had no idea you were sitting in here in pain, Sir Michael. We had thought—that is Mrs. Peterborough and I assumed that you had tired of our company, not that anything was wrong."

"Not tired of the company, Miss Stapleton, just a trifle indisposed."

"But that looks—" She shifted her weight from one foot to the other, and he could see that in the bowl in her other hand, there was water and some tea towels. "That looks painful, and I don't want to importune you, Sir Michael, but I would like to help."

Her last words dropped in volume till she was nearly whispering.

Something in Michael's chest felt odd.

"Miss Stapleton, it is beyond improper for a young lady to be alone with a man in his bedroom, much less in the state of undress in which I am here."

"I know, and I am sorry, but I am finding it difficult to leave if I might help."

Yes, that was definitely Michael's heart, feeling that odd way. He couldn't help that his voice was lower when he said, "How had you planned to be of assistance?"

Her ears flushed pink again and she scowled, and Michael couldn't help it, he had to laugh.

"Oh, you—I'm not trying to be forward, I can't just leave when you are in such pain. That would be absurd."

"I'm just wondering how to plan to minister to me when you can't even look at me."

At that her eyes came straight to his. Not his bare limbs, not his wounds. His eyes.

"I can look at you," she said simply.

And the laughter drained out of Michael as he realized that she had never been in any danger; it had been him in danger, all along.

* * *

LETTY COULD FEEL her skin burning with embarrassment—right up to the moment she met his eyes.

She knew those eyes, green as the trees and always with a hint of laughter in the corners even though Michael laughed so seldom. She knew that.

And she knew she wasn't supposed to be here. But he hadn't thrown her out, and no one else was offering to help him. And Michael needed some help.

"Just let me—"

She waited after she moved forward a step, but Michael didn't say or do anything, so she pushed herself to step closer, then closer again.

By the time she was kneeling before him, steadfastly ignoring the intimacy of seeing his bare foot, and the light sprinkling of hair on his shin, she knew she was blushing so fiercely he must be wondering if she were actually going to burst into flames.

But Letty ignored that and placed one of the damp, cool tea towels across the angry red and blue marks across the skin of his thigh.

Michael hissed between his teeth.

She bit her lip. "Is that noise because it hurts, or it feels better?"

"Better," he bit out, and paused with the last of his scone clutched in his hand uneaten to let his head fall back against the chair.

It was easier to look at him while he sat there relaxed with his own eyes closed. His arms were so long, still draped in that snowy linen crumpled from his wearing it all day, and they fell across his chest, draped across his lap. And the shin rising from where his long, straight foot met the floor had such interesting lines to the bone and curves of muscle.

She noticed him shift slightly in the chair and the knee that ended abruptly moved away from the other. It was odd, seeing the stump of the leg just below that knee move slightly as the knee bent, even though it ended so suddenly, and the rest of the leg she could easily imagine simply wasn't there.

But the oddness went away as fast as it had come, and she felt like they were clearly just Michael's legs, one different from the other.

She met his eyes again, and he wasn't smiling.

"Such sights are not for tender ladies' eyes," he said, gruff and something else she couldn't name.

"I can see why," Letty said, clearing her throat. "Such sights are bound to inspire extremely inappropriate behavior in young ladies."

Michael's eyes darkened.

Still blushing bright red, Letty leaned over and plucked off the tea towel, now warm to the touch, and exchanged it in the bowl on the floor for a fresh one. She wrung it out and laid it over the strip of angry marks, imagining that they almost looked better already.

She had to clear her throat again to speak, something was making her hoarse. "If you lay on the bed, I could see if the wounds go all the way around."

"If I lay on the bed, Letitia, you'll have to come with me."

Her eyes flew to meet his. He looked hungry, and he was looking at *her*.

"You said you didn't want me." She couldn't help but sound a bit accusatory; his rejection had hurt.

"I never said I didn't want you. I said that I must not have you. Those are very different things."

Letty supposed she should be insulted or affronted or some such thing that ladies were supposed to be by innuendo. Instead she felt lighter.

Softly she said, "I'm right here."

Michael's hands, bigger, darker than hers, reached forward to take her own. "I admit I would like you closer."

He drew her towards him and she stood between his knees. Letty felt awkward again for a moment, not sure where to look, but then she remembered how heavenly it had been to sit on Michael's lap and let him hold her.

"Wait—"

Letty ran to the bed and snatched off a pillow.

Michael nodded toward the slightly open door. "Lock it."

Blushing again, Letty did so, returning to lay the pillow across Michael's damaged thigh. How quickly they had gone from sharing awkwardness to sharing secrets.

She immediately settled herself upon the opposite leg, swinging her own legs up to rest on the pillow.

She wiggled closer and Michael's arms closed around her. What a perfect fit.

"Does that hurt?"

"I don't feel any hurt," Michael rasped before his mouth came down on hers.

His lips were so warm on hers, so plush and yet plundering; he was tasting her lips, and then when she sighed, the tip of his tongue tasted hers, and Letty wiggled closer, clasping her arms, one around his chest, one around his neck, trying to hold all of him the way he was holding all of her.

Michael seemed to have lost his restraint somewhere along the way. He kissed her temple, his nose stroking her hair, he kissed the shell of her ear, his breath gliding along her neck. Letty shivered and his arms only tightened. When she moved a hand up to slide her fingers into his thick hair and hold him tighter, he made a hoarse, hungry noise into her mouth and hitched her more tightly against his body.

In the days since they'd kissed before Letty had convinced herself that she had made too much of it in her imagination. She was untried and inexperienced, that was all. She had inflated the quality of his kisses in her mind.

Not so, Letty decided now, running her hand down the muscle of his arm, feeling it bunched tight as he pulled her body against his. She had, if anything, forgotten quite how good this felt. She felt at the same time tiny and very powerful, as if he could put her in his pocket and take her away with him, while at the same time, at any moment, she might fly.

"God, Letty, you feel so good," Michael said into her hair.

Letty pushed herself closer and sighed.

He worried the shell of her ear with his teeth and murmured, "May I touch...?"

"Anywhere. Everywhere."

One of his big hands slid over her shoulder and around her back, crushing her to him for just a moment before gliding around her ribs and up.

Letty *wanted* him to crush her, wanted to feel every inch of him wrapped around her. She was so focused on the need to be closer that she barely registered the feel of his hand stroking gently upward until it came to rest under her breast.

She gasped, the sensation surprising her. It was nothing like touching herself; her breast felt heavier just because Michael was holding it, and she felt the peak contract, anticipating him somehow.

Instinctively Letty let her head fall backward and she heard Michael growl, his arms half-lifting her so he could fasten his mouth on the spot where her neck met her shoulder, his thumb just brushing the nipple he could see hardening through the fabric of her dress.

"Oh *my!*" Letty cried out and if she had put away her embarrassment before, now she simply gave herself over to urgency. Her hand grabbed his and held it against her. "Do that again."

She couldn't know what that did to him, Michael thought only half-consciously as he throbbed in the confines of his underclothes, rocking himself just a little against the delicious soft roundness of her behind, because if he pressed any harder, he would explode. She was as clear and direct here as she was everywhere else, but this was something he wanted much more.

He obliged her, brushing his thumb back and forth across her nipple until it felt diamond-hard to his touch and she was positively writhing in his arms.

In *his* arms. He, Michael Grantley, lacking all manner of social graces, the ability to string words together prettily, and half a leg, had somehow become lucky enough to get *here*.

He would have to practice telling her how temptingly luscious she was like this, Michael hazily thought. Later.

"Letitia," he whispered in her ear while crushing her to him with one arm and continuing to tease her aching breast with the other, "you are beautiful like this."

"Like *this?*" She panted against his chest, turning her face into his skin where she had somehow managed to coerce her fingers to unbutton his shirt. His skin was warm, so hard and warm just like the rest of him, and dusted with more of the coarse hair that was so different from her own. She ran her fingertips across it, put out her tongue just to taste him there. He tasted slightly salty.

Michael groaned.

She felt his groan in his body, in his chest against hers. He seemed to mean it. She couldn't imagine being beautiful right now; she felt like she was on fire, she could feel sweat trickling down the nape of her neck and the backs of her knees, and she was wet, even more wet between her legs and her hands couldn't stop pulling at his arms, his shirt, trying to get him closer while she twisted against him.

"Very much like this," he growled against her throat and used both his arms to lift her against him and fasten his mouth around that beckoning nipple.

"*Michael!*" Letty let out a cry and grabbed his head with both hands. The pleasure was exquisite, shooting down her body, and she would not have been surprised to see lightning explode from her toes. Hazily she managed to open her eyes and check. Goodness, she still had her shoes on!

It was too late to try to move in any way except at Michael's bidding.

"Please," Letty heard herself beg, in a voice she'd never used before in her life. "Please. I need you."

"What do you need, my sweet?" Michael murmured, his teeth still worrying at that peaked nipple, which felt as though it had become the throbbing center of Letty's body except that she had an ache between her legs that was begging for its own share of attention, competing with the bone-melting pleasure from Michael's mouth against her breast.

"I don't know but I need it," Letty half-sobbed, feeling her hips thrust into the air, looking for something, needing something very badly, hoping to goodness Michael knew what it was.

Michael had never had more trouble pulling his thoughts together, not even in the heat of battle. Letty was magnificent like this, she was asking for *him*, he wanted to do this for her. Yet even as badly as he wanted to sheath himself inside her, something in the back of his mind still held him back. It would be a poor way to treat a young woman with no one to speak for her unless he intended to marry her. And he did not intend to marry her.

But he couldn't simply walk away from her either.

More than his own release he needed this from her, needed to see her come apart with desire for *him*, wanted, more than anything, to know that she had been completely his simply because she wanted him.

He wanted her to be his.

"I can touch you, just with my hands, rather like this, if you want," he rasped, still holding her against him with one hand while the other smoothed down the front of her dress and pressed against her between her legs, just lightly.

Letty startled and her hands grabbed him again, hard. "*Yes.* Whatever you can do, please, do it."

"Tell me if you want me to stop," Michael murmured, his hand moving to slide her skirt out of his way.

When Letty realized what he was doing, she wiggled again on his lap, this time to loosen her skirt where it was pulled tight around her thighs and hips, her hands frantic to loosen the fabric and pull it up over her knees to give him room for whatever he wanted to do.

Michael chuckled against her, his cheek sliding against her ear, even the sensation of the slight stubble of his beard after a long day eliciting a sigh of pleasure from his sweet woman in his arms as she moved her legs apart for him, and he obliged her by gently smoothing his free hand along the inside of her knee, caressing her inner thigh.

"*Yes*, that's good, yes," Letty sighed for him and spread her legs wider, and Michael had to clamp down on the desire to roll on to the floor with her and simply slide himself inside her.

She was his, he thought to himself with a primitive satisfaction he'd never felt before, not over anyone or anything. Half-consciously he realized that this was how men felt about land, or gold. This desire to keep, to own, to hold.

To hold.

"Please," Letty half-whimpered and Michael wanted to do as she wanted.

His hand slid against her curls, pressing and kneading the slick warmth he felt there, and Letty shuddered all over in his arms, against his body, her head completely fallen back now as she gave herself up to him entirely. "Yes, please, Michael!" she moaned out loud.

Glad they'd locked the door, unwilling to stop now for anything, Michael tentatively slid a finger inside her just because he couldn't do it with the rest of his body.

That made his Letty draw in a breath and hold it, her body arching backwards till he could barely hold her.

"I've got you," he told her, and she felt his voice rumbling against her through the wall of his chest as his second finger slid inside her and then the heel of his hand ground down against her.

Letty just barely knew she was digging her fingernails into his arm, she was holding him so hard; she couldn't breathe, forced herself to drag in a breath and hold it, and then, every fiber of her being concentrated on the sensation he was causing to flood through her, the hot clenching pleasure that was pulling tight every muscle in her body, centered around his hand, and she felt his fingers press deeper inside her, and the heel of his hand circled against her and pressed in too, and then she was lost.

Her body felt like it might fly out of his grasp, but Michael held her against him even as she felt every muscle clench, and shake, and a keening cry came from her throat that sounded unlike any noise she had ever made before. "Michael!" she gasped as she held him and wave after wave of body-dissolving pleasure flooded through her, completely taking her over and wringing her out. She felt her body squeezing the fingers he had inside her, felt herself shaking, felt both her nipples drawn up into tight nubs brushing almost painfully against the fabric of her dress, and wondered if she could die from this, because it was impossible to take a breath and surely she must breathe sometime.

Finally, finally she felt her muscles relax, sagging as if all her bones were gone now, the hot sweat trickling behind her knees echoing the feeling of wetness all around where his fingers were joined with her.

Michael's breathing was ragged and loud and Letty felt unspeakably shy as she felt him removing his hand. From *inside her*. But he said nothing, only held her close. She could feel his heartbeat slowing gradually.

Perhaps she should say something about how they shouldn't have done this, but that would be lying. She felt as though she had never inhabited her own body before. And she felt, still, unaccountably shy. But she did not feel regret and couldn't pretend that she did.

Finally she just said, "What do we do now?"

Apparently surprised, Michael gave a harsh laugh. "I have no idea."

Her hands crept back up to steal around his neck and she held him, too.

Michael swallowed. "I suppose we... You should get some sleep."

Leaving him had never seemed less appealing. "Will you sleep too?"

He had to decide first what to do about the raging tumescence trapped under her bottom. "Eventually."

Letty rubbed her nose against the skin on his chest where it was bared by his open shirt. "I feel like I should say... thank you?"

Michael could feel himself sinking in his own estimation second by second. In the dictionary under "corrupting innocents" they would place his name. "No, you shouldn't. You should clock me over the head with something heavy and run screaming away."

Letty just blinked at him. "Why on earth would I clock you in the head for giving me such pleasure?"

No, his stand wasn't going down anytime soon. He could claim that she should hit him because he'd taken her maidenhead—but as he'd suspected given her reports of horse riding, she didn't have one. He could say it was because he'd abused her trust, but he wasn't stupid; she was far more pleased that he had taken her up on her innocent yet luscious offer than she had been the other night when he had turned her away. He could claim that it was because he was soiling her maidenly ignorance, but who prized ignorance?

Michael finally decided to go with honesty. "Because a gentleman does not so take advantage of a lady unless she is his mistress or some other woman entered into a paid relationship with him. Only scoundrels take advantage of young ladies this way."

Letty frowned. "Never? Not even married gentlemen?"

And that made Michael frown. "I'm not... I don't think men generally do that with their wives."

"How tragic," Letty told him, and snuggled closer.

Michael's bark of a laugh didn't make her jump this time.

Letty said drowsily, "I wish we could sleep right here."

"I do too, but I think my leg would go to sleep, as light as you are upon it, and you need to sleep in your own bed." Because the maid needs to find you there in the morning, he didn't say but thought.

"Michael," she said quietly. "Kiss me and I'll go. I'm afraid that you are angry with me."

He wasn't, though she had good reason to be bonelessly relaxed and he did not. He was going to have to take care of himself once she'd gone; he wouldn't subject her to that. "Not angry," and his voice was softer, sweeter than she'd ever heard it before. "Grateful. And I want you to sleep soundly too."

She just looked at him, and Michael didn't really need convincing, so he kissed her.

His mouth was warm and Letty thought it as strong and sweet as honey, but when he pulled away, he lifted her in his arms, leaning forward to put her on her feet.

She looked back once and left.

CHAPTER 12

LETTY PAUSED with her hand on the doorknob to the breakfast room.

What on earth would she say to him? What would she *do*?

When she'd gone up to her room the night before Letty had felt as though she couldn't possibly sleep. Instead, her traitorous body had drifted away almost immediately upon her climbing up into the impossibly high bed and between the sheets.

Sarah had had to wake her this morning, and the sun had been well up.

She'd wondered... well, would Sarah be able to *tell*?

But Sarah had just chattered on, laying out her pink dress, pouring her tea, brushing out her hair and wondering when Letty was going to make some proper risen bread.

"The rising needs a few more days to work," Letty had told her absently, letting Sarah pin her curls into a twist.

She'd let her mind completely drift away while Sarah had rattled on about a hairstyle she had seen in a magazine in Mrs. Allenby's shop. It seemed that Sarah *couldn't* tell. Was there anything to tell? Was Letty now automatically a fallen woman, a bird of paradise, a lightskirt?

She didn't know. But she did know as she put her hand on the doorknob to the breakfast room she couldn't imagine that her heart could pound any harder. She didn't know what Michael would say, wasn't sure she was ready for it, but was dying for it just the same.

It was the first time, Letty thought to herself as she went in, that she had ever had the slightest inclination toward romantic feelings, and Sir Michael Grantley, she felt, was the world's most eligible target for those feelings.

It was a thought that stayed with her for all of about eight minutes.

Just as in previous mornings, Sir Michael sat with mail next to his plate, sipping his tea, eating a scone and looking out the window while Mrs. Peterborough commented on an inventory of people they had seen and things they had done the day before.

When Letty approached the table, Michael pushed his chair back and rose, balancing with one hand on the table and nodding to acknowledge her presence, just as he always did.

When she seated herself with Griggs' assistance, she helped herself to some eggs while Griggs poured her tea, just as she always did.

It seemed that the rest of the world had not changed at all. Only Letty.

"How are your cats getting along, dear?" Mrs. Peterborough inquired with a mostly toothless smile as Letty slowly began to eat.

Letty gave her a full rundown of the process of closing them in a stall and giving them some of Mrs. Dunphy's leftovers to eat so that they would get used to the building before she gave them the run of it. "Maggie might recall that we used to have cats in the barn when she was young," Letty added absently, watching Michael's fingers as he lifted his scone to his mouth, "I am hoping she will get along with them."

Mrs. Peterborough just nodded, turning her attention to her tea.

While Mrs. Peterborough was looking down, Michael turned and raised an eyebrow, pointedly observing Letty observing him.

Then he gave her a most wicked smile, inappropriate for the breakfast room or anywhere else in public, Letty thought.

She caught her breath and Mrs. Peterborough looked up. Michael's smile disappeared, his attention dropping again to his mail.

Letty frowned. Whatever Mrs. Peterborough said next, she ignored it.

Was this what it felt like to be a mistress? Publicly ignored, privately... importuned?

Letty did not like it.

"Please excuse me," she said before disappearing rather suddenly in the direction of the kitchen.

Mrs. Peterborough observed Letty's half-eaten scone and untouched tea.

"Sir Michael, I wonder if your guest is quite well."

Michael looked up, startled by the formal address. "I'm sure she is, Mary."

Mrs. Peterborough fixed her watery, graying eyes on Michael's face. "I let you get away with too much informality. It comes from raising you from a baby. And raising your father."

Startled a second time, Michael put down his papers. "I didn't know that you raised him too."

"Most days I don't think I gave either one of you enough hugs. But I probably didn't hold you to high enough standards, either."

Michael was sure he, a Navy lieutenant, could not blush, but if he could he would suspect he was doing it now. Whatever Mary suspected, he would not confirm it. "I think your standards have always been very high."

"I'm sorry you lost your leg, child. But I'm glad you're home. Rose-ford needs you and you need to take care of Roseford. I expect you to be a grown man and take your father's place, you know."

Feeling something squeeze in his chest Michael just nodded. He knew that he needed to take his father's place. He needed to make sure the estate continued to have enough money to survive, even with the downturn in farming income. He needed to make sure this house survived, and he needed to take responsibility for everyone in it. That would not include propositioning young ladies, whether under his protection or not.

He said, "I know my mother and my father both were always glad you were here to look after me, Mary, even when they couldn't."

Mrs. Peterborough snorted. "Those two were so wrapped up in each other, they trusted you to come out the other end all right by yourself. Shame they couldn't have more children to give you brothers and sisters, child. Though not for lack of trying."

That startled Michael enough that he almost dropped his knife. "What?"

"Oh, I know young men don't like to hear such things, but you're old enough now. You must know how in love they were. Something unlucky there, though; your mother had several miscarriages after you, and I'm not sure but what she died of one."

"She had a fever. I remember."

"I know, son." Mrs. Peterborough was shaking her head. "I know."

Five minutes before, Michael's head had been full of the memory of Letty is his arms, when he might hold her again, and residual guilt because of his certain determination to do so.

Now Mrs. Peterborough was shoving out all those pleasant thoughts with this random gossip. His parents were in love? Michael didn't remember any such thing. And his mother had died of...?

Though now she said it, Michael could remember scenes of his childhood as if through a new set of eyes. He remembered his mother sitting in his nursery with him, but now he remembered the way her face lit up when his father stopped by. He remembered her reading to him, but now he recalled too how she stopped and ran to throw her arms around his father's neck when he'd come into the room.

He was soon to be thirty years old, for the love of all that was holy. He'd lost his mother when he was twelve, and he'd been away from his father for six years, and fought in a war. He'd known he had good parents who loved him, a good home.

But he hadn't thought about it in just that way. It had honestly never occurred to him that his parents had been in love. His father had never said anything of the sort, and it was not the sort of thing a mother would bring up in conversation. He'd been away at school for many years, too, before she died, and his time with her had been, it now seemed looking back, so limited.

His parents had been *in love*?

Michael had known a good many sailors in the Navy who were in love. Almost all of them were in love with the lass who had last sent them back to the ship happy. There were no examples there of years-long relationships, not years of being in love. The officers who wrote home to their wives seemed to bear little resemblance to the doe-eyed sighing of the fellows in love with their girls in port. Had those men been in love with their wives? How would he tell?

Michael, growing up with little interaction with neighbor children and then spending all his time with other boys his age, first at school, and later in the Navy, had no idea what adult love would look like.

He couldn't wrap his head around it. His parents?

Mary was still looking at him. Michael pulled his thoughts together from a long way away.

She said, "It's time you did what your father did: put this place in order, do what needs to be done. And look out for those that need looking out for. Like Miss Stapleton. And her groomsman."

"I will, you know I will," but Michael's thoughts were spinning.

* * *

"MISS STAPLETON, Will Staffer is here. He says you engaged him for some carpentry, miss."

"Oh yes, I did. Will you show him through to here, please?"

"I don't want any changes to my dishtub, I don't. I told you that before."

"I know, Mrs. Dunphy, but I am asking you to trust me. I can see how far you have to bend to do the dishes and I just want to make you a bit more comfortable."

Mrs. Dunphy narrowed her eyes. She had wide hips and soft jowls and she looked fairly unthreatening except for those eyes, but they held a look that it would be unwise to ignore. "If Sir Michael wants something done to his kitchen, so he will do it. But you've no call to be making changes that aren't approved, miss. You're only a guest in the house."

I'm his mistress!, Letty wanted to cry out, preferably immediately followed by a burst of satisfying tears, but Letty kept her careening thoughts to herself. "I know, Mrs. Dunphy, but Sir Michael did approve this, and I know you don't want to disappoint him."

When Will Staffer puffed his way into the kitchen, all red-faced and smiling, Letty showed him what she wanted and then beat a hasty retreat.

If Mrs. Dunphy wanted to take up arms in defense of her current dishtub, Will was on his own.

Letty was behind the house hacking at her bits of leather with an axe when Anthony appeared.

He looked dubiously at what she was doing, bent over the chopping block, axe head gripped in one hand, and frizzy blonde hair falling in her face.

"Yes, Anthony, what is it."

"What on earth. Let me help you."

"I have it," she said almost viciously, yanking the axe away from his hands when he tried to relieve her of it.

Anthony changed tack immediately. "Letty, what is it. What's wrong."

She was not about to spill the reasons for her upset to Anthony. He would only remind her that he had been right all along. She was in danger from Sir Michael and that was the extent of their relationship. Never mind that last night she had felt so close to him, closer than she'd ever felt to anyone else.

What an illusion desire could be.

She brought the axehead down on the leather, chopping off an irregular edge.

Anthony shook his head. "You're going to lose a finger. If you don't axe yourself in the leg."

"What do you *want*, Anthony."

"Your cats hate it here. Or they hate each other. Or maybe they hate me. I don't know, all I know is that they yowled all night in that stable and I didn't get a wink of sleep. Nor did the stableboy."

"Oh, the poor things. I'll be down to visit them soon."

Griggs appeared in the doorway. "Miss Stapleton, a Mrs. Allenby is here. I've shown her into the drawing room, but Mrs. Peterborough asked me to inform you."

"Oh dear." Letty smoothed her escaping hair back from her reddened face. "I'll make it down to the stable later."

Letty took the time to finish hacking up the edges. If she came back out here, she'd swing the axe with both hands, and she might not stop with leather.

* * *

Mrs. Allenby was examining her green dress closely.

"What can you do with it?" Letty asked her, self-consciously pushing at her hair.

"Turn it into a rug," Mrs. Allenby muttered. "I'm sorry, my dear, I don't mean to insult. But I can see it's already been turned a time or two."

"It fits well. Perhaps you can use it as a pattern for the dress you are making," Letty said with a sigh. The last possession she had, aside from her slippers and her boots.

"And a riding habit. Sir Michael said you needed a riding habit," said Mrs. Allenby absently.

"What? When did he tell you that?"

"On the way in, madam."

Letty felt her armhairs prickling. Kept women got wardrobes, she knew that. She had a hazy idea that they were usually for operas or something, wherever loose women behaved loosely, she supposed. But Sir Michael didn't go to the opera, he went horseback riding. Or at least he wanted to.

She'd earned the dress Mrs. Allenby was making. And the dresses Mrs. Peterborough's great-granddaughter had given her were a lucky gift. But a riding habit seemed too personal, too specific, and somehow suspect.

"I see," she said faintly, and that was all she had time for before Griggs appeared again.

"I'm sorry to disturb," and Griggs seemed to be showing signs of strain. "Mrs. Dunphy is having rather a vehement argument with Mr. Staffer, miss."

"Of course she is."

Leaving Mrs. Allenby with Mrs. Peterborough in the drawing room, she was stopped in the hallway by a young man.

"You should wait at the door, sir," Griggs said more than slightly reprovingly.

"I'm sorry, sir, my father said that I should speak to Sir Michael, that he wanted a secretary, sir."

Letty looked the boy up and down. He was fresh-faced and strawberry-haired. He couldn't be sixteen. "How old are you?"

"I'm eighteen, ma'am, with distinction from my school."

She'd asked Anthony to find out if there was someone suitable in town, but this boy... "What do you do now?"

"I'm the magistrate's oldest son, ma'am," and he bobbed his head.

He didn't look eighteen to her but Sir Michael was not going to be able to go on the way he was. "Do you write quickly? And what's your name?"

"Blake Leighton, ma'am, and I'm pretty quick with a pen."

Letty offered her hand and a smile. "I'm Letitia Stapleton, Mr. Leighton, and I'm pleased to make your acquaintance. Griggs, take him through to the library, introduce him for me to Sir Michael, would you? I'll take care of the kitchen."

"Gladly, miss."

* * *

"Who sent you, now? What's your name again? And you're to do what?"

The young man didn't let Michael's gruffness faze him. "Blake Leighton, sir, and Miss Stapleton had sent an inquiry into town regarding a secretary. My father thought I might do."

"Griggs, where is Miss Stapleton now?"

"The kitchen, sir, but I can't recommend that you go there right now."

* * *

MICHAEL WAS grateful for his quick-rolling cart as he zoomed past Mrs. Allenby and Mrs. Peterborough in the drawing room, but felt it was less sanguine as he approached the kitchen and the noise therein.

When he opened the door, the increase in the noise level was considerable.

"I've had that dishtub since I came here! It's been that way in the Grantley house for as long as anyone can remember! You've no reason to go and change Sir Michael's house, you trumped-up—"

Before Michael could interject, Letty interrupted very smoothly.

"Mr. Staffer, you see what's needed here—perhaps you can please do the rest of the work in the garden? It's right through there and outside. Thank you. Sarah, please stop waving your apron around your head and go back to cleaning. Yes, please tidy the rooms upstairs. Mrs. Dunphy—how do you feel about cats?"

That stout woman paused and half-hissed, truly as if the air had been let out of her. "Cats?" Her tone was half-suspicious, half-yearning.

"I have two new arrivals in the stable, and Anthony tells me they are unhappy with their new home. They need more food, Mrs. Dunphy, and perhaps you'd be willing to spend a little time with them and help them get settled in."

"I like cats," said the cook, eyes darting about the kitchen. The breakfast being over, she was already ready to serve a light lunch at any time and the dinner was well on its way, simmering on the hearth—and she couldn't wash dishes from breakfast without her dishtub.

"Would you please visit the cats and help them get settled? Whatever time you think you can spend. There's no hurry. They're not going anywhere."

Something about the way Letty said that made Michael feel as though perhaps Letty meant more by it. As though those cats were going to be permanent residents, and that she would damned well see to it.

Which gave him a curious feeling but he didn't have time to name it before she was turning her attention on him.

"Sir Michael. I assume you are here regarding your new secretary."

"Indeed." The boy was gawking at the scene in the kitchen past his shoulder even now.

"Mr. Leighton. I'm sure your father told you this position would only be per Sir Michael's approval, and on a trial basis, as it were. You do understand, do you not? You will not hold it against Sir Michael if it becomes clear that his work methods do not admit you as a secretary?"

"Oh yes miss, no hard feelings," said the boy, who was practically climbing up on Michael's rolling cart to see more of the kitchen.

"Then why don't you two repair to the library to try responding to this morning's correspondence, and discuss salary while you are there. Yes, Mrs. Allenby, I will be there to discuss the riding habit in a moment. Meanwhile, Mr. Griggs."

"Yes, miss." Michael hadn't seen the old butler snap to like that in years.

"Please go to the stable and find me a spare nail, a wooden block, and a hammer. And ask Sarah to bring me down the needle and thread I brought home yesterday. I will be in the drawing room."

Letty nodded to everyone and slid past Michael and the boy behind him and marched straight down the hall to the drawing room. Mrs. Allenby, who had been standing in the hallway looking toward the source of the ruckus, fell in behind her.

Will Staffer disappeared into the garden with his armful of wooden parts for the new dishtub. Mrs. Dunphy muttered something under her breath but followed him out the door and Michael saw her passing the window on the way to the stables. Griggs followed.

Michael was left standing in the hallway with Blake. He gave the boy's narrow face, topped with a shock of reddish hair, another look.

"All in all, Blake, we might as well give it a go," was all he could say.

* * *

LETTY WAS USING a scrap of the leather as a thimble.

"Don't stab yourself, child."

Letty looked up, a snappish retort on her lips, but she just couldn't be angry with Mrs. Peterborough.

She set the nail against the edge of the leather again, finished punching holes. Then she wrapped the piece around the hand grip on Sir Michael's wooden crutch.

It was not perfect; she didn't like how the seam made a ridge. But it would be a gentler surface for him to grip, if he didn't wear the gloves, and she had a feeling he wouldn't wear the gloves.

Why she cared whether or not he wore the gloves, she didn't know.

No, that was a lie, she knew. She cared. Michael was not just the type of tall, handsome man that silly girls dreamed about. She thought he was a good man, at least he had been kind to her—

—*kind*, she thought angrily, whacking the nail through the leather, that's what she could call it—

—he didn't deserve to have his hands scarred up or infected when he needed to use the crutch.

"Don't stab anyone else, either," Mrs. Peterborough added mildly, just as Michael rolled into the room.

She couldn't help but look at him when he came in. She knew she always would. Sailing through in his shirtsleeves—at least his shirt was tucked in, she thought acidly.

It made her angrier, seeing his warm green eyes turning from her to the crutch in her hands. It made her angrier that she couldn't stop her own eyes from following the curve of his neck, the muscle there, down into the open hollow of the neck of his shirt.

He rolled to stand over her, put out his hand.

She gave him the crutch.

He examined the stitches closely. "You must give up hounding Miss Stapleton about her needlework, Mrs. Peterborough. Her true talents lie with leather."

Mrs. Peterborough just snorted. Letty stayed silent.

Michael looked down, the expression on his face softening the angles of his cheekbones, his jawline. "Thank you, Miss Stapleton."

"You needed it," Letty said brusquely. "Now I must—"

"You left breakfast early."

She had stood but he'd stopped her from her planned exit; they were only a foot apart.

She could see his throat move when he swallowed. Why *must* she find that so fascinating?

He went on, "I wanted to tell you, we must make sure to have a lesson with the horse—with Maggie today."

At least he remembered her name. "Must we?" Her tone implied that she knew nothing of the sort.

"My neighbor the Marquess of Faircombe has written to me. He will visit this week-end; he wishes to see this mysterious horse trainer I have written to him about."

Wide-eyed, Letty suddenly sat back down.

"Are you quite well, Miss Stapleton?" Michael put out his hand.

She didn't take his hand. But when she looked at him again, her expression was very different.

"Thank you, Sir Michael. How good of you."

Michael waved his crutch. "You have been very good to me, Miss Stapleton, for no reason at all."

Her eyes darting to Mrs. Peterborough, who seemed to be involved with her embroidery but who was, Letty was sure, following every word, Letty just gave a tiny shake of her head. "You know my reasons."

"Shall we meet in the stables in an hour?"

Letty shook her head. "I will skip luncheon, and if you will as well we can get started. I think we can make great headway today."

And then she launched herself back to her feet, going past him at speed—Michael would have said she was nearly running.

"Skipping luncheon, Sir Michael?" Mrs. Peterborough asked innocently from her seat on the divan. "In such a hurry to get out on the horse?"

He just shrugged. "It's a madhouse in here, Mrs. Peterborough. You only wish you thought of it first."

CHAPTER 13

"You're punishing me."

Letty did not look back over her shoulder to where Michael was perched on Maggie's bare back. She was punishing him, and she was enjoying it, but she didn't wish to discuss it.

Michael, however, did not let the topic drop. "How long do you plan to continue the punishing?"

"You're riding a horse, Sir Michael, hardly being whipped at the mast."

The sound behind her seemed to indicate that Sir Michael had smothered a snort, or something like that, but Letty kept on.

She was leading Maggie by her reins, leaving Michael to balance on the horse's back, gripping Maggie's mane. It seemed worthwhile to try riding bareback, and Michael had proposed the path rather than simply lunging around the paddock.

They had already gone down the hill from Roseford and were walking along the road, slowly, as Letty was on foot.

"The worst part of being whipped at the mast is the humiliation, Miss Stapleton, and humiliation is what you are accomplishing now."

Letty looked back to see Michael spread his hands wide.

"You are literally holding the reins. I have no say in our direction at all."

"See how you enjoy it," Letty muttered, slowing her pace not at all. These boots were well broken in, and she was used to walking nearly everywhere. He could damn well get used to riding at her beck and call for a few minutes.

Michael seemed to contemplate this, and then said in a quieter voice, "Did I hurt you last evening, Miss Stapleton?"

Her breath escaped in an exasperated burst. "You know perfectly well you didn't hurt me. You know perfectly well you pleasured me and then sent me off to bed like a plaything you had tired of."

She didn't look back.

Finally Michael said, "A little louder, Miss Stapleton, there are undoubtedly people in the village who did not hear you."

"And I was not angry till this morning when you pretended nothing had happened at all."

Michael sat back, and Maggie took his signal, pulling back to stop despite Letty at the reins. She did not want to confuse the horse; Letty stopped. Maggie whickered.

When she looked up over Maggie's shoulder at Michael again he was looking down at her. "Did you want me to announce over breakfast that we had shared a precious few moments of lovemaking the night before that kept me awake most of the night wishing for more?" He frowned. "To Mrs. Peterborough and Griggs?"

Lovemaking. Her heart skipped a beat.

"I would have preferred that you had said something to *me*," she finally told him. "I was the one left confused."

Michael wanted to take her hand, but she stayed by the horse's head, holding the reins, just out of his reach—frustrating him, perhaps on purpose.

"Letitia, I am just as confused as you are. Please don't imagine that I know what I am doing. I don't. I do not seduce ladies, much less send them off to bed alone afterward."

Letty frowned. "I don't care how rare it is, Sir Michael. I did not enjoy falling asleep thinking of you, and waking thinking of you, and then finding you in the breakfast room looking as if nothing had changed." She had changed, she wanted to add but did not say. She felt as though *they* had changed.

Michael shifted. Maggie felt it and shifted too, her hooves kicking up dust in the road.

"Letitia…" He had no idea how to explain to her that he was in unknown territory. He didn't know what to do with a lady so unconcerned about protecting her virtue. He didn't know what to do with a woman he wanted this badly. Of all the things he should probably be concentrating right now, Letty should not be on the list. But she was. In fact, Michael was worried that she was becoming the whole list. He needed to visit his warehouses in London, and instead he was here riding this damned horse bareback because this girl said she wanted a job as a horse trainer.

It was madness.

"I have been considering what it would be like to be a kept woman."

Something went down Michael's throat the wrong way and he choked.

When he was finished coughing, Letty narrowed her eyes up at him. "It seems to be one of the few positions available to me."

"A kept woman by anyone in particular?" Michael choked out while wiping his eyes.

"That was cruel," and Letty turned away to continue leading Maggie down the road.

Michael was forced to pay attention to keep his seat. "You are right, Miss Stapleton, that was uncalled for and I apologize."

Letty sniffed, though he probably couldn't hear it over the sound of Maggie's hooves on the road, and went on, raising her voice so he could hear her. "I decided I would not like to be a kept woman. I do not like the feeling of being a nasty little secret for someone I had allowed to become close."

Inside Michael had a sinking sensation in his stomach that he had felt very, very few times in his life before. Once was when his mother had discovered him fighting in the street with a ripped shirt; once was when he had almost accidentally cut loose a ship's anchor.

He was making an awful mistake. And he had no idea how to correct it.

"I'm glad to hear that you feel that being a kept woman would be an unsuitable profession for you."

She turned to glare at him over her shoulder.

Michael spread his hands. "Did you think I would urge you the other way?"

Perhaps, said a small and traitorous voice inside her. But she squashed that voice ruthlessly.

"I've made no secret of the fact that I think you should find an honorable husband."

"Who would own me and dictate my life just as my honorable father did." Letty managed to get quite a bit of sarcastic bite into the word *honorable*. "I would prefer to find a way to remain independent."

"Being a kept woman is very far from independence," Michael pointed out, then added, "Turn here."

Letty did so, not really looking where they were going. "I have very few options."

It was on the tip of his tongue to suggest that he take her to London for the season in the fall, introduce her to the eligible bachelors there who gathered there like honking birds looking for a spouse. She had no fortune to recommend her but she was pretty, and there were always husbands on the lookout for a pretty young wife. Especially older lords and gentlemen who had already lost a wife or two and were ready for the next one.

But he didn't, because he hated that idea. He could not picture himself squiring her to a ball where she would be bait for that sort of cold fish. "You might still marry," he said unenthusiastically.

Letty shook her head. "That is too chancy a business to count on for survival," she reminded him.

"Only if you are determined to marry for love." Michael was watching the back of Letty's head, waiting to hear what she'd say.

"I think... that I am quite determined," Letty said quietly, and

Michael just barely heard it over the sound of Maggie's hooves hitting the packed earth, and the soft rustle of the leaves that brushed him overhead.

Before Michael could even decide how he felt about that, they were there.

"How pretty!" said Letty, tossing him the reins and running ahead, her boots pattering up on to the wooden boards of the little footbridge.

"It's June," Michael said, seemingly apropos of nothing, but Letty knew what he meant.

The heavy heads of cabbage roses nodded down from their purchase on the tree branches that stretched over the footbridge, making a floral archway to the footpath as it led over the bridge to the other side.

"This has been here for... oh, hundreds of years," Michael said, smiling despite himself as he took in the picture, all the prettier for Letty in the middle of it, wisps of golden hair flying in the breeze.

"Not really."

"Yes, this is the ford the estate was named after when my ancestor bought the baronetcy."

"One buys a baronetcy?"

"At the time." Michael gathered the reins, felt Maggie shift beneath him but settled his weight so she would settle too. "Perhaps one still can."

"Roseford." Letty looked up at the hanging roses, laughing at them, then down to where their petals landed on the slow-moving water. "Are there fish?"

Michael shrugged. "When I came down here to play as a boy, I never caught one. I thought I saw one from time to time, but until you catch one, how could you prove it?"

Letty looked dubiously at the little footbridge. "Will it hold Maggie's weight?"

At that he flashed her an actual grin. "I doubt it."

And leaning forward, Michael squeezed both his knees, and Maggie took the hint, splashing through the water that barely came up to her knees even in the middle of the brook, and out the other side.

Letty ran across the bridge and followed them, clapping her hands in delight. "Look what you did, Michael!" she called without thinking.

And Michael realized that indeed, he had guided the horse here under his own power.

He patted the horse on the neck.

"Look what *you* did," he told her, because it was only true, meaning both Letty and the horse.

* * *

LETTY KEPT ON AHEAD, thinking Maggie might be more inclined to follow her.

But inside she was dancing. It *was* working. Sir Michael was riding, even only bareback. She felt confident that, once the saddle was sorted out properly to both Maggie's and Michael's taste, they would be unstoppable.

She could give up her horse, to him. Especially if she managed to keep her own heart.

Around the next corner in the path, she stopped short.

Maggie continued walking, past her. "Go ahead," Michael called. "You can look. It's the cottage for the manor. I think some ancestor of mine had a mother in law that he wanted to keep at some distance."

Cabbage roses hung heavy, scenting the air in front of the little cottage so that it seemed otherworldly fresh and sweet. Several were half-denuded, their petals lying in heaps at their feet.

"No one lives here now?" Letty approached the cottage almost on tiptoe, it seemed so quiet and so pretty. Surely it wasn't real.

"Mrs. Peterborough lives here now, with a girl to help her that she's sent up to her granddaughter while she is back at the manor house with me."

Letty stepped on each one of the gray, flat paving stones that led to the stoop. It was not such a sweeping grand house as Roseford, over-whelming in its size. It was a people-sized cottage, just one level, with many-paned windows at its front overlooking the path and the swaying grove of trees that surrounded it.

Letty looked up at Michael, and her mood must have improved, because her dimples were showing again. "You brought me out here to a secret cottage just to have me alone to yourself, didn't you?"

Yes. "Not at all. As you can see," Michael lifted the reins, "I am consigned to remain a-horse. Otherwise I cannot remount. And I have no crutches out here."

She nodded. It must be nearly a mile back to the manor, at least by the road they'd come. Sir Michael would not want to use his crutches to go back all that way.

Creeping up to the door, Letty tried the knob.

The door easily pushed open.

Michael frowned. "It should be locked up while Mrs. Peterborough is away. Go ahead and take a look inside, would you? And perhaps look out back."

Letty pushed the door open and stepped inside.

The door opened straight into the cottage's little parlor. It was wonderfully cool and dark inside, and smelled of dry herbs and slightly musty carpet. Letty wanted to explore all the rooms of the little place; she ran her fingers over the top of the beautiful inlaid table there before turning to look in the kitchen.

The flagstone floor was a bit uneven under her feet, but that wasn't the reason Letty tripped, nearly falling on her face as she went in.

There were dishes on the shelf over the stove, used dishes.

Mrs. Peterborough would never have left used dishes.

Feeling as if she were falling down a long, long way, Letty walked over and examined them closely. Several china plates with remainders of egg on them, the one on top sporting a few crumbs of bread and a greasy smear of what could only be butter.

She turned, feeling as if in a dream, and lifted the lid of the butter dish. There was a small pat of butter, half of it used, the corner cut and irregular as if its owner had just left that morning after breakfast.

Letty turned back and looked at the plates.

They were stacked largest to smallest, with used cutlery on top:

two spoons on one side of the topmost plate, and a used fork on the other.

She had seen such a pattern many, many times before.

Vividly Letty remembered her father stacking the dishes just this way as he'd left to go she knew not where. She was younger, she couldn't remember how young, but she remembered his speech one day as he'd placed a spoon on what was becoming a precarious pile.

"Wash the dishes today, Letty, or I'll break them over your head," her father had told her, not looking at her as he did so.

Letty was used to such threats from her father; he seldom lost his temper and he didn't seem close to it now, so she knew he meant it only as a last warning before he *would* lose his temper. She knew the process.

"Why haven't you washed them?" she asked innocently enough. He had had the time to cook and eat the food, after all. None of *her* dirty plates were in the pile; she had rinsed them and wiped them, returned them to their places as he'd taught her to do since before she could remember.

"Because that's what I have you for," he'd said, turning and looking at her so that she knew that he meant exactly what he'd said.

And then he'd left, and Letty had washed the plates, because she believed him.

That's what I have you for.

"Miss Stapleton," Michael's voice was calling outside, but Letty's feet were rooted to the spot.

He was here. Her father was here. In this house.

"Miss Stapleton!"

Letty made her feet move. They were heavier than lead, each step requiring tremendous force, but somehow she made it out of the house, stood before the little cottage that had seemed so charming just a moment before.

"Letitia."

She looked up at him.

"Letitia! You're white as a sheet."

"Yes," she said faintly. He seemed very far away.

He was here. Her father was here, in this safe little world that she'd thought so very far away from him. He was here.

That's what I have you for.

"Letty, don't faint." There was a note of command in Michael's voice, and she looked up to see that she was frightening him. "I can't pick you up if you faint."

"No," she said, and shook her head, but she still felt as though she were falling down a long, long well.

She'd thought she'd left that life behind. She'd thought she had choices.

How few choices there really were in the world.

"Letty. Give me your hand."

She let him drag her up over the horse's neck, turn her in his arms. It was so where she had wanted to be, all night, all day. But now she felt nothing but cold.

That's what I have you for.

"I have no choices at all," she whispered.

He had followed her here. He would follow her anywhere. Because he wanted her for whatever she could do for him. And he had the legal right.

"Letty, please." Michael shook her, just a little, as he slid back and made room for her sitting sideways in front of him on the back of the horse. "You're frightening me. What happened."

And Letty looked into those leaf-green eyes of Michael's that she loved—yes, she loved them—and knew that she had been wrong all along. There was nothing of her own that she could have. Nothing.

"He's here."

CHAPTER 14

LETTY DIDN'T REMEMBER RIDING BACK to the house on Maggie's back in Michael's arms. She remembered Michael calling for Griggs as they approached the portico, his voice was so loud, even though she wasn't really paying attention.

"Griggs, take Miss Stapleton into the library and have the footman light a fire," Sir Michael barked as he carefully slid Letty down from her perch in front of him. "And get Anthony up here."

Letty found herself sitting in the library in another of those large heavy Grantley wing chairs like the one she had inhabited with Michael, in his room, just last night. She had a cup of tea by her knee, but ignored it, staring into a fire. Surely it was too warm this time of year for a fire, she thought absently, but at the same time she herself felt chilled to the bone.

It wasn't long before Anthony arrived at a run. "What, what is it."

Letty just shook her head.

Michael arrived just a few minutes later, sweat on his brow from the speed at which he'd used the crutches to climb the hill to the house and up the front stairs. He hadn't bothered to switch to his rolling cart, just swung himself inside the room.

Anthony was sitting wedged into the chair with Letty, his arm around her shoulders. When Michael entered, he jumped up.

Michael couldn't deny that he felt something odd seeing the two of them sitting so close, but he ignored it; it wasn't what was important at the moment.

"Letitia," he said, startling Letty; it was the first time he had addressed her so familiarly in front of anyone else. He swung himself down into the chair opposite her. "Tell Anthony what you saw. Please."

She turned her pale blue eyes up to where Anthony stood next to her. "My father has been living in Mrs. Peterborough's cottage at the bottom of the hill," she nearly whispered.

She expected Anthony to be as shocked as she was.

Instead, he swore.

"That bastard. The runner couldn't find him at home, I knew he'd left the village. I had no idea he'd followed us here."

"What runner?" Michael barked out. "Tell me what you know, man."

Anthony paced. "I approached the magistrate about... my suspicions that Mr. Stapleton might have... committed crimes elsewhere."

"Don't spare me, Anthony, you know I have no illusions about my father." Letty's voice was getting stronger but still shaky.

Michael reached for a crystal decanter next to him, poured a splash of whisky into the glass and handed it to her. "Drink this."

She sniffed it, wrinkled her nose, but tossed it all down as though that would keep her from tasting it.

Michael didn't care if she enjoyed her spirits or not. At least a little color was coming back into her face. She'd been deathly pale for so long he had been truly frightened.

"What did the magistrate say?" Michael prompted.

"It wasn't what he said, it was what he found out. He sent runners to the city and found court cases with your father's name on them, both his real name and—and the one he'd used here. A runner to the county seat also found other complaints sworn out against a similar name, for fraud and thievery."

"Good lord." Letty's voice was a bit stronger but she was still wide-eyed. "So he has gone beyond inconveniencing the neighbors to—"

"Far beyond inconveniencing the neighbors, princess. I'm sorry." Anthony took Letty's hand in both of his, squeezed.

"Mr. Leighton, the magistrate," Michael pushed again. "What did he say?"

"He's got orders out to arrest Stapleton on sight, though under the name of Watsford. It's a name he's used before, and he didn't want the runners or the villagers to connect this with Miss Stapleton."

"Kind of him," Letty said, but her voice was still thin and papery.

"We thought he'd be using the empty cooper's house on the other side of the village," Anthony said, dropping Letty's hand to continue pacing. "Or sleeping somewhere like the mill at night. I've been checking both places every night. But he'd got past me somehow. Or, it turns out, found another option."

"Closer to me."

"Letitia. Listen to me." Michael's voice was like rope, pulling her unwilling back into the present. "Your father is not going to take you away from here unwillingly."

"But he has the right," she told him, and the look in her eyes hurt him somewhere inside his chest.

"He will be arrested as soon as he is seen," Anthony reminded her, both his hands clenched into fists. "He will not escape."

"But he has the right."

"But not the means." Michael's voice was cold and hard as iron. "He cannot enter Roseford and I will not let him take you. Do you hear me?" Michael reached across the space, leaning precariously out of his chair so that he could take her hand and squeeze it. He wished they were alone so he could fall to his knees in front of her and give her all the assurances he wanted to give her. As it was all he could do was squeeze her hand, which felt ice-cold in his, and repeat. "I will not let him take you away."

Letty didn't seem to be focusing, her eyes still looking at something far away. Michael had seen battle survivors shocked into somewhere else, afterwards, their eyes looking as empty and as lost.

Anthony didn't seem to feel the same restraint. He dropped into a crouch next to Letty's chair, holding her other hand tight. "Listen to me, princess," and she turned her eyes to him. "This is a fight we can fight. And we are going to win. You, me, and all our friends. This is that fight."

Michael saw tears start in her eyes, the first time he'd seen tears there since the day she arrived. He felt an even stronger urge to draw her into his arms and soothe them away.

But there was Anthony holding her hand right in front of him, and Letty was nodding. "All right, Anthony," she said, and he squeezed her hand and smiled.

Letty released both their hands and leaned back in the chair, her face still uncharacteristically blank.

"I can send you to a townhouse in the city with guards." Michael's brain was already ticking over the options. If her father was here, and it upset her, she should be somewhere else. Even if he'd rather have her here, he needed to think about her safety.

Letty's head whipped back toward him. "The marquess is coming to see the horses I've trained."

"Horses?"

"Strawberry has been learning."

"Letitia, be reasonable. If—"

"I have only one even slightly salesworthy skill," and here Letty's voice was rising over Michael's. "As you both have so kindly told me. I cannot miss this chance at a life where I might provide for myself."

"Letty—" Anthony, too, tried to cut her off.

But now Letty had found her feet. "I am going to the kitchen to find something to eat, Sir Michael; I have felt rather unwell, I think I need some refreshment. I'd like to see you at the stable in an hour; I have some drills for you and Maggie to practice."

Michael blinked. She certainly seemed to have pulled herself together from somewhere. She bent down to pick up her teacup and saucer, drained its contents, and then set off for the kitchen.

Anthony followed her but only to the door.

Closing it, he stepped back to the middle of the room and stopped a few paces away, hands clasped behind him, somehow failing entirely to look like a servant.

Anthony said, "If you intend to make a whore out of the woman who has been my sister, I will feel obliged to call you out, sir, even if it is a poor way to treat a man who is shy a leg."

Michael might have thought his capacity for astonishment had been exhausted by the past hour, but he found he was wrong.

Hauling himself to his feet with one crutch under his right shoulder, he step-hopped over to where Anthony stood in the middle of the floor, unmoving.

"Boy, you forget yourself," Michael growled at him.

Anthony's eyes only narrowed. "I have not had occasion to fire a pistol in quite some time, sir, but I suspect my skill has not disappeared."

Michael took him in, arrogant chin in the air, black hair raked back and tied back from that unyielding face.

He said, "Whoever you were before you came to this country, you are a stableboy here."

Anthony did not move. "Letitia Stapleton is the closest thing I have to a sister. I will not see her abused. Not while I live."

Well, he wasn't to be cowed, Michael had to give him that.

"I'm not going to hurt her, man. I can send you with her if you want to be sure. I offered her a townhouse just because it's the first place I can think of that is not here. What would *you* suggest?"

Anthony's black eyes narrowed. "You might think you are not hurting her, but—"

"I will not importune her, I will not bed her, there, have I been blunt enough for you, sir?"

Michael felt like backhanding the boy, who still stood several inches shorter than he himself did, leg or no leg.

But Anthony's posture softened only slightly. "You seem to be a gentleman, sir. But I know *noblesse oblige* has its limits. And it is just becoming clear to you how friendless Letty is."

"Not at all." Michael refused to smile, and he still felt a coal of anger somewhere deep inside at the way Anthony took liberties with

Letty himself, but he was trying to ignore it in favor of the larger truth. "It is becoming clear to me what a good friend she has."

Anthony could not help the upturn of one corner of his mouth at that, and Michael turned his back on the younger man to crutch over to his desk, drop down in the chair.

"What does the magistrate need in order to apprehend this miscreant who calls himself a father?"

"More men," Anthony did not hesitate.

Michael nodded, pulling a sheet of paper towards himself and dipping his pen. "I'll give you a letter to take to him and authorize that he engage as many as he needs. Take the footmen; George and Gerry will be extra hands at least. He'll want to draw from other villages. But this must be done, and quickly."

Michael didn't like to think of what Letty might look like after days of knowing her father was out there, somewhere close by.

"I agree. And Sir Michael. The magistrate has enough evidence of the things he's done... if we can find him, he'll be convicted and he will hang."

Michael felt his lip curl from distaste. If it didn't bother Letty... "That's for the courts to decide. Hanging or transporting, I don't care, as long as he never bothers Letitia again."

* * *

LETTY DREW on her gloves slowly. She was not going to give Michael another reason to criticize her. She was going to behave perfectly from now on around other people, because she had to, because there was no other way anyone would give her the chance to do any work that would be useful, that would be valuable enough to keep her fed and housed.

That was her entire problem, Letty had decided as she'd washed her face and hands and put on a dress that was without horse-sweat. She'd been running around behaving like a baby, trusting people she didn't know, like Sir Michael. Anthony had always tried to warn her,

her Anthony, but she was the one tripping through the grass like a toddling child putting her arms up to hug anyone she met.

Of course she'd gotten too excited over Michael Grantley. He was the first eligible man she had ever really met. There hadn't been too much opportunity to meet strong young men capable of swinging themselves around by their arms before she'd left her home village. Perhaps the world was full of them.

No, she knew that the world was not full of chestnut-haired men who had beautiful eyes even if they never smiled and who tasted better than berries in summer.

But she could pretend that it was, if it would keep her from embarrassing herself yet again, keep herself pulled together till she could get her first real employment, find her own way of keeping herself at least a few feet ahead of the grasping hands of her father.

Her father. She'd never resented him before; she'd never had the time. Now she felt resentment swelling up under her breastbone, and it made her want to scream. Why couldn't he just leave her alone? Why couldn't she have any sort of a life of her own, even for a little while, without him hanging over her head?

Because he always had been, she realized that now. Even when he'd been away, she'd always been waiting for the next axe to fall. It was exhausting.

And Anthony thought she was afraid of being alone in the world, thought she blamed him. She only blamed herself. She should have realized years ago that she had to leave that house, get away from that person, and do something, anything else with her life, no matter how long that life was.

She had given Michael exercises to do with Maggie until he probably hated her, and she'd worked Strawberry no less tirelessly. Strawberry was a flighty, silly thing compared to Maggie, but she had some patience too, and she let Letty drill her until she knew the signal to come. Then she had Strawberry practice standing.

The horse was a bit nervous. Perhaps she had had a bad owner. Letty had led her away and then back to stand, repeatedly, yanking on the ropes dangling from the treetops to make them rustle and showing Strawberry that there was nothing to fear. Someday Michael would work out what was the correct saddle for him, and Strawberry might be needed to give Maggie a break. Michael was a baronet, for goodness' sake. He would need more than one horse. He had things to do. Just like she did.

Letty set her jaw. She'd worked herself and the horses and Michael all afternoon, and she felt much more stable, as if she had rediscovered how to stand with her feet underneath her.

Sliding her gloved hand down the bannister, Letty walked sedately down the steps, still determined to behave herself for once. She needed to be more careful. Michael Grantley was not a bad man, but he was the sort of man who would make love to her, and buy her riding habits, and ultimately tuck her away into some mistress cottage somewhere to have children that he might or might not let her keep. She couldn't chance that; she wouldn't do that. He might be beautiful, but that was all the more reason she needed to keep her head. He was a better man than her father was, but he still thought in terms of controlling her, and she was done with that sort of person for good.

As she came down the final stairs, she glanced toward Michael's room, half disappointed, half relieved to see his door was shut. He could at least see that she was properly dressed, even if she was glad to escape another biting remark about her person in general.

"I've beaten you to the door," said Michael's voice out of the cool dark foyer, and Letty's eyes flew to him there.

He was shifting out of his wheeled cart on to crutches. He wore a plain blue waistcoat, and a coat, and a *hat*.

He offered her an elbow. "I apologize I cannot take your arm, but if you'll indulge me?"

She slid a hand through the crook, over the dark fabric. "I can walk." But her expression didn't match the brusqueness of her words, and she looked up at him inquiringly.

"I realized that if I objected to a lady visiting out of doors without an escort, I should be providing the escort," Michael said, clearing his throat. "Griggs, I've no idea when we will return so please do keep a lantern out here."

Still blinking with surprise, Letty accompanied him out. "I don't..."

"Miss Stapleton, I am determined that you shall be safe at Rose-ford, and as it happens, following the rules of propriety at this time aligns with the goals of your safety."

"You should send me with someone, I suppose," Letty said, for she also did not want to meet her father lurking about the grounds in the dusk, and it was entirely the thing that man would be likely to do. "If there were anyone who wasn't busy."

"I think I'm going to take your advice and hire a few more staff."

"Oh, not because of my wretched father!"

"No, because it was good advice. I need a stablemaster, and some more footmen about the place; Sarah and Griggs and Mrs. Dunphy have enough to do."

Letty agreed; she'd been carrying bathwater for herself lately, it had seemed so foolish to ask for it when everyone was so busy, and it took a lot of time. It was nice, thinking that Michael had been listening to her after all.

"And will you keep Mr. Leighton as a secretary?"

"Surprisingly, yes. The boy is quick with a pen, as promised." He looked down at her bonnet; he couldn't see her face. That ugly sensation he was quickly learning to identify as jealousy poked him in the chest. "Will you be sorry to have another marriageable man about?"

She did look up at him then, and smiled, and just the sight of her dimple flashing and disappearing made Michael feel better. "Blake Leighton? He seems half my age."

"Two years younger than you. Not so distant."

"The same category as the boy who chopped off my braids back home. Not interesting, thank you."

Then she looked down at their feet. "Not even if you would wish it, I'm sorry to say."

But I wouldn't wish it, not at all, Michael wanted to say; but he was determined to rein in his baser instincts and behave with Letty Stapleton as a gentleman should. He kept his mouth shut and his too-personal remarks to himself.

In the stable, Letty tossed her bonnet down on a hay bale. And she needed to keep her gloves nice for the party, she told herself, excusing herself for peeling them off as well.

Maggie snorted and whickered, and as always Letty felt better running to her side and patting the square strong length of her nose.

"Letty, I—" Anthony, walking past the stall, stopped when he saw Michael.

"My protector Sir Michael," Letty said with a laugh, which for some reason made Michael's brows draw together in a bit of a frown, but Letty just went on. "I've come for my dance lesson, Anthony, as promised."

Right behind Anthony, Mrs. Dunphy appeared, with her apron draped up over her arm and inside it, two small, purring, sleepy cats.

"Never tell me so!" Letty dashed to examine the cats curled up in Mrs. Dunphy's arm, and only one even deigned to open an eye before continuing on purring. Letty rubbed the crown of its head; it butted her hand slightly, then back to snoozing. "You are a miracle worker, Mrs. Dunphy."

"Not so much. I just fed them everything they could hold, then cuddled them up a bit when they got sleepy." The cook's eyes met Letty's frankly admiring gaze and amazingly, Mrs. Dunphy smiled.

"Genius," breathed Letty, unwilling to startle the cats.

"Don't you fear, they won't budge for the devil himself this evening. You're down here for a dance lesson? Not with the horse!"

Letty felt herself starting to scowl, stopped. How much could she trust Mrs. Dunphy? "No, I must accompany Sir Michael to the vicar's house and I am told there will be dancing and frankly, Mrs. Dunphy, it is not something I have often done."

"Everybody dances," said Mrs. Dunphy, and while Letty stood gaping in amazement, the cook shouted over her shoulder at the stable boy, "Jim, run up and tell Griggs to bring down his pipe and we'll all have a go."

"Griggs plays the pipe?" Letty asked, astonished again.

"Griggs plays the pipe?" echoed Michael from his seat on a comfortable hay bale. This was turning out to be a more educational evening than he'd expected.

CHAPTER 15

"Good night, sir," Griggs bowed slightly and let Mrs. Dunphy precede him out of the stable.

Anthony had drilled them all in various *contredanse* forms, partnering with Letty and forming squares with, amazingly enough, Mrs. Dunphy swinging Jim the stableboy around quite vigorously.

Michael hadn't minded sitting out the dancing. He had never cared for dancing but found himself enjoying watching, especially Letty's golden hair coming free of its moorings and starting to fly all around her head. Letty gradually lost the grim set to her jaw that she had had all day, and Michael was glad; it didn't seem to suit the Letty he had gotten to know, however briefly. And Anthony threw in odd directions just to make her laugh.

Michael noticed himself watching Anthony for the meaning of his looks, his eyes on Letty, and it surprised him how glad he was to see Anthony treat Letty like the sister he called her. He'd never been jealous before. He didn't feel it suited him, either.

Now Letty was pulling her bonnet back on and holding her gloves, readying to make the trip of several dozen yards back to the house in ridiculous formality, because he had pushed her to do so, and that didn't suit either of them.

Michael had the definite feeling that whatever it was he should be doing, he was doing it badly.

But Letty smiled as he nodded toward her, and he felt that, after all, the dancing had been a good idea, forgetting that he'd had nothing to do with the idea.

And Anthony nodded toward both of them as he turned down the lamp. "I'm off to the village," he told them, giving both Michael and Letty a meaningful look as he said it. "I'll be back by morning."

"Don't stay out all night... doing anything," Letty admonished him.

"Only what I'd like to do, princess," Anthony said, giving her a smile before slipping out the door.

Maggie snorted in the dark behind them and the cats were in the next stall where Mrs. Dunphy had settled them, still sleepily purring.

Michael followed Letty out the door and let her close and latch it behind them. "I haven't seen those cats do any work to date. I hope they do something besides sleep."

"They'll earn their keep," Letty said, with a quick smile that faded just as quickly.

Michael missed it immediately. As he swung himself toward the house, Letty walking uncharacteristically quietly next to him, he tried to think of something he could do, anything, to make her smile again.

As they crossed the drive, he said, "Would you—if you would like to come with me, I am going to walk around the house before I go in."

Letty frowned. "That doesn't seem efficient. If someone were watching, would they not simply walk behind you until you went in?" Then immediately remembering that he had served in the military, "I'm sorry, how rude—"

Michael made a tsking noise, making Letty think she had said something wrong till he finally said, "Miss Stapleton, I shall leave all my tactical considerations to you in future."

Then he smiled down at her, and she realized she hadn't irritated him at all.

He went on, "There are many reasons to walk a camp's borders, including simply letting anyone watching know that you don't intend to be taken unawares."

The smile drained away from his eyes and she saw the corner of his jaw twitch.

Feeling a familiar sinking sensation in her stomach, the kind of sensation her father's behavior had caused for her all her life, Letty said, "I wish you wouldn't go to any bother."

Michael's frown pulled down the edge of his hat. "Miss Stapleton, I would go to quite a bit of bother to keep you safe. Walking around the house is no bother."

Letty considered the house enormous, and the work of swinging around it on crutches to be quite a bit of bother. "There really is no danger. My father has never been violent, he just... convinces people to do what he wishes."

But Michael had already turned, and was making his way toward the kitchen garden, tucked between its corridor and the kitchen, which had been built a short distance from the manor proper.

"Then you should be as safe as you say, since whether or not he wishes you to return with him, you wish to stay here." He looked down at her walking next to him. "Do you not?"

Letty watched her feet for a while, her slippers darkening with the evening dew, her bonnet off again and trailing from the fingers of one hand. It was hard to look up at him when surrounded by its brim, and she wanted to look up at him. "I do not understand the manners of society, Sir Michael, as you well know. My understanding is that I am damaging my reputation by residing under your roof, and by extension endangering yours. I need a means of supporting myself, but you cannot employ me as an unmarried woman, beyond my insistence that you allow me to help you retrain my horse for your needs. If I gain a reputation as a trollop, I have no hope of convincing other gentry to employ me in their stables, do I? So it is not a question of whether or not I want to stay here. You are kindly walking a fine line of impropriety for my benefit already by allowing me to be here."

Michael wished that he could take her hand. It might not be appropriate, but he would feel better. "I enjoy having you here."

Letty flashed him a more rueful smile than he had yet seen her wear. "It is kind of you to say, especially given my poor... behavior."

"Behavior?"

Her dimple did appear for a second, even if it immediately disappeared. "Importuning."

"Miss Stapleton," Michael nearly whispered.

"What?"

Impatient with his crutches, Michael sped up to reach the brick nook behind the kitchen garden before her. He leaned himself and his crutches against the windowsill so he could offer her his hand. She offered the hand with the gloves; he took them and stuffed them unceremoniously into his pocket so that there were no barriers to their touch.

"What?" she asked again.

He drew her closer, rubbing his thumb over the back of her bare hand. "What can I say that will convince you that the poor behavior has been all mine?"

Letty scoffed. "Perhaps you have been importuning some other girl in your spare time, Sir Michael, but when you and I have been together, I have been appallingly... importunistic. Is that a word?"

"I have encouraged you, because I enjoyed it," Michael said, moving his thumb up to stroke the back of her wrist, feeling her pulse speed up against his fingertips. "I have done just as much importuning, because I wanted it." *I wanted you*, he almost said, but stopped himself. "As a host I have been horrifically remiss, failing to protect an unmarried young lady under my roof."

"I'm not a lady, Sir Michael," Letty insisted again.

"Society claims you must be that or a lightskirt, Miss Stapleton, and you are no lightskirt."

Letty scowled a little. "How do you know *that?*"

Michael let out a huff of air. "Miss Stapleton," he whispered again, and his voice, so close in the dark that it was more intimate than a kiss, "I could explain, but it would require another most inappropriate demonstration."

She looked up at him, his eyes dark in the shadows, and moved towards him till her skirts brushed the leg he was using to brace himself upright, his hips against a brick windowsill. She dropped her bonnet beside them. "I do like your demonstrations," she said very quietly.

Michael's brain exploded into a chaos of thoughts like *So do I* and *You asked for it*, and he groaned, giving up the battle as he pulled her tightly to him, his arm sliding easily around her waist, the other supporting her shoulders. She came to him immediately, flowing full against him more softly than a featherbed, fitting against him perfectly. His mouth came down over hers, her soft lips opening to him instantly, the taste of her affecting him like honey. She was *delicious*. He held her more tightly still, tasting her kisses until she sighed and rested her hands against his chest, and he felt himself harden against her belly.

Michael lifted his head and looked into her half-closed eyes.

"I thought that did make me a lightskirt," Letty told him softly.

"Have you ever kissed anyone else like that before?"

"No."

"Have you ever even thought of kissing anyone else like that before?"

She shook her head just a little. "No."

"A lightskirt, Miss Stapleton, would have kissed several men that way by the time they had reached your age."

No one has ever kissed a man like that before, Letty thought to herself, but out loud she said, "Perhaps I've simply never had the chance."

"You would have found chances."

Letty considered. Perhaps she had grown more observant, but she felt that she simply had never before met a man who drew the eye quite the way Michael did. It was probably not ladylike, but she had not failed to notice, for instance, the excellent shape of what she could only think of as Michael's backside. She let her fingers slide boldly over its curves now.

Michael raised his eyebrows at her.

"Perhaps I'm simply a very choosy lightskirt," Letty told him.

"And how many men have you importuned, Miss Lightskirt?" he teased, kissing the tip of her nose.

"Just the one," she breathed out, opening her mouth in hopes that he would kiss her again.

"It appears that the object of your … advances, then, is limited to me."

Letty frowned, closing her mouth. "I have very little experience of men at all, sir. But it has seemed to me that without my … poor behavior, you would have left me entirely alone."

Michael crushed her to him, his voice whispering in her ear as he traced its edge with his lips, "If the burden of society's disapproval would not fall so disproportionately on you, my lady, I would have importuned you day and night since practically the moment that you arrived."

"Really." Letty's smile sparkled at him even in the dark, and her delight was so evident that he could not but kiss her again.

And again.

"I would have importuned you in my bed, and in yours," he muttered harshly, rubbing his cheek against the side of her neck and then, when her head fell obligingly to the side, nipping at the base of her throat with his teeth.

She moaned and raised up on tiptoe, pulling him closer to her as well.

"I would have importuned you in the library, the breakfast room, and very likely on the stairs and in the kitchen."

"Oh my," Letty breathed into his neck, and tried copying him by biting him on the shoulder, just a little, through his shirt.

That caused a deeper groan to tear its way out of Michael's throat, and he pulled her hips against his, settling her between his thighs. "I would have importuned you until we were both too tired to move, and then I probably would have tried to importune you more," he admitted hoarsely into her hair, his hands sweeping down her back to pull him more tightly against him.

"I thought it was only me," said Letty against his earlobe, worrying it a bit with her teeth.

"Not just you," he said, trying to keep his voice from cracking as he pressed himself into her softness, nudging her sideways in his arms so he could kiss his way down her neck.

"I would have importuned you in all those places as well, except that I would probably have burst into flames from the embarrassment if I even tried," she admitted with a laugh, and Michael thanked everything he held holy that she seemed more herself again, more his indomitable, laughing Letty.

"I like the thought of that," he muttered into her skin, bending down and rubbing the stubble of his chin against the soft skin of her decolleté, delighting in her gasp.

"Really? I had thought that gentlemen... did not like such behavior," Letty managed to get out, then gasped again as he closed his lips over her nipple through the fabric of her gown. "Michael! Please do that again!"

He did, and felt himself grow impossibly harder as she unthinkingly grabbed his head and pulled him to her. He applied a tiny bit more pressure, then scraped his teeth over the hard point, and the cry she made nearly caused him to spend in his trousers.

He had to loosen his grip a little on her or they would end up on the grass with him inside her. She pulled him, like a magnet. It was hard, physically hard to open his arms a little and give her space he did not want to give.

"Letitia, I would not risk giving you a child you did not want. Aside from that, I would be at your disposal to importune at any time you like, were we free to do as we pleased. Would that I were only at your disposal, my lady."

She blinked, seeming to come from someplace far away, and regarded him dubiously. "Truly?"

It was difficult, but Michael could prove that to her, at least. "Truly," he said, settling her on her feet and leaning back against the brick sill, spreading his hands wide as if to offer her an open field. The only thing he wanted more than to touch her, was to have her touch him, and that was only the truth. "The truth is, whenever you touch me, I always want more."

Letty licked her lips. "How much more?"

Michael couldn't tear his eyes away from the way she was looking at him, all of him. He felt seen in a way he had never been seen before. And just like the night before, the way she looked at him pulled at something inside him. "All you like," he said hoarsely before he even realized what he was saying.

It was too tempting an offer for Letty to resist. She was aching, and felt herself ready for him to do whatever he would to her; but she had been so longing to touch him for what felt like a million years, she was not about to miss the chance.

Her fingers flew to unbutton his waistcoat, and then to pull his shirt tails from his trousers; Michael laughed at the eager quick way her fingers flew about his clothes.

Then she unbuttoned his trousers, and he stopped laughing.

"Letitia," he warned, his voice dropping low as she pulled at the edges of the things, revealing his smalls.

"Only touching you cannot ruin me," Letty reminded him, freeing him from his clothes. Her hand stroked his length, and Michael's head thumped backward against the window. "Is this not what we did in your room?"

"Not exactly," he gritted through his teeth as her fingers squeezed the tip of him, causing his hips to jerk forward. His hands flew to the windowsill to keep himself braced.

"I would have liked to stay and try this," she admitted, "but you seemed eager for me to leave."

"If you had stayed, and we had done this, I would have had an extremely difficult time avoiding pulling you into my bed and sliding inside you," Michael told her, using his hands for balance, thrusting into her tight hold.

"Well, sometimes one must do what is difficult," said Letty, twisting her grip on him even as she leaned against him, sliding her arm behind his waist.

Letty could feel wetness from his tip spreading over the length of him as she moved her hand along his length. She had not expected it, and found it extremely interesting, not least in the way that it made it easier for her to stroke her hand up and down him, in a way that made Michael gasp much like she had done just moments ago.

She was going to kill him, Michael thought wildly, and he was going to enjoy it.

"Michael, let me kiss your ear," Letty whispered, and he dared not risk his balance by lifting his hands to hold her, as much as he wished to; his groans grew louder as he leaned toward her to let her do whatever she would.

Letty traced the edge of his ear with the tip of her tongue, then bit his earlobe as she squeezed him tightly.

With a shout, Michael drove his hips forward, his seed shooting out into the darkness.

Breathing hard with her own sense of triumph, Letty came back to awareness slowly, realizing as Michael put an arm around her waist again and drew her close that they were simply standing outside the house in the dark, even hidden in their little corner as they were, and that anyone could have wandered by.

Michael leaned back, drawing ragged breath after ragged breath, and Letty saw his thigh muscle trembling with the effort of holding himself upright. "Oh my," she said to herself, turning herself to shelter him a bit though there was no one else to see, and tucking him back into his clothes even as he softened, and buttoning him up.

He sighed and pulled her closer, his face in her hair, breathing in the scent of her and his own scent on her hands. "Letitia." His voice was low, quiet, somehow almost reverent.

"Thank you," she told him, pressing herself against the solid muscle of his side, wrapping her arms around his neck.

"Thank you, my lady," he said raggedly, and then with a little laugh. "Thank you."

His lack of composure, and the evidence of how she had affected him, gave Letty strength and composure she had been struggling to feel all day. She had her own abilities; she had her own effect. She felt more stable on her feet, even as she too was trembling.

She wanted to tell him that she had wanted to importune him just this way many times, and would like to do it many more. She ached to lay him down on the grass and wrap her legs around him, press herself against him as he had done with his hands before until she reached her own completion.

Instead she lay her head against his chest where they stood, breathing in the scent of him and the damp grass and the night air, and felt good.

* * *

CHARLES STAPLETON HAD BEEN EXTREMELY inconvenienced by the number of men that the magistrate had zipping back and forth along the roads.

He had no reason to believe that they were looking for him, but he also had no reason to believe that they were not, and his freedom to date had resulted from his policy of remaining overcautious rather than the opposite.

Damn his daughter. When had she gotten so inconvenient? He was not used to having to sneak around the countryside looking for her. She should be at home, where a girl belonged, waiting upon the needs of her father.

Instead she seemed to have gotten herself tucked in very cozily at Roseford Manor, and that didn't suit his plans at all.

Charles F. Stapleton knew his daughter very well, and he knew that she was no fool. If she had gotten herself a place at a comfortable manor, however she had gotten it, she was unlikely to give it up. He himself had nothing at the moment with which to lure her away, except any remaining sense she had of filial duty, which must be waning rather thin or the girl would be at home where she belonged.

His only hope lay in the possibility that Anthony had convinced Letty to run away from their village and somehow take up residence here. In twelve years, he had never had a reason to mistrust Anthony or his motives, but the boy wasn't his blood, and the boy was a foreigner here, alone for God knew what reasons. Charles Stapleton had not survived as long as he had by trusting people.

It was just possible that Anthony had simply grown tired of the village and had taken the opportunity somehow to convince Letty to leave with him. Perhaps he'd felt guilty at the idea of leaving her on her own. That sounded like the sort of idea the boy would get into his head.

If that were the case, Charles should have a simple matter in front of him of finding a way to see Letty and convince her to come home.

If it wasn't that simple a matter, well, Charles would have to have some alternative plans in mind as well.

All these dratted men were making it awkward for Charles to even organize his day. He couldn't go back to the Roseford cottage, and the damned young men, as he thought of them, from the village were checking the cooper's and the mill two and three times a day.

Charles was having to stay on his feet, stealing the odd morsel of food from a windowsill here and there as he stayed out of sight but within shouting distance of the cottages outside the village's main street. With his collar turned up and his hat crushed on rather awkwardly, he could easily be mistaken for the miller, the red-faced Will who was constantly running about on one errand or another, and he counted on that somewhat.

He spent much of his day ducking under the bridge that held up the road on its way away from the mill, and sleeping against trees with one ear cocked for approaching shouts. It was uncomfortable and difficult.

It would be easier if he had an associate he could trust, but this would have to do for now.

Perhaps it would be easier once he convinced Letty to go with him.

CHAPTER 16

WHEN LETTY COULDN'T SLEEP, she slipped down to the kitchen to mix up a batch of risen bread dough by the light of the banked hearth.

Though Mrs. Dunphy hadn't said anything, the new washtub was sparkling clean. It made Letty smile just a little. She hadn't seen Mrs. Dunphy struggle to stand up last night, either.

Forcing herself not to walk to Michael's room, even if only to watch him sleep, Letty turned instead down the long hall of the formal dining room. She knew where it was, as Sarah had identified its door, but she had barely entered it before.

The tall portraits of stern older men stared somberly at her as she crept along by moonlight, the starlight from outdoors flickering and splitting in the faceted glass panes of the long narrow windows. Even in the warm summer night, it felt cold and unwelcoming in that room, and Letty felt a prickling sensation between her shoulder blades.

The Grantley men, she strongly felt, disapproved of her presence here.

Trying to hurry past the rear door, she almost tripped over Griggs, lying rolled on the floor in a quilt.

"Griggs! What on earth!" Letty caught herself from falling just in time, hands outspread, her nightgown flapping like a wide linen cloud.

"Keeping an eye on this door, ma'am," said the butler, blinking his bloodshot eyes. It couldn't have been that long since they'd all retired; was he sleeping at all?

"This cannot be the best plan, Griggs. Perhaps Jim can sleep here, if Sir Michael really feels it is necessary?"

"Jim is sleeping at the front door, ma'am, and Sarah has moved down into the room next to yours for the evening."

Letty felt tears coming to her eyes. "You are all wonderful people, Griggs."

"Well, ma'am, I..." Griggs didn't seem to have a ready answer for that one. Perhaps his own eyes were looking a bit damp, at that.

"None of this is necessary, not just for me."

"Well ma'am, there's two things, if you don't mind me laying it out for you. One is that we like you, and that's the truth. Two is that we don't much care for people coming to Roseford looking to cause trouble."

Letty nodded, trying to dash away the tears before he saw them fall. "I agree with you, Griggs, I don't care for that either."

"So you go get some sleep, ma'am, and it will be morning before you know it."

"Thank you, Griggs, I will."

Letty found it easier to go back up to her room without looking in on Michael now. The house seemed warmer now, and with much less of a disapproving air.

But she couldn't ignore that fundamentally, the stern portrait Grantley men were right. It was clear that she couldn't stay here, if even the threat of her father was causing this much trouble. She needed to make some plans to move along, and soon.

Nearly silently, she opened the door to the room next to hers, but Sarah was still awake too, or a very light sleeper, because "Is that you, miss?" came out of the dark as soon as she did.

"Yes, Sarah, I didn't mean to wake you." I just wanted to know you were really here, Letty thought silently. How distressing.

"Go to sleep, miss; you need to look pretty for the party tomorrow, and I have a very clever plan in mind for your hair that Mrs. Allenby has already approved of."

"Good night," said Letty softly and closed the door, creeping back to her room, knowing she wouldn't sleep much; she would go down and see to the bread in a few hours, and let it rise again before morning, and now she was absolutely terrified of whatever Sarah planned to do to her hair.

* * *

LETTY FULLY EXPECTED YET another cold welcome from Michael this morning; in fact, she welcomed the idea. It would help firm up her spine about the need to leave. He was always going to be the sort of man who shared intimacies at night and ignored her during the day, and that was just the way it was. Better to cut herself loose.

She was *not* expecting him to meet her eyes as she entered, and smile—a complete, eyes-crinkled at the corner smile, first thing in the morning and straight at her.

It made the memory come back to her, almost as if she were reliving it, of leaning with him against the brick of the garden wall, his hot skin under her hands and his moans in the air, and she felt herself flush beet-red from her face down to her toes, and she could not help but smile back.

Mrs. Peterborough, who had been picking at a buttered scone, dropped it as if a shot had been fired, and immediately said in tones of iron, "*What have you two children done?*"

Letty felt the flush stay on her face as she settled in her chair, but Michael looked absolutely unabashed. "Mary, that is a very accusatory tone for such an early hour of the morning. Neither one of us has done anything yet today."

And Letty decided to follow on Michael's nonchalant tone, adding, "On the contrary, I have baked some bread that I am bringing to share."

Michael seized a thick slice from the basket she was putting on the table and immediately began to slather it with butter.

"My apologies, Miss Stapleton, I am most happily corrected."

"Children." Mrs. Peterborough was sitting up ramrod straight in her chair, eyes flipping back and forth between the two of them. "This is not a game."

"No one here is having any fun right now, Mary, I promise you," Michael said with his more usual expression, making Letty glad that perhaps the smile really was just for her, and simultaneously sad that it was gone.

"Children," Mrs. Peterborough said again. She rapped a spoon on the edge of her teacup, as if she needed to get their attention with its ring. "You are going to attend the vicar's party tonight and demonstrate to the entirety of the town that you are distant relatives only faintly acquainted with one another and not the least bit interested in the fact that you are currently, scandalously, living together under the same roof. It is *vital* that you convince everyone in the town of this. It is vital for both of your reputations, but it is far more important for the reputation of Roseford Manor, which, I must tell you, means far more to me than either of yours."

"I quite agree, Mrs. Peterborough, I—"

But Michael cut Letty off.

"Mary, I find that this morning, I am not in the mood for a lecture. I will attend this party, as will Miss Stapleton, as you insisted. You will attend too, and damn the proprieties. I'll come home when I please, and leave as I please, because, as you like to remind me, I am the baronet now and this estate is mine."

Letty wished that she could shrink as Mrs. Peterborough's eyes narrowed at Michael.

Michael, who ignored her, and bit into the bread.

The moan he let out made Letty jump. Then flush again. She'd heard him make similar noises before, but not at the breakfast table.

"Miss Stapleton." The baronet was now rudely chewing and speaking at the same time, and he pronounced her name as if he were addressing a bishop. "This bread is sublime."

"Thank you, I—"

Caught between Mrs. Peterborough's glare and Michael's ability to ignore the glare completely while praising her bread in tones usually reserved for princes and kings, Letty found herself for the first time without anything to say.

* * *

LETTY ENJOYED WATCHING Michael enjoy the bread, but she couldn't eat much, not with Mrs. Peterborough glaring at her so.

She excused herself from the table as soon as she could, slipping away into the hall but not before she heard Mrs. Peterborough's voice again. "Think of your business prospects, Michael," but she ran outside, *sans* bonnet or gloves, before she could hear any more.

* * *

"WE SHOULD SKIP LUNCHEON AGAIN."

"We will not." Michael wiped the sweat from his forehead, patted Maggie's nose. "You must eat, as we've a long night ahead of us. And it will soothe Mrs. Peterborough's feathers somewhat."

Letty looked over at Michael, in shirtsleeves once again, then up at the sky where summer rainclouds were also threatening to gather. "You shouldn't have—" But she still couldn't find the right words.

"What? Contradicted her? I never like to contradict, but if the choice was between hurting your feelings again and upsetting Mrs. Peterborough, it was a pretty clear choice."

Letty's face was scrunching up in a number of new directions. "I didn't want to make Mrs. Peterborough unhappy."

Michael shrugged. "She's just looking out for us, Miss Stapleton. As you may have divined, the rules of the game of polite society are stacked against us no matter what we do. My patience was bound to run out."

"But that's—I don't understand. If we fail to be convincingly uninterested in each other this evening. Will there—won't there be consequences at all? Or is Mrs. Peterborough misinformed?"

Michael kept his eyes on Maggie's soft nose. The horse had snuffled up his sleeve as soon as he had approached her, and she was staying with him throughout the morning, rather than looking longingly after Letty as she often did. It was reassuring, in a way, that Maggie's regard for him this morning was so positive. He had rather a dim view of himself again this morning, but also the growing realization that he didn't care. He had never felt, never expected to feel, as Letty made him feel, and he was realizing slowly too that he had no intention of letting go of that feeling.

He had no intention of letting go of Letty.

Nonetheless Mrs. Peterborough was right about one thing. A man with a reputation for poor moral character was unlikely to run a successful business. He needed others to invest in his and his partner's plans, and he needed to appear above reproach.

He despised that only the appearance of being above reproach was required.

Society's answer was to put Letty safely in a townhouse somewhere and visit her when he pleased.

He didn't please. He wanted to wake up to her every day, and see her every night. He didn't want his lady love tucked into a townhouse somewhere far away. She wasn't a lightskirt, but they way they reacted to each other was the way men treated their mistresses, and one didn't keep mistresses in one's home. It was insanity.

Letty stomped her foot. "How unhelpful! Don't leave me wondering, Sir Michael. You know I am not familiar with society. Simply tell me."

Michael sighed, and clicked his tongue to have Maggie walk forward, balancing himself with a hand on her neck. The horse walked him, hopping but stable, to the fence, where he could grab on without his crutches.

Inwardly Letty cheered, but she said nothing for fear of derailing his answer.

"Well. Consequences always start with gossip. The vicar could spread the word around town, or farther, that I am up to immoral behavior at my own house. Theoretically village businesses could refuse to do business with me—but they won't, both because there is no other manor and because I am fair with them."

"All right..." Letty waved a hand to indicate he should continue.

"Local neighbors could refuse to receive me, but I don't care because I don't socialize anyway and I don't invite them here as it is."

Letty's brows knit together. "The young ladies in the area would stop being... eligible for you to court?"

Michael looked her in the eye. "About which I also would not care one fig."

That made Letty feel peculiar. She ought to be glad, she thought, but it felt more complicated than that. She went on, "And the fathers?"

"Would think me a villain and denounce me publicly, and privately would probably congratulate me in a completely hypocritical fashion."

"Publicly...?"

"Oh, wherever," Michael said airily. "Wherever my name might come up."

Letty nodded slowly. "Regarding your marriage options. But also regarding the men you need to hire. And your business dealings. Your business in the city?"

Silently he damned his Letty for being so intelligent, but Michael kept his expression nonchalant. "Possibly."

"You could be known as a dishonorable man... just in the places where you are trying to launch a business that requires other men to trust you with their investments in order to pay for goods you are trying to bring into this country."

"Miss Stapleton, I assure you, of any ten men who might impugn my honor, five of them would be supporting mistresses."

"But not under their own roofs. Because they are married."

Michael looked bored by the entire discussion. "You should marry me and cap off the whole mess."

Letty felt that like a punch in the stomach. He wasn't even looking at her. Any opportunity to be pleased with his attentions this morning evaporated in the sunlight, leaving Letty feeling cold. It felt hard to move.

"That is not funny, Sir Michael."

"It's a proposal, Miss Stapleton. It's not meant to be funny."

If he hadn't called her Miss Stapleton just then, she might have felt, somewhere inside her, like he meant it.

She was proud that she held her voice firm. "Your need to put all this unpleasantness behind you is driving you to bizarre conclusions. We will go to this party, with any luck at all, I will engage a new position tomorrow training horses for the marquess, and your problems will be solved."

Frowning, Michael made the sign to Maggie to lay down.

Surprising both of the humans, Maggie did.

Letty was still trying to decide what to say when Michael shook the reins, making a bit of a chuck-chuck noise, and with just a bit of a rocking motion, Maggie stood.

And on one crutch, Michael led her horse away.

* * *

LETTY WANTED to work with Strawberry, but she didn't have the time. She had strict instructions of when to go inside and begin her bath, and indeed she was late because Sarah had it ready, the water already cooling, when she arrived. Though it wasn't cooling much, because there was also a fire going in the room, albeit a small one. An iron—an *iron?*—was in the coals and there were scissors and other wicked-looking tools set out on the bed.

Sarah looked as if she were the one going to a party.

"I'm that excited, miss, I can't wait to see if my plan works," she said as she helped Letty sluice water through her wet hair.

Letty looked at the bedraggled yellow strings falling down in front of her eyes and dripping into the tub. "But what if it doesn't?" she half-wailed.

Sarah was not interested in the possibility of failure. Letty soon realized that she would need a book or something to do if she wasn't going to expire of boredom while Sarah fussed over her hair.

Sarah massaged a bit of oil of something fresh and fragrant into the hair while it was still wet, and set Letty to tossing the curls to dry a bit while she went to get the hairbrushes.

Left to her own thoughts, Letty was barely able to choke down some of the bread and butter that Sarah had brought up for her as she had, after all, forgotten about any luncheon.

She also decided to simply give up ownership of her head to Sarah for the rest of the afternoon. It would be simpler.

Sarah brushed, and pulled, and tugged. At one point she had Letty lay her head on a table full of linens, and used the iron on Letty's hair. Letty just kept her eyes closed and tried to ignore the whole thing.

The toughest part was when Sarah left her for an hour laying on the bed, hair spread all around her, and warned her not to move much.

This, thought Letty, this was enough of a reason never to get involved with a member of the gentry, if attending someone else's dinner entailed this much effort.

* * *

MICHAEL WAS SCRAPING the beard from his chin when Griggs knocked on the door.

"In a minute," he groused.

Unaccountably, Griggs appeared anyway over his shoulder.

"Good lord, man, I'm—"

"Miss Stapleton asked me to make sure you had this before you dressed."

Michael's frown faded a little as he took the wad of linen from Griggs' outstretched hand. "What …?"

"She explained there are two layers, sir, and that you should treat it as a stocking for your—for your leg."

Michael saw what he meant. It was like a huge sock, with an inner layer and an outer, and he was sure it would fit with room to spare over his knee and up his thigh.

"Miss Stapleton felt that it would render your leg more comfortable, sir."

Michael couldn't help himself from smiling, just a little. So completely inappropriate, and yet so very practical—and relayed through Griggs, poor man.

He smiled at Griggs, who looked taken aback.

"Understood, Griggs. And thank you. For everything."

The older man just nodded, his eyes misting a bit, as he stepped back. "We'd all—we're happy to do for you, sir, not just for the memory of your father, but, y'know, for you."

He nodded again and left Michael silent.

Michael had never proposed to anyone, and he didn't expect himself to be good at it. Nonetheless, Letty's extremely firm refusal had hurt. She didn't even seem to care about it. Michael hadn't really expected her to follow him, but he hadn't seen her since he'd returned to the house, either.

He was left with the lowering understanding that the girl simply did not want to marry him. It blackened his mood and he hadn't wanted to go to this bedamned party in the first place.

What was wrong with the prospect of being Lady Grantley? What was wrong with Roseford?

Of course he knew the answer. The problem was that the title and the manor came with a bad-mannered, stutter-tongued, half-legged bilge-rat, namely, himself.

The thought of Letty leaving Roseford was pulling at some place under his ribs, as though there were a hook set into his flesh and pulling him very slowly apart. He loved his home, but it would be a cold, hollow place if she really left.

He was going to have to figure out what it would take to convince her to stay, that was all.

* * *

MICHAEL WAS DETERMINED to get through this evening as unscathed as possible, so he was sitting in the drawing room resting the leg, in its leather and metal strapping, when Letty came in, rushing as always.

"Oh no, Sir Michael, don't get up, surely we are at least past that." She was fussing with her gloves. "Mrs. Dunphy whitened these with lemon juice and now I smell like a cake. Sarah?" she called back down the hall. "Are you helping Mrs. Peterborough?"

Michael had stopped in the act of attempting to stand, jaw dropped.

Letty looked back at him. "Oh for heaven's sake, is it not all right?"

Letty looked like a polished ray of sunlight. Mrs. Allenby's gown was of a watered silk that was just slightly darker than Letty's sun-kissed skin. A plain ribbon edged the neckline and arms, but satin-side out, to give it some texture but in the same color, and long streamers of the ribbon trailed down from her decolletage, where they were caught up in an exquisite ruby and diamond brooch.

It was a perfect dress for Letty—modest but becoming, very well tailored and yet somehow prettily practical.

But her hair—

"What on earth did you do to your hair?" Michael couldn't stop himself from saying gruffly.

Letty's hair was smooth, the pale gold of it sleek to her head and caught into several tiny braids at the back, wound around a large smooth chignon of golden hair. Not the least bit of frizz escaped around her face; he could see every inch of her flushed cheeks, the tilt at the corner of her sky-blue eyes, and the stubborn line of her chin.

Red rosebuds and three half-blown roses were artistically arranged around the shining arrangement of her hair, setting off the pale gold with a flush of riotous color. Not little-girl pink, but full-blown red, as suited a woman too old for virginal coming-out parties. They suited a woman who had been kissed.

They suited Letty.

"I did absolutely nothing to my hair. Sarah did it all, and I can only assume she's been possessed by some hair-obsessed demon," Letty said testily. "If it is not all right, I cannot take any blame—"

"It's lovely."

Letty paused in the act of breathing in, and breathed out. She looked hopefully at him. "Really?"

And then Michael felt a little more on stable ground, because this was after all his Letty, emotions changing like the summer breezes and covered with freckles from the horse yard.

"I think I prefer your look when we are out working with the horses, to be honest, but yes, it's lovely. You are lovely."

Letty's smile glowed, her dimple practically glowed, as she relaxed a little. "So are you," she said, and her cheeks flushed slightly, just as Mrs. Peterborough came into the room, with Sarah following her carrying a bag for her.

"Miss Stapleton, very pretty, Sir Michael, well done, are we going to this fooforah after all?" Mrs. Peterborough looked tired, though her Chinoise scarf was exchanged for a silk velvet wrap and her delicate cap for one of silver-edged lace.

"Heavens yes, the sooner we go the sooner we'll have it over with," Letty said fervently, and Michael burst out laughing as he offered Mrs. Peterborough his arm.

CHAPTER 17

As THEY SETTLED in the barouche, Michael frowned at Letty's dress.

"The brooch looks well on your gown, Miss Stapleton. My mother's, is it not?"

"Oh!" Letty's hand flew to cover it, pressing it into her chest, which Michael also enjoyed. "Sarah said I should wear it, I wasn't even listening, I should not have—"

"It's fine," said Mrs. Peterborough, who was arranging a lap-rug over her knees with her bent, blue-veined hands.

"But I recall I don't believe I should have borrowed your mother's jewels before, I was so distracted—"

"It's fine," said Mrs. Peterborough again, as though completely uninterested in whatever Michael might think.

Letty was scowling, that wrinkled-nose scowl that always made Michael want to laugh. He didn't feel as uneasy this time, for some reason, seeing his mother's jewel on Letty. "Truly, it looks very well on you, Miss Stapleton, and I have no objection. It should be enjoyed."

"If it won't distress you?" Letty still looked unsure.

Michael felt something settle inside him. He simply nodded, enjoying the way Letty's curves and skin were outlined by the soft color of Mrs. Allenby's dress. That woman deserved every penny she made, Michael decided. "No distress at all," said Michael, leaning back in his seat.

* * *

AT THE VICAR'S, Michael handed both the ladies down from the barouche before turning back to Anthony in the driver's seat.

"You'll keep an eye open outside?" Michael said softly.

Anthony nodded. "You can trust me. Like I'm trusting you."

Raising both eyebrows, Michael nonetheless bowed his head in acknowledgement, ever so slightly.

* * *

LETTY WAS ASTONISHED to see that the vicar's house was but a largish cottage, with its rooms all on one story.

Had she become so accustomed to the grandeur of Roseford Manor so quickly?

Within minutes, however, she became more accustomed to its more people-sized scale, walking through the foyer to the parlor where she could see the vicar had removed some furniture and rearranged things to make more room for guests.

There seemed to be a dizzying number of guests, but in fact once Letty took a deep breath and looked again, what had seemed to be dozens calmed down to a few handfuls. Aside from herself, Michael, and Mrs. Peterborough, there was a bevy of terrifyingly pretty young ladies who seemed to be about her age; the vicar; three or four of the better-off merchants in the village and their wives; Mr. Leighton the magistrate and his son Blake; and...

"Miss Stapleton, Grantham Eliot, Marquess of Faircombe," said the vicar, his hand leading Letty up to curtsy in front of what must be a wall. No man could be that wide and square.

"Miss Stapleton," said the sun-weathered marquess, touching Letty's fingertips in a mere formality. "Pleasure. Ah, Sir Michael, good to see you again."

Surely this luck was the good kind. And Letty had been drilled in how to address him. "Lord Faircombe, I'm so delighted to make your acquaintance, I have been looking forward to speaking with you about—"

Michael's hand closed over hers and placed it on the vicar's arm. "I think Mr. Herrings wanted to show you the garden before we join the party, Miss Stapleton."

"But—"

Michael gave her the faintest of head-shakes *no*.

Puzzled, but determined to be nothing but appropriate this evening, Letty took her cue.

She turned to the vicar. "I'd love to see it, Mr. Herrings. It must be lovely."

"Please. I'd enjoy showing you my roses, though I'm sure you've seen many better around the village."

Letty looked over her shoulder and it seemed to her that Michael and Lord Faircombe immediately fell into serious conversation.

Without her.

She hoped it wasn't about horses.

* * *

ADMIRING the garden had been a snap compared to being introduced to the other young ladies at Mr. Herrings' dinner.

"This is Lady Charlotte Eliot, Lord Faircombe's daughter," he said, and Letty curtsied to the elegant young woman with flawlessly glossy brown curls, and the slightest golden tint to her skin, possibly from sunshine. Letty could believe that the girl cared about horses; she carried herself like a thoroughbred. "Charlotte," said the girl, bobbing her head in return, and yet Letty somehow had the feeling that the intimacy was actually a formality.

"And this is Miss Delina Farsworth, visiting Lady Charlotte with her parents for this part of the summer, and Miss Virginia Díaz de la Peña."

The vicar seemed much less interested in these two young ladies, but to Letty they seemed at least as interesting as the tall and elegant Lady Charlotte. Miss Farsworth was Letty's idea of a princess in a picture book: golden-haired, with a perfectly heart-shaped face and a delicate manner that was only slightly contradicted by her lush, pink-flushed lips.

Letty would have thought Delina Farsworth the most lovely girl she'd ever met, except next to her Virginia Díaz de la Peña was a beauty of a type Letty had never seen before, or even imagined. Her skin was darker than polished wood, darker than Letty had ever seen even for those who worked all day in the sun, yet completely free of sunspots, and her rounded figure was lush and not the least bit girlish. She had red roses too, full-blown ones, setting off her shining thick black curls and one at the dip of her décolleté, and Letty immediately felt like a small, young, pale imposter standing in front of someone who was so clearly sophisticated.

"Miss Stapleton," said the marquess' daughter Charlotte, and Letty almost failed to recognize *her* name, she was so caught up and probably staring. "How are you enjoying your stay in our little village?"

"Oh, please. Call me Letty. Roseford is lovely." Internally Letty felt on the verge of panic. This was exactly the sort of situation that would lead to disaster: her talking with sophisticated young ladies.

"It is." Delina Farsworth nodded enthusiastically, and Letty smiled. "The light is often perfect."

"Perfect? For what?" Letty had never heard light being complimented before.

"Delina is mad for her drawing and such," said Charlotte, waving a hand in a bored fashion that conveyed exactly how uninterested she was in Delina's drawings and such. "I'm hoping to encourage her to do something out of doors besides draw it."

"What is your recommendation?" Letty had a suspicion that was confirmed in the next moment.

"Riding, of course; it is the only profitable outdoor pursuit in these parts," said Charlotte with a dismissive shrug.

"Charlotte would say that about any part of the world." Virginia's black eyes twinkled as she ducked her head in mock conspiracy toward Letty. "She has yet to find a pleasure to match horse-riding."

Giggling a giggle like a tumbling silver stream, Delina leaned towards Charlotte and said in English-schoolgirl French and half under her breath, "*Because you haven't managed to saddle the baronet yet.*"

Charlotte frowned and responded in the same language. "*So taste-less, Delina. Please don't encourage my father's matchmaking plans. After all, the man is only half a man now.*"

Something furious swelled inside Letty as she realized that they were speaking of Michael.

Letty said, in flawless Parisian-accented French, and loud enough for all three girls to hear, "*How premature a description. Entirely a man, I think, and not inclined to be saddled or ridden, at least not by a horse-rider.*"

Letty's perfect accent seemed to mock their English-tinted French pronunciation, and the sentiment, once its meaning settled on the group, brought the entire group to a frozen stillness.

Groaning inwardly, Letty realized that this was why she should never have agreed to leave the house. Though they'd made sense in her head, once the words had hit the air even Letty could hear how scandalous they sounded; and though she didn't understand why, it was also clear that the pure French accent she had learned from Anthony as a child was not appropriate in this company either.

The girls stood in shocked silence for several moments while Letty wished the ground would swallow her whole.

Then Virginia laughed, a full-on, deep in the belly laugh, and she grabbed Letty's hand and tucked it into the crook of her own arm. "*What delightful company to meet in such a rustic place,*" she said, in French that had a rounded, lilting accent new to Letty too, "*we must talk further on this fascinating topic. Walk with me.*"

"Excuse me, Lady Charlotte, Miss Farsworth," and Letty was happy to put her golden head closer to Miss de la Peña's and quietly murmur as they walked away, "I know nothing of men amusing enough for party conversation, I'm sorry to say."

"But I'll wager you know something about Sir Michael, and since that's what those two are going to be discussing, you and I can discuss him too," said the woman, with her eyes still sparkling with mischief.

* * *

MICHAEL WISHED that the damn marquess had written to let him know that he'd be at this little party. Michael had hoped to see him first at his stables, and impress him with the horses' useful capabilities before he introduced the horse trainer.

Of course he should have expected this. It was a social triumph for Mr. Herrings.

Just a disaster for poor Letty.

And just as predictably, the marquess wanted to dive straight into the topic of horses. "Looking forward to seeing the performance of that new filly of yours."

There was only one topic Michael knew that the Marquess of Fair-combe liked as much as horses. It was a topic he himself preferred to avoid. But he'd introduce it now before he'd introduce the idea of a woman horse trainer.

"Lady Charlotte is looking well," said Michael.

Instantly the marquess was all beaming fatherly pride. "Isn't she though. She is a champion at following the hunt with her latest horse, you must see her some time. She needs a better-devised saddle so she can jump like the lads but side-saddle. My boys are all champion jumpers. Don't suppose you go in for jumping any more yourself."

"Not at the moment," said Michael, inwardly vowing to begin training with Maggie to jump.

"Charlotte a quite good hunter. Not one of those ladies who slows a party up, always asking for help with gates and the corks of their bottles. A proper hunter. You ought to come with us."

"Thank you, you're kind to think of me." Polite but noncommittal; how could he get the man on the topic of something other than horses? Horses were, Michael knew, all that Charlotte cared about, but Charlotte seemed nearly the only other conversational topic to hand. He knew nothing about any sort of politics that might interest Faircombe, and he refused to resort to talking about the weather.

He went with, "I suppose your sons ride with you?"

That turned out to be a relatively safe gambit, and soon Michael was nodding regularly to a long report on the benefits of son One, son Two, and son Three, none of whose names Michael ever managed to keep straight for long.

As was his goal, he let Lord Faircombe drone on while keeping an eye on Letty.

She looked subdued as she accompanied Mr. Herrings to the large French doors that opened on to his garden. Lovely, in the golden wheat-colored gown that shifted in the light as she moved, and with the red blooms in her hair reflecting their color on to the pale golden strips of smooth hair that had been tamed into glossy braids and dainty ringlets.

With her hair pulled back the expressiveness of her cat-shaped eyes seemed overwhelming; they drew his attention from everywhere in the room. The freckles on her cheeks provided a dusting of color there, with one or two dark accents that weren't that far from purposeful beauty marks he knew ladies made an effort to apply to themselves.

She didn't look much like his Letty, though.

And she didn't look happy.

If he could just keep Lord Faircombe off the topic of horse training, thought Michael, this evening wouldn't be a total disaster.

* * *

"Would you like to sit down, Sir Michael?"

"Thank you, no," Michael said absently, one ear still listening to a series of accomplishments one of the marquess' sons had reached at school, though as near as he could tell it amounted to continuing to eat, breathe, and attend classes.

There were two older ladies there and a gentleman perhaps in his seventh decade, seated on chairs around a settee where Mrs. Peterborough was holding court. It was the gentleman who had asked him to sit.

Belatedly Michael realized that it was a pleasure to be able to keep standing for a while. The sock Letty had made for this leg seemed to be making it vastly more comfortable to wear. He knew his stump would swell, but if he could avoid the abrasions and contusions, he might stave off his loathing of the leg for hours yet.

Yet another way in which she had improved his life.

When he looked over again, she was seated at another side of the room, with the dark young lady whose acquaintance Michael hadn't made yet. She looked desperately unhappy.

They were all too close for Michael to make any comments to Mrs. Peterborough that the others wouldn't hear, but nonetheless he bent over the settee from behind her to say quietly in her ear, "I hope you're satisfied with the evening so far?"

"I am," she said brusquely, not even bothering to look up at him, much less interrupt her lecture for the ladies in her audience on how to play a proper game of whist.

* * *

LETTY WANTED to hide entirely behind her hands. She limited herself to just pressing them against her cheeks for a moment.

"I assure you, Miss de la Peña, I have no interesting gossip about Sir Michael."

Virginia just raised an eyebrow as they settled themselves on a couch side by side. "Boring gossip then?"

"I have no gossip at all. He has been kind due to a distant relation-ship, and has allowed me to train his horse."

"Truly?" The young woman looked genuinely more interested in this news than in gossip. "I am in the neighborhood to buy a horse from Lord Faircombe. He is supposed to have very gentle horses for ladies."

"Does Charlotte train them?" Letty leaned forward, hopeful of gaining a colleague.

"Charlotte rides them," said Virginia wryly. "But you actually train them?"

"I've trained one very thoroughly, and I'm training a second for Sir Michael. I believe I am learning quite a bit. I'm afraid I will have to stop there, as he has a stallion who will not be amenable and two fat carriage horses who are uninterested in anything but their feed."

"If I were a horse that would seem to me to be eminently reasonable. If my job is to pull a carriage, start and stop are surely all I need to know. Perhaps going faster and slower."

Virginia wore a broad grin that told Letty that she was teasing, but Letty bowed her head in acknowledgement. "Sir Michael's mount knows a great deal more. I have been training her for years. She may be the smartest horse in England."

"Do tell."

Letty launched into a long description of Maggie's brilliant performance as a horse to date.

* * *

"You're not truly going back on your decision to marry Sir Michael just because he's lost half a leg."

Delina was walking along the edge of the garden with Charlotte, the short pacing steps providing both of them with an annoying pastime. She'd rather be sitting inside drawing the guests, as Charlotte well knew; and Charlotte would rather be out racing a horse, as Delina was aware.

"It's a tiresome problem." Charlotte tossed her curls back over her shoulder.

"He's a baronet and he's practically a neighbor."

"I still expect to find a better catch in town."

Delina looked askance at her friend. "Your first two seasons were not a success, Charlotte. You turned down four bachelors who were not repulsive, and at least two old men that I know of who were completely repulsive but also very rich. What on earth are you trying to accomplish?"

"If Mama were alive she would have made me choose, but Father doesn't care if I spend the rest of my life with him."

"Is that really your plan?"

Charlotte made a tsking noise with her tongue against her teeth. "I don't have a plan, Delina. I just—you have no idea, when I look at those men my palms itch. I need to get reins in my hands and ride away as fast as I possibly can."

"Oh, I think I understand."

Delina's dry, bitter tone was at odds with her fairytale face.

"I'm sorry, Del, I didn't mean that. Of course you understand."

Charlotte and Delina had shared those two seasons together, and Delina hadn't had the luxury of turning down four unrepulsive bachelors. She'd been hounded by good-looking rakes, and men over fifty who wanted a second wife, but she had had no offers. Her family's lack of funds, and her own interest in art to the exclusion of almost everything else, made her an unsuccessful debutante despite her looks, at least by her own standards.

She too just wanted to run away from those appalling suitors—but she didn't usually have a horse to carry her.

"What on earth is the girl so animated about?" Charlotte muttered under her breath as they were taking a turn closest to where Letty sat with Virginia.

Delina, whose hearing was better, said, "Apparently, training horses."

"Training horses? Never tell me so!"

Without any further preamble Charlotte marched up to where Letty and Virginia sat so closely on the couch.

"Horses are one of my favorite topics, Miss Stapleton, I hope you don't mind if we join you."

Subdued, Letty watched as Charlotte and Delina sat on tiny chairs facing her and Virginia on the settee.

She felt like a barn animal that had just been penned in.

* * *

WHEN ANTHONY HEARD dinner being announced, he slid in through the open door, seeking out Mrs. Peterborough.

He got to her just before she started to lever herself up, appearing magically at her elbow and lifting.

Mrs. Peterborough looked up at him, startled.

He put on his best country English tones. "I just wanted to ensure that you were not left alone, madam. When there is a party, people tend to overlook those of us who just need a hand here and there."

Mrs. Peterborough's chin went up. Her eyes narrowed at him. "Do they."

"Indeed."

Her face creased into a thousand wrinkles as she grinned at him. "Used to go to a lot of parties, did you, boy?"

"I, uh, did."

"Mm-hmm." She took his arm and he began to walk her, shuffling slowly, toward the long table the vicar had assembled along one wall of the room. "Someday, you will have to tell me who you used to be, my lad."

Smiling ruefully back at her, he patted her hand, gently. "No, madam. I won't."

As he helped her to her seat, Mr. Herrings looked suddenly confused at the appearance of the slim young man with his long dark hair tied back at Mrs. Peterborough's elbow. "What what?" He was sufficiently flustered that he couldn't even formulate a question.

Michael looked up. "That's my man," he said shortly. "Here to help Mrs. Peterborough if she'd like."

Anthony just inclined his head silently.

"Of course, of course. Go on through to the kitchen, boy, cook will find you something to eat," said Mr. Herrings dismissively, turning to ensure the rest of his guests were seated.

Letty's eyes were wide as she looked toward Anthony, but he did not look toward her.

He helped Mrs. Peterborough get settled then, with a brief bow, withdrew.

CHAPTER 18

THE SOUP and a vegetable course had gone off smoothly and Michael was beginning to think they would all get out of this alive when the conversation lagged and Charlotte changed the topic.

"Miss Stapleton is a great trainer of horses, Father."

"Is she?" Lord Faircombe looked down the table with slightly squinting eyes, as though to capture an elusive image of something as rare as Letty.

Michael sighed inwardly and cursed silently. Damn the girl. Damn this.

"Yes, she was regaling the rest of us with her stories of training Sir Michael's new horse."

"Really."

Again the marquess sounded surprised, as though someone had suggested that ducks could play card games.

"I wrote you about her abilities in that area, Lord Faircombe, you recall that prompted the visit you are making to me tomorrow," said Michael calmly, sipping half of his glass of wine in one go but otherwise appearing very nonchalant.

"Really. A girl horse trainer. Remarkable. I don't—"

"I think we had better speak further of that tomorrow, sir, don't you think?" Michael interrupted him smoothly.

"Oh yes," Mr. Herrings immediately agreed. "Not conversation that will entertain the ladies over the dinner table, surely?"

Despite the fact that all four young ladies at the dinner table looked more interested in discussing horses than anything else, the four older people immediately agreed with the vicar, with Mrs. Peterborough leading the way. "Quite right, Herrings, no need to bore everyone with that discussion."

Silently Michael recited a prayer of thanks and finished the glass of wine.

Charlotte was silent for a moment as there was a general rustle of people picking up their silverware again.

Then before anyone else could introduce a new topic, Charlotte said, "It seemed odd to me, Sir Michael, because Miss Stapleton said she's been training your new horse for years. But you just acquired him, didn't you? I thought it had something to do with that court case, Mr. Leighton, that I remembered you mentioned just a few weeks ago. Something to do with a fraudster stealing from the villagers, wasn't it? And didn't you receive that horse as a settlement?"

Michael swiftly put down his wineglass so that it would not shatter in his grip.

Deliberately resting an elbow on the table, Michael looked steadily across and down the table at Lady Charlotte Eliot, spoiled rich country child, someone to be pitied more than hated, because Michael felt that he needed a moment to remember that or else the rage that was beating in his ears like a battle-drum would burst out and wash over her, and that would be a bloodshed that they would not easily recover from.

He breathed in, and out, and in and out again, reminding himself, as he had when he'd just been about to order the firing of a cannon, that in battle things move faster than you realize, that it had only been a few seconds since the woman had unloaded that appalling broadside.

The older people were looking around, confused, but the young ladies, savvy to the art of the drawing room war, were already taking up sides. Delina had leaned slightly toward Charlotte, her eyes expectant as she looked at Michael, also daring him to make an explanation. Virginia looked disgusted and was glancing toward Letty, who might have turned to stone she was so still and pale.

"Lady Charlotte," said Michael, pronouncing her name very slowly. "It does not become a lady of your station to even imply an insult like that. I believe that, for the sake of the relationship between our two families and for the sake of our host, the best course of action I can suggest is that we all ignore your behavior." He looked levelly at Charlotte and let her see the expression in his eyes, which he assumed was most likely murderous.

Charlotte's chin went up, but she did draw back in her seat slightly, as though a weapon had been drawn.

"Oh I say!" Mr. Herrings had turned nearly purple. "Not at all the sort of conversation for a dining table with ladies present! Not at all!"

"No, of course not," said Charlotte quietly but clearly, keeping her eyes on Michael.

Virginia lifted Letty's wineglass and handed it to her. "Miss Stapleton, do take some wine. You look astonished."

"I am astonished," Letty said and took the glass, sipping from it.

Letty did not look around, not at any of the guests, and certainly not at Michael. She felt stupid, and embarrassed, and incredibly sorry. She had underestimated that anyone else would want to hurt Michael through her, for any reason, and this was how her foolishness played out.

Michael and Mrs. Peterborough had given her no choice about attending this party, but that, Letty now saw, was as much to protect her reputation as to protect Michael's. And that, she should have told them, was a fool's errand, because she had no good reputation to protect.

She had a thieving con man of a father and nothing else.

She dared not look at Lord Faircombe, whose voice had gotten louder, as if he wished to be heard over the general murmur. "Of course you want to keep a civil table, Herrings, but I daresay—"

Michael interrupted him with a tone he'd learned commanding sailors that was not loud but was harder than steel. "I'll certainly accept your apology for an insult to a guest of mine, sir, and nothing further need be said about it."

The marquess looked as though he might yet decide his beloved daughter deserved a bit of defense. As he was frowning, perhaps about to speak, Virginia leaned toward Mr. Herrings and said quite loudly enough for even the oldest of the older ladies to hear, "My grandfather, Lord Gourgaud, intends to acquire a good gelding for me this fall, and I so wish I could use the horse to jump. Lady Charlotte's brothers are all ripping good at jumping their horses. Do you think that jumping is a skill that resides in the horse, Mr. Herrings, or in the rider?"

Unavoidably placed in the position of answering, Mr. Herrings, predictably, deferred to the most senior titled gentleman in the room, thereby engaging him in conversation. "I myself have never jumped, Miss de la Peña, and I'm sure my opinion is not the one you want. You trained your children's horses regarding jumping, Lord Faircombe, did you not?"

This time no one objected to discussions of horse-related topics, and everyone ate silently while Lord Faircombe held forth on the need to train a horse to jump but also to have a talented rider in the saddle. This gave him the opportunity to praise his offspring without engaging the topic just previously at hand, which seemed to mollify him as well as distract him.

Michael reminded himself to unclench his fists. The anger, the *fury* he felt at Charlotte's open attempt to sabotage Letty still pounded in his heart, and he had to let it go or he would not be able to get through the rest of this thrice-bedamned evening.

He regretted ever subjecting Letty to this, regretted listening to Mrs. Peterborough's advice on his business reputation, regretted ever starting his business venture in the first place. This was why men needed their own property, this was why they built *castles*, so they could raise their own food and live by their own means and not be beholden to the rest of damned society which was made up of petty, small-minded people with petty, vicious goals of their own and no sense of kindness to others who were less fortunate than they.

Mr. Herrings' cook, who was serving as maid and footman as well tonight, appeared with another bottle of wine, and Michael gratefully accepted another glass.

He didn't drain it, because he'd need to keep his head if he was going to get through this night and not kill anyone.

He hoped Letty realized how sorry he was.

* * *

"WOULD you like to walk again through the garden now that it is a little cooler?" Virginia said quietly as they arose from the dinner table.

"I would like to sink through the floor to the other side of the earth," said Letty just as quietly. "But if you cannot arrange that, then yes, let's take another look at the garden."

Virginia laughed softly as they walked down the small pebbled path. The light from the sconces in the vicar's living room followed them out the open French doors and two beautiful mullioned windows, casting diamond shapes on the rose bushes.

The rose bushes had not been tortured into any fashionable shapes, but had apparently been well cared for, because they burst with fat blooms in many colors, and their scent filled the warm humid summer air.

Virginia walked close enough to Letty that their skirts brushed.

"I take it you are not out in society, Miss Stapleton."

"I am not, and as you see, never will be," said Letty in the same tone, pitched to stay between the two of them.

Virginia just nodded. "Here is a rule of the game that many girls never discover. What they say about you matters less than how you take it."

Letty nodded, bending her head near a full-blown rose, rubbing her cheek against its petals. "If I were a lady, I should learn to withstand such assaults, Miss de la Peña. But I am not. I'm only sorry to bring disgrace on those who have befriended me."

"Well," sighed Virginia, "I often find that ill will does more harm to those who spread it than to those at whom it is targeted."

"You are extremely kind," said Letty. "Extremely."

"I'm a little kind," said Virginia, her smile flashing quickly and then disappearing behind a more serious expression. "I'm also well versed in the art of being insulted."

"Please don't let me keep you from the party." Letty felt as if her feet were made of lead; she could barely move, and the task of being light-hearted and entertaining felt far from possible.

"I prefer the company here," said Virginia, turning to follow Letty as she strolled farther down the garden.

Though neither of them noticed, in the trees at the edge of the garden there was a movement, as of someone rustling among the leaves there, shadowed from the moonlight. Then there was silence.

* * *

AROUND THE END of the dinner table, Mr. Herrings broke out his grandfather's humidor and distributed the cigars inside to the gentlemen, the ladies having withdrawn to the other side of the room together while Letty and Virginia toured the garden.

"What's all that rubbish about then, Grantley," blustered Faircombe, lighting his cigar. "Too dry, Herrings, these will go up immediately."

The vicar turned a bit red and Michael shook his head. Had he never before noticed how unkind the marquess was? Was this something Michael had learned to notice from Letty?

"Nothing worth upsetting a lady about," Michael said, shrugging and leaning back in his chair. "The horse I got in the legal settlement is a big black bruiser, a stallion. Worth something, no doubt, but no good to me as a mount, which was what I had hoped for."

Across from him William Leighton puffed on his own cigar. "The horse you just had delivered is a filly, isn't it, Sir Michael?"

Michael thanked the magistrate silently with a crook of a smile.

The magistrate had become one of his new favorite people. "Sweet-tempered little filly. Far more useful."

"You are referring to the horse and not the girl, I presume," said Faircombe absently, brushing some tobacco ash off his waistcoat.

There was no way he was going to get through this evening without killing someone, Michael thought, not bothering to hide his expression as he looked across the table at the marquess.

Next to the magistrate, young Blake Leighton was sitting with his back very straight and an expression on his face that for the first time made him look like his father. "You don't know Miss Stapleton, Lord Faircombe," said the young man, slowly and distinctly enough that the marquess looked up to pay attention. "I think you had better judge her by the quality of her friends."

"Well, I daresay," the marquess said, leaning back in the delicate chair and making it creak. "Don't get on the high ropes, lad. You're not the one travelling all the way here with high hopes only to have it all dashed over foolishness."

"I gave you news to help your business endeavors, my lord, no foolishness," said Michael, still evenly; the marquess apparently did not notice the muscle ticking in his jaw.

"What *are* you on about, man. You cannot seriously be expecting me to take the girl off your hands. What do you think would happen to her if I took her back to my estate? I have three grown sons, or nearly."

"I would expect that she would work with you to train your horses," Michael ground out. "What else do *you* expect would happen? What sorts of animals are you raising there?"

The marquess had the grace to look at least slightly abashed. "All right, I see what you're driving at. My boys are well enough behaved. As well behaved as any I know, I'm sure."

"I doubt it," said Blake Leighton quite clearly, and inwardly Michael scored another point for a Leighton.

The marquess wrinkled his nose. "Don't think I don't know when you're having a laugh at my expense, boy. All right, I should be easier on the girl, I take your point. But what about this fellow pushing off his used goods on me, eh?"

"Faircombe," Michael growled, too quietly for any but the men around him to hear him, "retract that comment immediately and do not make another like it. I'd hate to have to kill you."

"Eh?" As if suddenly waking up to the danger he was in, taking in the red glare of Michael's eyes and the cold hard looks of the rest of the men, even Mr. Herrings and the fellow who owned the properties on the other side of town, the marquess sat up in his seat, making the delicate chair creak ominously again. No one moved.

Finding no support in any of the faces around him, the marquess appealed to the magistrate. "What hey, man, do you allow threats like that in this godforsaken village?"

"In the practice of the law, I find that my own judgment often comes to bear as much as any legal interpretation," said William Leighton, who leaned forward next to his son. "Bad judgment is its own punishment as often as not."

Realizing the magistrate was not going to help him, Lord Faircombe finally seemed to grasp that his safest course of action was at least another careless apology. "My mistake, apologies, Grantley, no offense intended. If you're that desperate to expand your stables, I'll house a few horses with you, you can train them if you like." Faircombe looked as if he intended this to be a genuine olive branch.

"Keep them." Michael concentrated on breathing to keep his temper. It was a trick his mother had taught him, he remembered now. Breathe in, breathe out, twice, before you say anything. Then say what you have to say. "You've just decided me on another business venture. I believe I'll expand my stables and offer extremely well-trained horses. I think there are buyers out there without good options."

He intended to keep the horse trainer too. But that, as he very well knew and which Faircombe didn't seem to grasp, depended on the good will of the horse trainer.

* * *

As LETTY and Virginia turned into the living room, Letty heard Michael's voice cutting through the murmur of general conversation. "I'll expand my stables and offer extremely well-trained horses. I think there are buyers out there without good options."

"Take me up on my offer and take some of mine too," said the marquess.

Letty couldn't hear the rest of the men's conversation. They looked serious, even as they were mostly puffing cigars and sipping their spirits.

The thought of Michael taking on the business idea that had been Letty's made her feel a little sick to her stomach.

It was a good idea, she couldn't argue with that. That was why she had had it. She couldn't picture Michael training horses himself. He didn't have the touch she had with horses; he didn't really extend himself to them the way she did. But that probably wouldn't matter; perhaps he intended to hire a stablemaster after all.

It would only matter that he be all right. He needed to support Roseford and he deserved to undertake any business he could.

Before she knew where her steps were taking her, she was out in the kitchen.

Anthony was sitting there on a stool, eating from a bowl that he swiftly set on the table upon seeing her face.

"We've got to get out of here," she told him fervently, heedless of the cook.

Anthony took her arm, walked her out through the kitchen to the drive of the little cottage. Michael's barouche was there, as were several of the other visitors' horses and carriages.

Letty walked up to Major, the complacent carriage horse, and leaned her forehead against his neck.

"These sorts of parties are dreadful, I know."

"If you'd really told me what I was in for, I would have drowned myself in the brook before coming here."

"It's twelve inches deep."

"I would have made the effort."

"Princess, just a little while longer. I'll have you home soon."

"It's not our home."

Letty just rubbed her forehead against the horse's neck, fearful that she would smell of horse when she went back inside and yet heedless, since that seemed to be the least of her current problems.

When she turned, Anthony was looking at her, biting his lower lip.

"Don't worry, Anthony, I'm not going to cry." She felt too empty inside to cry.

"Princess... would you like to go to London?"

I'd like to go anywhere I didn't have to feel like this, Letty wanted to scream at him. Anywhere I didn't have to worry about my awful father following me, and anywhere I could forget falling in love with Michael Grantley.

"Should I go to London?"

He patted her back. She felt stiff and unmoving. He frowned.

He said, "Mr. Leighton has a friend in the city who's been helping us in the investigations about—about Watsford. He's offered me a job. Says he could use a man of my talents."

"You're a talented man, Anthony."

"But if you wanted to go with me."

Letty just looked at him. "And do what. Be... what?"

Anthony huffed out a big breath. "What do you want to do, princess?"

She wanted to go back to Roseford and sit on Michael Grantley's lap, in his arms, for the rest of her life.

That was too foolish to even think about.

She said nothing.

Anthony said, "If it would help you to be married, princess, we'll get married."

Numb and exhausted, Letty just shook her head, unable to give Anthony even a full smile. "No more proposals, thank you. They don't suit me."

Anthony took her hand. "Are you all right, Letty?"

"I'll be fine."

Over her shoulder Anthony thought he saw some movement out

in the trees. A slender man carrying a thick staff stepped out of the trees. One of the men he'd hired at Leighton's direction.

"Letty, go back in the house. Right now. I'll walk with you. It's only two steps to the door."

"What?"

She barely knew what was happening before Anthony had her inside and the door shut and latched after her.

She looked around at Mr. Herrings' cook. "What's happening?"

CHAPTER 19

VIRGINIA DÍAZ DE LA PEÑA approached stocky, bristle-haired William Leighton as the floor was being cleared for some dancing.

"Sir," she said, stepping close to him and smiling as if she was flirting with him. "There is a man skulking around the base of the garden outside."

He looked over her shoulder, favored her with a half-smile as if he were actually listening to outrageous suggestions from a beautiful woman half his age. "You saw him? What did he look like?"

"Like someone who should be engaging in a fistfight in a public house," said Virginia, smiling and fluttering her eyelashes at him. "He had a large staff in his hands and he was looking at the house."

"That's one of my men, but you shouldn't have seen him. Thank you. Stay inside, would you?" He nodded ruefully as if turning down her suggestion of a dance, then disappeared out the garden doors very quickly for a man of his size.

Virginia followed him and closed them.

"Oh no!" said Delina but the older ladies sitting with Mrs. Peterborough shushed her. "It's getting cooler out, it's better not to have drafts in the house," said one.

Charlotte arranged herself on a small chair next to Delina and stared at Virginia with almost no expression.

"Shall I play something gentle before we start dancing?" said Virginia, looking over the ladies' heads to where Letty reappeared from the kitchen.

"Do, child," said Mrs. Peterborough and held up her hand, beckoning to Letty.

Letty took it gratefully and sat next to the older woman, smiling at the other ladies in the circle.

Michael grabbed his cane and headed outside.

* * *

"LEIGHTON, WHAT IS IT."

William turned to face the baronet. "My men spotted Watsford, lost him again."

"Not here, surely."

"Not a hundred yards into those woods, sir."

Michael's eyes scanned the treeline. It was impossible to make out anything other than a blur of dark shapes except right at the edge where the moonlight outlined specific branches. And that just wasn't much.

"Should I take Miss Stapleton home? No, I don't want her exposed in the carriage for any length of time," Michael muttered and then answered his own question.

"I think you're right, sir. Stay here. We'll make a full sweep of the woods just here and work our way over to the cooper's on the far side and Roseford more nearby. Odds are he's got to be going one of those two places."

"Roseford." Michael's chest clenched at the thought of Griggs and Mrs. Dunphy and Sarah and Jim.

"Sir Michael, honestly, this old cutpurse is wiley but he's not magic. He's got to go somewhere to get food and shelter eventually, or he's got to leave the neighborhood. I'd rather he's here; we have a better chance of catching him."

Michael understood the sentiment, but... "I need my household safe, and they won't feel safe with him at large. We need to apprehend him."

"I do understand, sir. We could try to lure him out of hiding by asking Miss Stapleton to—"

"No."

William Leighton shrugged as if he hadn't really expected that plan to go anywhere. "He's not a young fellow, and he's got to be feeling the pressure. Your George there nearly caught up to him and grabbed him, and Frank Briarly chased him into the trees faster than a rabbit can run. We're going to get him."

Michael cleared his throat. "Very well. I'll keep Miss Stapleton inside for another two hours, most likely. Let's hope for all we're worth that you catch him by then."

Leighton nodded. "If we don't, I'll have two carriages of my best men escort you home, before and after your carriage."

"As you say."

Michael turned, using his cane to work his way back into the house and somehow tell Letty that they just had to survive two more hours of what had to be the worst dinner party in the history of England.

* * *

LETTY LET Michael's whispered explanation wash over her like water. Of course her father was somewhere outside. The only thing that could make this evening worse was the person who'd ruined her life before she'd even had a chance to live it.

She wished that Anthony were here, but apparently he was out with all the rest of the men.

Her task was to stay inside with all the party-goers who knew nothing of the manhunt happening outside, and pretend to be entertaining and happy.

How utterly insane.

Virginia made it unnecessary for anyone to pretend to do anything for some time. She was good at playing the pianoforte, and she had several songs that she said were from her home that were fresh to Letty's ears, and sweet.

Eventually Delina insisted on the promised dancing, and Charlotte, who had been silent since her disastrous dinner speech, simply nodded and prodded her colleague on.

With far more young ladies than mobile men, it was not difficult for Letty to sit out the dances, perched on one end of Mrs. Peterborough's settee, with Michael on a chair nearby.

"You should at least dance once," he said to Letty at one point, leaning closer to her.

She looked at him and smiled a blank, polite smile. "I'm fine here with you and Mrs. Peterborough," she said quietly, her hands folded in her lap.

It should have been a perfectly appropriate speech, but it was so *not Letty* that it made Michael frown.

There had been no dimple in that smile.

"I should mention," said Mrs. Peterborough, leaning toward Michael over Letty's lap, "that you two are doing an excellent job of convincing many people here that you barely know each other, and certainly don't like each other."

"I hope that's all right," said Letty in the same not-Letty tone, and Mrs. Peterborough just shook her head.

"You children are going to kill me," she muttered at them both.

* * *

It seemed to Letty a million years before Anthony reappeared, nodding to Michael.

"We must be going," Michael said out loud instantly.

"Yes, I'm quite tired and I must take the young people with me," Mrs. Peterborough added just as instantly.

There were goodbyes all around, and when Letty said goodbye to Virginia, the other young woman kissed her cheek. "It was so lovely to meet you, Letty, I hope we get to talk about horses again," the beautiful girl whispered, and Letty tried to give her a real, though small, smile.

Michael had both the women in the barouche with Anthony driving away before he reached down and took Letty's hand, heedless of Mrs. Peterborough on his other side. "Are you all right?" he asked her, quietly.

Letty said, "I think, if I were wearing riding boots instead of these slippers, I would unhitch Major and just ride him away across the countryside till I came to the edge of England, then I would dive off and swim away."

Michael hummed deep in his throat. "A more Letty answer than I've heard all night, my lady, but not truly an answer."

Mrs. Peterborough grabbed Michael's cane and used it to poke Anthony in the back. "Were you saying something about parties never having killed anyone? Do you admit what a liar you are? Do you?"

"None of us are dead yet," Anthony said cheerfully from his spot up front, and whistled. An answering whistle came from the wagonful of Leighton's men in back of them, and a similar one from the front.

"This is insane, this cannot go on." Letty just shook her head no, repeatedly, one hand over her mouth.

"It won't," said Mrs. Peterborough. "Eventually we'll be home, eventually we'll sleep, eventually it will be morning."

* * *

SARAH GREETED them at the door along with Griggs, all a-bustle and wanting gossip of the party, and Letty felt like the bottom of a used shoe for disappointing her, but she could not bring herself to rehearse any of the party she had just left. It had felt mostly like leaving a funeral.

"Oh but..." Sarah watched as Letty trailed into the drawing room and just dropped unceremoniously onto the settee.

"Should I—would miss like a fire?" Griggs seemed dubious; it was still warm out even as it was nearly dark, but Letty looked so color-less, and couldn't seem to take her eyes off the fireplace.

"No thank you, Griggs," was all she said, quietly.

"I can take down your hair," Sarah offered, taking a step into the drawing room and then stopping just inside the door instead of approaching.

Letty didn't look up for that either. "No thank you, Sarah," was all she said.

Sarah and Griggs looked at each other, and Griggs just shrugged.

But then as Sarah started to turn away, Letty started. "Oh wait—"

She unpinned the ruby brooch and held it out.

"Do take this back to Mrs. Peterborough, won't you? I couldn't stand it if something happened to it."

"Why I... of course, Miss Stapleton," said Sarah softly, looking at the jewels winking in her hand, and, brows drawn together in puzzlement, followed Griggs out.

"It's just Letty," Letty sighed at the empty fireplace.

* * *

WHEN MICHAEL ROLLED up to the drawing room half an hour later, he found Letty in just the same place where the others had left her.

She had picked at the pins in her hair, apparently, and they glittered in a small pile on the tile table next to the settee. Her hair, usually a crown of golden fuzz, lay shimmering around her neck and shoulders, small curls and braids here and there studding the silken mass and making her look like a shadowed painting.

She was not moving, and she said nothing as he rolled in, but she did look up.

"My lady," he said, his voice sounding too brusque and loud in the otherwise dark and empty room. He cleared his throat.

"Not a lady," Letty said, shaking her head again.

Michael rolled over to take the spot on the other end of the settee. He couldn't bear to be farther from her even as he knew he ought to maintain his distance. She didn't look like his Letty, and to be honest that almost helped; she didn't look like the sunny young woman who had captured his days and his trust and, he feared, his heart. That helped him stay on his side of the settee, leaving her the space a lady ought to be able to keep in the presence of a gentleman.

On the other hand, she looked older, and sadder, and Michael was still chewing over his anger at the way she'd been treated that evening.

This was why he had never cared about society, *this* was why he had never bothered to take up the social duties of his father's office when he had inherited it, *this* was why he didn't bother to go out. He didn't care about anyone making remarks about his leg, and anyway, when he wore the false one, people barely seemed to notice. It was that they were such uncaring, inhumane people.

Michael leaned back against the arm of the settee and watched the shifting play of Letty's straightened, gleaming hair and hated it. Why had she had to go through all that rigmarole in the first place? She'd rather have been outside with the horses. Why did anyone have to live up to those people's expectations of them? Especially her?

"I cannot find the words to say how sorry I am that you were subjected to this evening, Letitia," Michael said heavily.

She paused in her contemplation of the empty, dark fireplace to look at him, startled. "It is I who ought to apologize, Sir Michael," still sounding not at all like herself. She sounded proper, and quiet, and restrained, and Michael hated that too. "You should not have been in the social position that I put you in in the first place. You have been nothing but kind to me and I am grateful."

Michael snorted, making her jump a little. "That's not true and you know it. I have several times been unkind. You, on the other hand, have been the soul of patience with a cranky old sailor and you were poorly repaid for it tonight."

"I have never done anything to be paid or repaid for," Letty said, shrugging one shoulder. She did not look back at the fireplace, but kept her eyes on her hands.

After several moments of silence Michael felt forced to break it again. "Are you all right?"

"Of course," she answered immediately.

But she did not look as though she believed her own answer.

And Michael certainly did not believe it.

"Letitia, please."

Not even knowing what he was asking for, he put out his hand.

After what seemed to him a long moment, Letty took it.

As soon as her fingers were within his, his grasp tightened.

He could feel now that she was not truly still, she was practically thrumming with tension. He could feel the trembling in her fingers, in the palm of her hand, and now that he looked, he could see it in the pulse of her throat too.

"Please," he said again, more raggedly. "Don't be afraid."

Something in her seemed to snap. She pulled her hand from his and shoved herself forward, beginning to pace on the small oval of rug that lay between the settee and the cold hearth.

"I am afraid. I should be afraid, I *need* to be afraid. My father is out there haunting Roseford and I am sure that it is because of me. And I am furious about it. I must *do* something about it. Your life is upended because of me, your livelihood in danger because of me, and it is all because of him, this whole ridiculous torture is because he is a horrible human being who doesn't have the decency to let me go and let me live *my own life!*"

There was his Letty. Michael would have felt a bit better, but he had never seen her so on edge. She *was* furious, he could see that now, and pacing like a tiny lioness in his parlor, and Michael needed to do something about it.

"The men will find him. He will be turned over to the law. I *promise* you."

"When? How?" Her arm waved as if to indicate a wide expanse of unpleasant future. "This is absurd, all of it is absurd. I was only supposed to bring you my horse. I did that. What a wretch I am to bring all of this distasteful cloud around your home—"

"Please. Please." Michael couldn't think of what to say except that. He reached forward, his hand stretched out towards hers again, but she did not move towards him.

He let his hand fall.

"You brought me the horse. You brought me *your* horse. And you brought me the way to ride her. You brought me outdoors again, and the freedom to ride my own lands, and you brought me leather gloves and cats and a much better washbasin and some very good advice and *you*, Letitia, you brought me you, and God forgive how I've treated you but I can't be sad about that. I can never."

She looked at him, the reddish-brown wave of his hair against his sun-golden forehead, and the lively eyes so like the trees of his estate, and the big square hands with which he could haul himself into the air, and she just… Couldn't imagine a world where someone as beautiful as he was had to adjust to a life with her and her odious father in it.

"I can," she said, and he flinched.

"Please don't. Please—" Michael stretched out a hand toward her again and again Letty ignored it.

In a low fierce growl Michael said, "I have not since I lost my leg been more desperate to cross a room under my own power." If he could go to her and pick her up and carry her off to his bed right now, he thought wildly, he could shake her out of these doldrums and make her realize how much he needed her, how happy she made him.

Hell, if she would only touch his hand again, that would make him as happy as he ever needed to be again.

Letty shook her head, the oddly straight gleaming strands of her hair falling around her face. "I can't," she said, in a fierce whisper.

Michael went on. "I am so sorry I put you through that nightmare of a party. I never want to see any of those people again, I swear to you. Even Mrs. Peterborough can go hang if she can't adjust to living without the good graces of a petty world. I'll engage a house in London, we can go there tomorrow. Tonight, if you like. We can do whatever we like, if it will only never put us in a position that awkward again."

"You can't just go hide in London, Michael." She kept shaking her head no.

Surely, he thought desperately, if she were at least willing to use his given name without the title, surely she didn't actually hate him. "I want so very little right now. I want you in my arms, I want so badly to take you right now, and I want really nothing else."

Blinking, she stepped back. "That's—"

"Is it too much?"

Feeling stunned, Letty stepped back again. Michael didn't look like himself, or not the Michael she knew from the horse paddock and their breakfasts and the moments alone here at night. He looked hungry, older, his face drawn somehow and his eyes lit with a fire she didn't recognize. The muscle in his cheek jumped and she realized he was clenching his jaw, perhaps with fury.

She was very afraid she loved him but she did not want to be *taken*, and whatever it was that she wanted right now, she felt like this was the moment that Anthony, that Michael himself had been warning her about all along. She could take one of two paths right now and one would not only be dangerous to herself, she now realized; it would be dangerous to him.

And looking at him, as much as she wanted that feeling again of being wrapped safe in his arms, as much as she wanted his mouth on hers, as much as she wanted to know what it would be like to be loved in his bed, with his complete attention, with his whole body, the risks involved in that were not just risks to her future. They were risks to his future as well. Maybe risks to everyone in this house, this beautiful house she had come to love with the people in it who cared about her in a way no one else ever had except Anthony and it was too much. She couldn't risk that much.

"Sir Michael, I must be going," said Letty and she swept out of the room.

CHAPTER 20

MICHAEL MADE two circuits of the house on his wheeler before he even bothered to try to lie down.

He'd frightened her, he'd been unable to do anything for her, he was a useless ox of a man who had been unable to tell her what she meant to him at the most important moment of his life.

It was intolerable.

He was almost glad, too, that she had rushed away, as he felt his temper roiling worse and worse, and he was afraid that he couldn't say anything that wouldn't make her even more upset than she already was. His history was rather more being upsetting at key moments than the opposite.

He'd snapped at Frank Briarly to pass along to the rest of the men that the manhunt needed to be wrapped up, and quickly. It was useless expecting Letty to calm down when she knew her father was lurking out there waiting to frighten her—damn it, he was frightening her without even seeing her. The man had to be stopped.

And as he'd looked out the back door for the last time, he'd seen Anthony in the flower bushes, and snarled at him too.

"What are you playing at, man?"

The younger man hadn't stepped out of the shadows at all; instead his long black hair seemed to become one with them as his lightly French-accented English came out of the dark to Michael. "This is no game to me, sir."

"She won't rest until he's found." In another five minutes Michael felt like he would have to be on horseback himself, looking for the reprobate, and he owed any ability he had to do that to Letty, and that just made his temper spiral up again.

"Nor will I. Rest assured, our friend Watsford will have a reckoning with me tonight."

Michael growled. "She's frightened."

"I doubt it," Anthony's voice sounded low and sure from the shadows, "I suspect she is more angry than frightened. I am not frightened, though, and I am determined, and I am ready for him."

Michael just nodded.

Back in the house, he checked all the windows in the portrait gallery again, leaving Griggs to the cot he'd made up there, just grunting as he went past.

Griggs had known him for many years; Griggs knew when he was in a foul mood.

Why the hell hadn't he courted her from the first day? When she had landed on his doorstep, so pretty and sweet and looking like an armful of happiness, why hadn't he been smarter from the beginning? Why hadn't he offered her presents and kind words and the pleasures his money could provide her? Why had he ever wasted a minute, when he realized now that he would spend the rest of his life waiting for the next minute with her?

He was a fool.

As he ripped off his cravat and his boot, laying down on his coverlet, intending just to nap briefly before going out again, Michael was struck with an intense memory of his mother crossing one of the rose-covered carpets that had lined the hall when she was the lady of the house, her simply elegant coppery gown and her hair shining atop her head and his father, beaming with pride, waiting at the door to escort her out.

He remembered the look of affection, of attentiveness, and—he now realized—of possessive glee on his father's face as he'd taken the hand of the woman he loved and tucked it into the crook of his arm before going out together to face the world.

That's what he should have offered her from the first day, he realized. Because from the moment she'd alighted from that carriage, his small hard-working frizzy-haired stubborn darling, his heart had belonged to her and he'd just been delaying the inevitable.

He had to work harder to be as smart as his father had been; he'd turned out to be just as lucky, and he hadn't had to wait forty plus years to find his lady.

I MUST GO, I must go, I must go, Letty was chanting to herself in her head as she swept into her room, unable to think beyond the pounding of the words that kept repeating in her head and the sick feeling in the pit of her stomach that she had done something irreparably bad to Michael's life by staying here so long that her father followed her.

In the dark it was impossible to pack, but then she'd need to leave with pretty much what she came with, and that had been pretty much nothing. She could leave the party slippers, they were too light a fabric to be any use from now on; she needed her horse-training gown and she needed to put her good boots on. She'd do it at the door, so she'd walk more quietly.

Oh, and her pretty blue and pink dresses. They were hers now, she'd earned them, like the wheat-colored silk she was wearing, and she would take them.

She couldn't even really unfasten the buttons of the silk without Sarah's help, but she daren't try to fetch Sarah now. Breathing out, she wiggled uncomfortably, terrified she would rip the thing, until she managed to slide the waist of the dress up above her breasts, and slid free.

Fortunately the other dresses buttoned much more practically in the front, and she slid on the blue one in nearly seconds flat.

Three dresses wouldn't fit into her reticule, but she managed to wrap them into her sunbonnet with her shawl and gloves, and realized that she would look bizarre on the road but would have her every earthly possession with her.

Everything except her beautiful horse, which she was gladly leaving to Michael. And the friendship of the wonderful people who had changed her life in just a few days. And her heart.

Anthony would follow her, she knew that the way she knew that the sun would come up in the morning. Perhaps he would help her write a letter back here to tell everyone how sorry she had been to have to leave them.

But she wouldn't write to Michael, because she wouldn't know what to say; and anyway, she wouldn't have wanted Anthony to help her write how she felt about that.

Anthony would follow her, he would figure out where she'd gone, he always did. She had one person in the world who knew her well enough that she didn't have to explain herself, and that was more than many people had in a lifetime. She had nothing to cry about.

She reminded herself of that as she wiped off the tears and tiptoed down the stairs, wishing she had the ability to turn towards Michael's room and Michael's arms. But if she did that, she didn't know if she'd ever have the courage to leave. She knew she would not be happy as the mistress of her beautiful, gruff man, and she did not want him to marry her without loving her when she loved him so very desperately. Nor did she want him to have to suffer the social put-downs and financial set-backs that would come from having someone like her in his house. She could picture the pleasure she would find in his arms, and she would not be able to tear herself away. If she found that pleasure with him, she might lose all hope of ever finding a life she could live on her own terms and not everyone else's.

And, she realized, she couldn't use up all her hope today. Young as she was, she felt that she must save a little hope for tomorrow.

Moving slowly enough that her feet made no sound on the wooden floor, she turned down the hall toward the kitchen, intending to go out that way so that there was no danger of Michael hearing her from his downstairs room.

* * *

MOVING through the kitchen garden quietly, Letty turned toward the close section of the trees where they came up to the lawns, on the side of the house farthest from the stable, the side she seldom used.

She could get the road there, she knew, and walk to the village. From there she would just need to ask the way to the Faircombe estate.

Letty refused to think about her father any more. He would most likely follow her, and she would ignore him. As long as he wasn't harming anyone at Roseford, she would ignore him.

She would go to Lord Faircombe and convince him to let her try helping to train his horses. He had been interested in the idea, he just needed to be persuaded to let her try. She did not give up easily.

And if Michael were going to begin a competing business, Lord Faircombe would have all the more reason to let her try.

She didn't care what he said about her or to her. She was past caring. She hoped the numb, cold feeling she felt now would last forever. She just needed to put one foot in front of the other.

She felt something brush her arm in the darkness, and jerked away, her heart pounding so hard she thought it might leave her chest.

Just a tree branch, she realized. She ought to find a path and work her way toward the road. The woods wouldn't be so thick there.

Just a tree branch.

"Scared yourself, did you?" said a voice beside her in the dark.

He was there, he was right there.

Letty didn't see his clothes or the dirt and scratches on his face and hands. She just saw that he was there. Just as she'd feared.

"Go away, father," she said in a voice just above whispering, not because she was trying to be quiet, but because she couldn't seem to breathe.

"Indeed, I've been waiting for you. I thought we'd go a bit north together. It's perfect weather this time of year for walking."

"Go away, father," she said a little more loudly. She still felt like she couldn't get any air. She felt a bit dizzy with it.

"Yes, I'm agreeing with you, you daft girl. I've been waiting for you. Let's go."

He had nothing with him that she could see, no bag. She finally registered what he was wearing.

"When did you steal Mrs. Dunphy's shawl?"

He ignored her. "We can't follow the road, they've got crowds of stupid youths with sticks patrolling up and down, we will need to stay in the woods and go quietly."

"Anthony." She drew a deeper breath.

"What?"

"Anthony has men patrolling the woods. They will find you."

Charles F. Stapleton, scratched and bleeding from being pursued through the woods and arguing with her in pitch dark in the middle of the night, greeted this news as if it were a bad joke. "Surely not."

She didn't care whether he was denying that Anthony was looking for him, or that he would be found. "Go. Away. Father. Go away from me. Go away from me now."

Letty picked up one foot and then the other. It felt good. She felt like she could breathe more easily with every step she took. Not following his advice to stay in the woods. She wasn't the one with anything to fear from patrols. She had done nothing wrong.

"Letty—" He tried to grab her elbow.

With all her strength Letty swung her sunbonnet-pack of clothes up and around, hitting him squarely on the side of the head.

He was knocked back a step, struggling to stay upright. The bundle was soft, not delivering much of a blow, but it had had force behind it.

"Go away from me. Go far away. I don't care where you go, just go away from me." Now Letty had her two feet under her and she was gripping her sunbonnet stuffed full of clothes like a club. "If you touch me again I'll kick you so hard your kneecaps will fly off into the trees."

"Letty! What has gotten into you. You've never been—"

"I've never been free of you, maybe not till this minute. What are you going to do, threaten me? It makes me sick I ever did what you said, it makes me sick that you only had to hit me a few times to get me to behave all the rest of the time. I'm done. Go away and don't you ever talk to me again."

Charles eyed her up and down. She somehow looked taller than he remembered.

It had been a difficult week for Charles and he had put a lot of effort into regaining his daughter, which was all he had left. Though he hadn't bothered to tell her, he had lost any chance of continuing to claim legal ownership of his house, and he was running out of ideas about where to get more money unless he went further north. If he did that without Letty, he was certain, he would lose track of her. And he never lost track of anything valuable.

"I can see you've developed a taste for a finer life; I had no idea you could snag the lap of a gentleman to get it. We can—"

Letty dropped her bundle of clothes and picked up a tree branch instead. She raised it at her father, who stopped talking, his jaw dropping open.

"Don't you ever speak of Sir Michael again. Not to me, not to anyone."

"I wasn't trying to upset your game, girl, I just—"

Letty could only see red. "You get away from me, you get away from Michael, don't you ever come back here, don't you ever—"

"Dammit, your mother wasn't half this much trouble," choked Charles, going to the actual physical effort of grabbing the tree branch and wresting it away from her, throwing it into the trees.

"What did you do to my mother?"

Grabbing him by the fabric around his throat with both hands, Letty, possessed with fury, shook him like a dog.

Rattled, Charles locked his mouth shut, clawing at her grip with his fingernails trying to get loose.

She threw him away from her with as much force as she could muster.

He was a vile animal, and Letty wanted to drag him to the road and put him in the hands of the magistrate herself.

But her first instinct took over again, and she decided to do what she knew she could do. He would fight her, and lazy as he was he might still win; she could already feel the energy of her fury draining away from her. She didn't want to fight him. She wanted him behind her.

Picking up her sunbonnet pack she said, "You'll get what you deserve. Go away from me. Leave this place alone. And never speak to me again."

And she walked away from him into the night.

* * *

IT WAS torture not to be able to pace, though not as much torture as trying to figure out what he should have said to Letty.

Michael scrubbed his hands through his hair, tucking in his shirt-tails as much to keep them out of his way as anything else. He hadn't bothered to change out of his formal trousers, and the empty leg flapped as he hauled himself out of the bed and settled his stump into his wheeled cart, but he didn't want to take the time to change.

He had to see her.

He'd startled or frightened her somehow, he was sure of it. He was haunted by the look in her eyes, that last time she had looked at him. He couldn't sleep until he'd seen her again. He didn't think he could *live* until he saw her again.

Everyone was asleep and he wouldn't send anyone to her anyway when what he wanted was to see her himself.

He sat on the stairs he'd been largely avoiding since he'd returned from war, and backed up them one at a time with his arms and his one foot. It went faster than he expected.

But then at the top of the stairs he realized he had no crutches and no cart and Letty's door twenty feet away seemed like miles. He knew it was her room, Sarah had told him where she was sleeping when she'd told him that she would sleep next door. He could just see the carving on the door in the night gloom.

This was his house, and he was the baronet of Roseford.

But no one could see him and he had no time for pride.

Moving as quickly as he could Michael crawled for the door, surprised that the knee of the lost leg didn't bother him more. Perhaps it would have been more of a problem if he'd had to support his weight on the actual stump, or if the linen sock Letty had made for him hadn't saved him from so many of the abrasions he usually got from his artificial leg. But it was fine.

At her door, though, he pulled himself upright with the doorknob and the door frame. He wanted to be standing when she saw him, if she was still awake.

He pushed open the door to her room, which was lit with starlight, the drapes open to the warm summer night.

It was empty.

She was gone.

In a flash he took in the still-made bed, the neatness of a room where the personal things have been removed. She was not there. She had not been.

"*Sarah!*" he bellowed at the top of his lungs.

The maid appeared in the adjoining door in a cloud of braids and linen. "*What!*" she screamed back at top volume. "Is it fire?"

"Where is Letitia?"

The girl took in the empty room, her hand going to her mouth. "Where has she gone? She's not been here?"

"Help me to the stairs."

Without preamble he leaned on her as much as he dared and hopped at top speed to the stairs. He nearly rolled down them in his haste to descend.

As he moved down the staircase the way he had ascended, he said, "Search the house. Get Griggs to help you. Make sure she isn't in here, hurt or something."

He could imagine scenarios where she was trapped in the house somewhere, perhaps if her father had managed to get in, but his gut told him that his Letty had left.

He threw open the front door and rolled out to the edge of the portico, wondering if he dared to simply try taking the cart down the hill to the stable.

No. He didn't dare. There were no brakes on the thing, and if he smashed into the stable wall at speed he could hurt himself too seriously to be able to get to Letty.

Throwing himself back through the door he grabbed his crutches, then back out to the edge of the portico, hopping a bit as he thrust himself off the cart and onto the crutches.

He'd never moved on them so fast as he did down to the stables, the main door cracked so he could just see a sliver of lantern light inside.

"Letitia!" he called as loud as he dared—he didn't want to frighten her again—as he balanced on the crutches, shoving the door open with one hand.

The stableboy Jim, twelve and skinny and dark-haired, leaped off his place in the straw, eyes as big as saucers.

"I haven't seen her here, Sir Michael, not all night!"

The boy was certain.

Michael swung toward Maggie's stall. The horse snorted and shuffled sideways, sensing his urgency.

He grabbed her bridle from the wall, dropped it in place in her mouth and over her ears and threw the reins backward over her neck. Quickly, he backed her out of her stall.

Should he try for a saddle? Dammit, he hadn't really ridden her yet, not more than a short distance here or there and always with Letty.

Always with Letty.

"Seen anyone else skulking around here?" Michael brusquely interrogated Jim as he backed the horse out of the stall, leading her toward the outdoors.

"No sir! Mister Anthony told me to keep a lookout and I have! I saw some of Mr. Leighton's men 'at I was introduced to, an' I saw

Mister Anthony, an' I saw Mrs. Dunphy go through the kitchen garden t'ard the wood about an hour ago, an' 'at's all!"

"Dunphy." Michael whirled on the boy, hopping on one crutch. "You saw Mrs. Dunphy outside an hour ago?"

"Yessir!"

"Not at all. Mrs. Dunphy would never go outside at night, not alone, and certainly not to the woods. Run and find the nearest one of Anthony's men and tell him what you saw. Do you understand? *That wasn't Mrs. Dunphy.* Tell him. Fast, fast as you can!"

The boy took off running at top speed towards the woods.

It had to have been Watsford. It had to have been.

Where was Letty?

The urgency in his chest, in his gut, was a palpable thing. He felt like he could feel his heart calling out for her.

He took a deep breath of the night air, cool and still. He tried to push back the terror he felt at the thought that she was traveling alone through the night with that man after her. She was tough and brave, his Letitia, but if she needed help—

"Maggie."

The horse whuffled as she raised her head to the sound of her name.

Michael stared into one velvety dark eye fringed with deep lashes. Letty always said that this horse was the smartest horse in the world. She always told him that he could count on this horse.

This was one of the times he was going to listen to her.

"We have to find Letty, Maggie, can you do that?" He swung himself out in front of her, to a spot on the green just beyond the barn door. He wouldn't injure Letty's horse for the world, but he had to find Letty herself and he needed the horse's help.

"We have to find Letty, Maggie, we have to go."

He gave her the signal to lay down.

Maggie's head dropped, and Michael had the bizarre sensation that the horse was going to nod to him. She didn't, just raised her head again, shaking it, breathing out with a "hoowhuh" sort of noise and looking Michael in the eye like she was thinking hard about what he was saying to her.

"Yes, Maggie. Good girl. Yes."

Michael gave the signal to lay down again, and though something in her eye gave Michael the sense that she was humoring him, Maggie knelt her front knees down on the ground, then bent her haunches and lay fully down at his feet.

"Thank you, thank you, you wonderful horse, you best of all possible horses."

Throwing himself over her back Michael let the crutches fall where they may. Praising her brilliance and perfection in more flowery words than he had ever used to any human in his life, he wrapped his hands in her mane and tried to stay relatively flat to her back, knowing how she would rock and tilt getting up. He shook the reins, giving her the signal to get up.

Which she did, lurching to her feet.

Michael took a deep ragged breath. He could do this. He could. Maggie was helping him, and Anthony and Jim and magistrate Leighton; there were decent people in the world and one of them was a horse and he could do this.

"We can do this," he whispered to Maggie, and leaned forward.

She started to walk.

CHAPTER 21

THERE WERE two directions in which to go when they met the road that wound past the estate and through the village of Roseford, and Michael wasn't guessing when he picked the one that went in the direction of Faircombe.

He knew his Letitia and he knew that she didn't give up on her plans easily. He bet that she intended to walk to Faircombe and convince that odious marquess to let her train his horses whether he liked it or not.

And when he and Maggie passed Frank Briarly standing watch on the road, he knew he was right.

"She went this way?" He didn't even bother to specify who. The man looked guilty as sin and chagrined from the moment Michael had come into view.

"I didn't mean to let her pass, Sir Michael, I swear I didn't, and not alone. She just—I don't—I can't rightly explain why—"

"Never mind, Frank, I know what happened. You're a woolen-headed barn door of a man to let her go alone, but I know what happened."

His heart swelled to think of Letty barging past the barriers of the world and never letting them stop her.

He just wanted to be with her while she did it.

* * *

ALERT to the sounds of men following her or preparing to block her path, what Letty didn't expect was to hear the clop-clop-clop of a horse's hooves on the dense dirt track of the road.

Especially not that particular rhythm of a horse's hooves.

But if it was Maggie, then...

She didn't want to look back. Maybe she was imagining this. Maybe he would be angry with her. Maybe it was her father again. Maybe it was just another one of the guards. Maybe it was Anthony. Maybe it was—

"My lady, won't you please let me take you wherever you would like to go?"

That voice. It stopped her in her tracks. Letty closed her eyes.

Maggie's hooves clop-clop-clopped right up to her in the night.

She looked up past Maggie's soft, understanding eyes, up, up, to see her partly-dressed midnight pirate, Sir Michael of Roseford.

He looked awful, his hair going every which way, the shadow of beard stubble starting to show on his chin, his rumpled shirt linen catching shadows in its wrinkles from the moonlight, and the full dress trouser leg dangling down Maggie's side, where the horse was being too polite to worry about it.

He looked glorious.

He surely was the most beautiful sight in the world.

He ran his eyes over her, taking in her tousled hair, still half-straight and braided from the party and tossed loosely over her shoulder, her worn green dress, her strong hands with their clever, square-tipped fingers clutching a clothing bundle, drooping at her side from fatigue.

When she looked up at him his agonies of worry were over.

She was here, she was safe, and he was with her.

"Michael, you don't—"

"My lady," he said softly, "I don't wish to interrupt you, but I was asking if you might permit me to take you wherever it is that you would like to go."

Letty closed her eyes again. She was so tired. "I would *like* to go home with you."

"That would be my eternal pleasure," he said, nodding. "Shall we go now?"

"I won't endanger anything you must do, I won't."

"Then I will take you wherever you'd prefer to go," he said in the same even, quiet tone, "As long as I have you in my arms while I do it. May I at least bring you up here with me?"

Squinching her eyes shut, Letty thought, *I want to.*

Almost against her will, she said, "I so very much want to be exactly there, with you."

"Letitia."

She opened her eyes and looked back at him.

He said, "Let me take you, me and Maggie. Wherever."

How could he melt all of her insides with so few words?

Letty shook her head. "You don't understand. I'm so in love with you and I won't—I can't live near you and not tell you, not touch you —" She broke off. It was mortifying. She couldn't regret loving him, but it was mortifying.

"You cannot imagine how inconvenient it is not to be able to dismount a horse at will. My lady. Letitia. Please. I'm begging you. Please let me bring you up here with me and let me hold you. Please."

"How embarrassing. I am—"

"Letitia. *Please.*"

Letty gave herself a little shake. She had decided to do what she wanted, hadn't she? And she wanted him to hold her so very, very much.

Slinging her little pack around her neck, she reached up her hands.

She was small, but she still marveled that Michael was able to lift her straight off the ground the way he did, bringing her up to his level on Maggie's back. She flipped herself over and wiggled while he slid back a bit, ending up ensconced in his arms just behind Maggie's shoulders and with one knee a bit pulled up Maggie's neck, as if she were riding side-saddle after all.

Letty sighed, a blissfully happy sigh as she settled into Michael's arms there.

"Thank you," Michael murmured into her hair. His arms were full of Letty, so soft and strong. Her skin was a little cold from the night air and he gratefully wrapped her in his arms, pulled her close.

When he thought he might be holding her too tightly, he let his arms relax just a bit, but Letty made a small noise of dissatisfaction and her arms went around his waist and held on tight.

So he pulled her close, his eyes closing as he breathed in the scent of her, felt her welcome weight against him.

"This is exactly where you should be," he whispered to her. "This is exactly where we should both be."

"On Maggie's back," she half-laughed.

"On Maggie's back," he smiled against her hair. "Or anywhere."

"It is a terrible plan," Letty sighed, burrowing her face in his shirt.

"Perhaps it is, my beloved, but as it turns out I love you too, so it may be the only plan available to us both."

"Not really." She pulled back to look up at his face.

He had those crinkles at the corners of his eyes she loved so much. She couldn't believe it. "No, but not really!"

"Really, my lady. I should have realized it sooner. I am slow to understand many things about other people, but even slower about myself." He leaned forward, kissed her forehead. "I wish I were a little shorter."

Letty reached up in his arms and put her hands on either side of his face, and kissed him, slowly, enjoying the feel of him, the taste of him, the way she always wanted him.

When she released his lips she said, "Or I could be a little taller."

"Since you are perfection just as you are, I cannot wish that."

"Does this change things? Oh, this changes things. Or perhaps it doesn't change anything. Michael, I believe it doesn't change anything. What a mess we are in. My reputation, my family—"

He kissed her again.

When he finally released her, she stayed there for a moment, eyes closed, lips parted for him. He very, very much enjoyed seeing her this way.

Then her face scrunched up in a scowl, and Michael felt laughter bubbling up inside him.

"That is a very poor argumentative strategy, Michael, and you should not think it will benefit you to—"

He kissed her again.

"Honestly," she breathed when he let her go, but her eyes were open and shining at him.

"I could do this all night," he told her, tightening his arms around her.

"I will not ruin your life," Letty said very firmly.

"You will ruin everything about my life if you leave me," Michael said with a shrug.

"But you saw how those people treated me, treated you!"

"Letitia, that party was an excruciating experience, but let me remind you. We put rumors about your family firmly behind us. You had far more friends than enemies in that room, my beloved. You have not damaged my reputation, and you will not."

"But if I stay..."

Michael had to take a deep breath, blow it out. It ruffled where the hair was starting to curl again on the top of her head.

He said, "I am reluctant to bring up the topic again, as my ego took quite some punishment the last time, but would you not be willing at all to marry me? I love you. Would you not be willing to make a home with me? At Roseford or anywhere. I am quite confident that anywhere you are, I would be at home."

"You're serious."

"Entirely."

Letty shook her head, hid her face in his shirt. "You did not sound serious, before."

"Do I sound serious now?"

Letty did not answer. Michael touched her chin and lifted her face. "Tears?"

"I am very happy."

"All right." It was unnerving, seeing the tears trembling in the corners of her lovely clear eyes, but Michael steeled himself. It wasn't the first time he'd seen her cry, and he knew it wouldn't be the last. "Well, I was serious, and I am serious, and I fear my ego is about to take another pounding because you have not answered me."

"You want me to live at Roseford with you."

"I want you to live with me. Full stop. Anywhere. If you prefer London, or Greece, or the far archipelagos of the world, I would be happy to be anywhere as long as you are there with me."

"I adore Roseford."

"Then we will live there. This is an excellent plan, don't you see?" He stroked her cheek with his hand, the other still holding the reins. He felt an urgency to get her home, get off this horse, and get her into his house. "I confess I would prefer if Roseford were a castle I could lock up and keep you prisoner in so I could be sure you would never leave."

"Michael!" Letty thumped his chest with a small fist. "That is an awful thing to say."

"I thought it and so I told it to you, my beloved, but I would not do it. I am nearly shaking with the worry that you will not at least let me take you home with me. You have not said yes."

"You would put me right back down on this road and let me go on about my business if I said no," said Letty, slowly.

"No I would not," Michael replied immediately. "I would ride on with you to Roseford, or the village if you prefer, and engage a room at a safe lodging for you. Then I would hire some of Leighton's men away from him to guard you if you went on to that absurd man's estate to train horses, or to the city, or anywhere else that you wanted to go. And I would make sure they wrote to me regularly to let me know that you were safe, as otherwise I would be unable to think of anything else."

"And you would go back to Roseford."

Michael swallowed. "I would go back to Roseford. But since I would be leaving my heart with you, I would not feel as if I were at Roseford. I don't think I would be able to feel anything at all."

"Michael." Letty sighed against him; he could feel the warmth of her breath on his skin, through the linen covering his skin and his pounding heart, and he could feel how strong her arms were as she tightened them around him again. "I could not bear it if I hurt you."

"How can I convince you that you would only make me the luckiest, happiest man in the world if you would marry me and be my lady?"

She was silent for some moments. Maggie shuffled on her feet, shifting them both.

"What if my father..." She trailed off.

"I think that situation is under control. I promise you, you need never worry about him again." Michael still searched the trees with his eyes but his attention was on her. "Do you... would you want to know what became of him?"

"No," she said instantly. "Only that he could never bother you, cause trouble for you, again."

"He will not cause trouble for either of us, my beloved, I swear it."

"Oh Michael. If I could believe that. I do want to live with you and be your love, I would love to marry you, I would."

Suddenly he could breathe again. "Thank you."

"I can't help feeling that something will happen to ruin this plan. It might not be the best plan. In fact I am sure it is a terrible plan."

He chuckled and nuzzled at the top of her head. "Is it not efficient? Since you love me and I also love you?"

Letty gave a little unladylike half-snort, half-laugh. "Yes, I suppose it is very efficient."

And Michael twitched the reins so that Maggie turned around and headed, slowly, with both of them, right back to Roseford.

* * *

THE MAGISTRATE WAS PROBABLY a hundred pounds heavier and certainly six inches taller than Anthony, which was completely apparent as the two of them stood in the road surrounded by three of the men Michael's money had hired.

But everyone's eyes turned to Anthony as George Willis and Blake Leighton, the magistrate's son, brought their captive forward.

Charles F. Stapleton, also known as Charles Watsford, Charles Eagleton, Francis Wallinford, and Chuck Eaves, his hands tied behind his back with rough twine, a stolen lady's shawl askew around his shoulders, had scratches on his hands and face and smelled like a man who had not bathed for some time. His clothes, once respectable, were covered with dirt and the stains of leaves, and the bottom of his trouser cuffs were soaked with mud. His shoes were wet.

His last attempt to hide under a bridge had failed him as the cordon around him had shrunk, making it impossible, in the end, to evade his captors.

William Leighton looked him up and down, and his upper lip curled.

He addressed Anthony. "That's the man?"

There was something emanating from Anthony in waves, some brittle mixture of anger and disgust and something like triumph. "Not much of a man. That's Charles Stapleton."

Leighton walked forward. "When you appeared in my court, you called yourself Watsford."

Charles said nothing.

"As it turns out," said the big man, withdrawing a folded piece of paper from his pocket and unfolding it with his thick fingers, "both Watsford and Stapleton have committed quite a few crimes, for several of which we have located witnesses who can identify you. And a few more names, hey? When you frequent some of the same establishments and use different names at different times, barmaids remember." Leighton folded the paper back up again, returned it to an inner pocket. "Barmaids are never as stupid as some people think," he told Charles softly.

"This is a campaign of harassment." Charles pulled his head up to look at all the men around him. He seemed taller, more regal, despite his physical state. "I made a mistake taking that boy in and letting him work for me. He is a Frenchman and we are at war; of course he is making accusations, he does not want me to reveal who he is."

Anthony stepped forward and all the hired men tensed, including both Leightons. Violence seemed imminent, even though the slight young man did not raise a hand.

His dark eyes looked like they could have shot fire.

"I am not afraid of you. I have never been afraid of you. You know that, you remember very well the first and last time I saw you hit Letty. You have never touched her since. It is you who fear me, as well you should, you insignificant snail."

Anthony pushed his face right into Charles' line of sight, and Charles did try to draw back.

"I had nowhere to take her so we stayed in that house but I have never worked for you. I worked for her. I knew you would manage your own downfall someday, and so you have. I am only glad to see it."

Charles still said nothing. Anthony nearly hissed, "You think I would let you prostitute my sister? Then you have never known who I am at all."

There was a moment when the men in the ring of firelight felt like there could be an explosion of any sort. Every muscle was tensed.

Then Anthony stepped back. "Mr. Leighton."

The big magistrate blew out a breath, as if he had been holding it. "They're waiting for you in Faircombe, and tomorrow in London. Your trial won't be here, Watsford or whatever name you want. It will be in London. And you'll either be transported or you'll hang. No one will care which."

The look Anthony gave the captive, it was clear which one he preferred.

The criminal with too many names said nothing as he was led away.

Leighton took a lantern from Briarly, stood next to Anthony as the rest of the men escorted the captured man to the jail. They both watched the light from their lanterns disappear down the road.

"So," said Leighton as the last of the group disappeared, "who are you then?"

237

Anthony shrugged, bit his lower lip and smiled up at the magistrate. "I'm Letty's groomsman, you know that."

"Mmm hmm," said Leighton, sounding unconvinced. "You didn't tell him that Letty told Briarly where to find him."

Anthony shrugged again. "Why on earth would I tell him anything about Letty?"

CHAPTER 22

THE LIGHT WAS STILL BURNING in the stable; Jim or someone must still be there.

Letty shifted. She did not want to leave this blissful spot. "You must be so uncomfortable, with all this unaccustomed riding, and without a saddle at that."

"As you perhaps may be too," he said, leaning back so that Maggie slowed to a very slow amble.

"I am the most comfortable I have ever been in my entire life, or could ever imagine being," Letty told him.

He made a pleased noise but then they were at the door.

"Jim, look who I've found."

"Miss Stapleton!" The boy sounded thrilled, and Michael realized that he had forgotten that he hadn't yet changed her name. In his head, she was already Lady Grantley and always would be.

"Carry my crutches up to the mounting block, would you? Then bed Maggie down as comfortable as you can, then take a message to anyone in the village who's still awake. Gerald at the inn should be up. Ask him to get a message to Anthony or William Leighton, whomever they see first, and tell them Miss Stapleton is safe at Roseford, and I will see them tomorrow."

"Late," said Letty firmly. "You need sleep. And so do you, Jim."

At the mounting block Maggie stood for them, good as always, while Michael eased Letty to her feet, then swung himself down and hopped down the steps to take his crutches from Jim.

He stopped to stroke the fine arch of Maggie's smooth nose.

"Thank you," he whispered to her, and her ear flicked at him to show she heard.

After Letty had also whispered her good nights and patted Maggie's neck and let Jim take her away, they found themselves standing alone in the dark, looking up at Roseford manor.

"I can't... I feel as though... Would your mother have liked me?" asked Letty in a rather small voice.

Michael smiled as he thought of his beautiful, elegant mother, and his beautiful, energetic Letitia. "She would have adored you."

Letty looked unconvinced. "I can't imagine anyone thinking of me as Lady Grantley."

Michael shifted on his crutches. "I already do. Letitia, my darling. Truly, we can do anything you like. I never want you to feel trapped, or owned."

Letty had her face half-scrunched up in confusion. "Is there—are there things people do other than... whatever the law allows?"

He nodded. "I can settle some money on you; people do." He didn't add that it was usually for mistresses; he didn't care if she didn't. "I can buy a house in your name and you can live in it and tell me whether or not I'm allowed in. But I would also happily live with you here for the rest of our lives whether we're married or not."

"Michael!" Letty gasped. "Can you just imagine what people would say?"

"No," said Michael bluntly, "and I care even less. We can make anything possible. I'm sure of it. What I *want*, my darling, is for you to marry me. And let me marry you. We will marry each other, very clearly, vehemently even, and if you don't mind being Lady Grantley, then I will revel in it. But there are any number of ways we can be together as long as we *are* together. Tell me what would make you happy and we will arrive at our own arrangement."

She was staring at him with those light-colored eyes; they were almost glowing in the starlight. "And you love me."

"Utterly, my lady. Absolutely."

"Then... I think I would like to marry you."

Michael's whole face split into a grin. "Thank you, my love." Then he realized. "Though I thought we had settled this already. Should I continue to ask you?"

"We should go inside. This night has been madness and we are both tired." He saw Letty look thoughtful. "In fact, we should discuss this again in the morning just to make sure we both still agree."

Michael was appalled. "Why? Are you going to change your mind with a good night's rest?"

"No!"

"Well, neither am I! What a notion. In fact as far as I'm concerned, you are already Lady Grantley and you should sleep in my bed with me."

"You're not serious!" she said again, aghast.

"My lady. Have I not been clear about how much I wanted you there?"

"You absolutely have *not*! It has been 'we mustn't' this, and 'I don't want to take advantage of you' that!"

Michael felt that laugh bubbling up again inside him at that scowl. "You make it sound as though I have been most unfair."

"You *know* you have!" Letty stomped her foot.

He couldn't help it. He laughed.

Letty grinned and slid her arms around his waist. "I love it when you laugh."

When he bent to kiss her again, she reached up to meet him, but then broke off the kiss almost as soon as it had begun. "Here I am keeping you standing when you must be exhausted. *I* am exhausted. We must go in, you need rest."

"And you, of course, are not tired at all."

Letty did yawn but didn't bother to hide it, keeping her hands around him, of which he thoroughly approved.

She said, "I quite like the idea of you carrying me off to your castle and locking me up in your dungeon and keeping me prisoner there, if it has a comfortable bed."

Michael felt himself throb. "My lady, I will happily build you a dungeon and furnish it with a comfortable bed." Just the images she brought to mind for him nearly unmanned him.

"Let's go *inside*," Letty insisted, and walked with him up the hill.

* * *

EVERYONE ON EARTH was still awake.

It took just a few minutes, though, to reassure Griggs and Sarah and Mrs. Dunphy that all was well, and let them disappear.

So that Michael could draw Letty into his room without them seeing.

She smiled at him with her dimple, and his universe was complete.

"Should we not wait until we are truly married?" said Letty, belying her words with the way she unbuttoned his shirt and spread it open.

"If that is what you wish," said Michael, his voice thick in throat, one hand curving around her neck.

Obligingly she tilted her head for him, and then his lips were on her ear, her neck, her shoulder, and he could hear his Letty nearly purr.

"I wish you to do exactly this," she told him, looking out of the corner of her eye at him.

Hurriedly he rid himself of his shirt and backed up to sit on the edge of his bed. It was too high; she was a little lower than he would like. Michael growled slightly in frustration.

Letty just smiled.

He hooked a finger into the front of her dress, savoring the way his hand brushed against the skin of her warm breasts and the way it made her tremble, and pulled her between his knees.

"My lady," Michael said in between kisses to her throat, running his fingertips down her arms and listening to the small gasps she made, "how fond are you of this green dress?"

Letty looked down. "I think I have hated it for a long while."

Hooking his fingers on either side of the dress' neck, Michael easily ripped the worn fabric apart.

Letty's laughter as she shrugged off the shreds of the dress made him feel as though there were music playing. He lifted her towards him.

She moved her knees apart to make room for him, sitting astride him as she would a horse, and leaned forward, pushing him back flat on the bed. "That was *very* efficient."

He wanted to explain that he needed to get her petticoat and shift off too, but Letty had melted against him, her hands tracing his ribs, ghosting softly over his nipples, and he forgot to speak.

She asked him, "Do these feel for you as mine did for me when you touched them?" One palm teased gently over the brown peak, before she went back to carding her fingers through the curls on his chest.

"Would that they did. But then," he added, arching his back, "you cause many impossible things, so who knows what may happen?"

Humming a pleased hum, Letty leaned down to flick her tongue over the same part of him.

The groan he made was deep, and Letty almost giggled with delight. She wanted to keep this up for hours, but she was aching and wet and needed more, something much more, immediately.

"We agreed to talk freely to one another, did we not?"

Michael was distracted by the way his body seemed to pulse to the sound of her voice, and a growing desperation to remove the rest of his clothing, but he was listening. "Absolutely, my lady."

"Then I must tell you that I am dying for you to touch me."

"Where?" His hands came up to cup her face.

"Everywhere," Letty said simply.

Taking her at her word, Michael rolled her over into his bed, his hands making short work of the rest of her clothing—removing, tearing, it was all the same to him, he needed his Letty naked in his arms right now, and she needed it too.

He tasted her skin, skimming the peaks of her breasts just as she had done to him, and she cried out.

"Too much?"

She looked so excruciatingly perfect, freckles dotting her flushing skin, all spread out in his bed, arching her back with pleasure because of *him*.

"Not enough," she panted, reaching for the buttons of his trousers and pushing at the waistband. The spot where the hair narrowed just before it disappeared into his clothing had her entranced.

He seemed to take that as an order.

When she understood where all their arms and legs were again, Michael had settled himself, thoroughly naked, between her knees, kissing the curve of her belly.

"I am going to kiss you here, my lady—"

"Michael!"

Her gasp sounded more encouraging than shocked, but Michael finished, "—and you talk to me as much as you like."

When his mouth dipped to touch her there Letty felt the pleasure jolt through her.

"It is like lightning!" she gasped, unable to prevent herself from writhing under him but held steady by his hands. "Is that how it should be?"

"Always," Michael murmured into the pale skin of her thigh, nearly free of freckles, before returning his attention to her core.

Letty lost track of the things she said then, or the noises she made. Michael stayed lost in her, the taste and sounds and feel of her, till he realized that he was rubbing himself against the bed and might spend if he didn't stop.

"Letitia," he murmured into her body, unwilling to stop stroking her with his hands, his lips, his tongue, "are you close?"

Letty had only time to think about asking him sensibly, close to what?, when his mouth closed over her again and he sucked lightly at her.

It blew her limbs apart like an explosion, her back arching of its own accord, her hands flinging outward to grasp and pull at the sheets. It might have been his name she wanted to scream, but her cry was unintelligible, drawing the last gasp out of her as all her limbs locked in a paralysis of pleasure that wrung her in waves, over and over, until at last she fell back to the bed, gasping out loud.

"Michael," she said weakly, her hands coming to rest upon his hair.

"Yes, my beautiful," he murmured, pressing his own urgent stand into the mattress, giving her a moment to breathe.

Letty took in a deep breath, then another, before she said weakly, "Are you going to do that again?"

"Yes," he said, leaning himself over her so she could see the bare hunger on his face. "But inside you. I want to be inside you."

"Yes. Oh yes. Please," she breathed, wrapping herself around him with all her arms and legs, holding him as close as she could.

She felt the muscles of his arms flexing around her as he leaned up. His eyes caught hers and stayed there. She looked sleepy and relaxed, his darling, with a halo of blonde hair starting to curl again from the heat they were making together, but he felt something like panic crawling at the edge of his blunt desire to be inside her when he thought that this might hurt her.

Slowly, slowly he slid himself home, nearly a quarter inch by quarter inch, and Letty just smiled.

"I knew that you would feel good," she whispered, leaning up to bite his chin.

"My darling," and to Michael it felt like a curse and a prayer as he wrapped himself around her in return and drove inside her.

For all his urgency, he wanted her happy noises and sighs to go on forever.

"Michael," said his Letitia, and when he looked at her face, beautifully flushed, she had a small scowl on it.

"What is it? Are you hurt?" Michael froze.

"I want the explosion again, I want to feel it again," she told him, her brows drawing furiously together. "I need it."

Michael felt the laughter bubbling up inside him that only she ever seemed to cause. "And you shall have it, my love," he said, rolling them both over so that she straddled him again.

"Oh my! How—" Whatever word she wanted seemed to elude her as she took in her new vantage, her hair streaming down around her shoulders over her breasts, and her hands now free to roam Michael's broad and welcoming chest. When his hands closed over her nipples and teased both rosy-pink peaks, she shivered.

When she leaned back, she discovered that it was she who was now driving him deeper into her.

The blush that climbed to her face started in his hands, Michael was delighted to discover. "How is that, my love?"

"I am suddenly understanding a great many inappropriate remarks about horse-riding that I have never fully understood before," gasped Letty, balancing her hands on the muscles of his belly and raising herself slightly only to impale herself upon him again.

Michael's laugh was choked off into another deep groan as she ground herself against him. "Letitia, you are brilliant." He wanted to wrap her in his arms again, drive himself into her furiously until they were both spent, but he let her discover this, let her learn what she might do for both of them, when he let her.

And learn she did. Letty could ride. She used the strength of her thighs to push herself up and then grasp him tighter when she lowered herself back down again, and now it was he who felt himself writhing and searching for that last little bit to push him over the edge he so desperately craved.

Endearments seemed to flow from him like water, as though once breached, he had a flood of affection he had never before tapped that was now all released for her.

And the smile Letty gave him as she made love to him, that smile locked up tight something deep down in his heart, into a place that had her face and her name and her love etched on it forever.

But then the tiniest shadow of the scowl came back. "Please," she gasped, driving herself faster, desperate for what he had already given her to happen again.

And he obliged her, reaching between them to find her rigid, aching nub, the feel of her slick smooth walls opening and closing around him making it urgent that he please his lady and fast, before he lost control of himself.

And as she rocked against him, gripping him everywhere with

everything she had, his finger stroked her there, again, again, and she felt the waves of hot pleasure washing out through her body as though his touch had lit her into explosive flame.

"Michael," she said silently as she shook, uncontrollably spasming, around him, and then he joined her over the peak, the dark angular lines of his face looking almost frightening as he drove himself up, up into the softness of her body, his muscles feeling hard and desperate against her.

They slumped together, wet, winded, and both of them stroking the other's hair, and face, skimming over the surfaces of their bodies where they were not joined, Letty making small noises of exhausted pleasure as Michael touched her, Michael holding her shoulders, her waist, her hips, her thighs as though he could not decide what he needed more and would never let her go.

* * *

THE SUNSHINE SEEMED to be teasing her. Letty opened one eye. That was not where the light came from in the morning.

Then Letty realized that she was not alone in the luxurious depths of the featherbed. A hard, long body was cradling hers.

When she moved her head, an arm appeared and wrapped itself around her, pulling her back against him. One of her feet cradled his stump, the other his shin. She was entirely surrounded.

It was bliss.

Letty closed her eyes again. She felt as though her body were glowing. Maybe that was what was so bright. Perhaps she would float away, were it not for the arm around her and the linen sheet holding her down.

Letty felt utterly peaceful. Safe.

At home.

"Good morning, my lady. Shall we still be married?"

Letty lazily rolled to look at Michael. "I can't stop smiling."

Michael stopped smiling. "Is that a no?"

She tsked at him. "Are you going to be this worrisome every day for the rest of our lives? Yes, we absolutely must be married. How could I let you go after a night like last night?"

He frowned a little. "Because you might have got a child?"

She looked at him through just one eye, as if focusing might make him more sensible. "Because I am greedy and want you all to myself. Every inch of you."

"Oh." Michael relaxed a little. "That seems to be a yes, then."

"Yes."

Then she took him by the ears and pulled him down to kiss him, and there were some minutes lost to rolling into each other's arms, feeling their bodies against one another, feeling their heartbeats speed up together.

Michael liked the idea of returning her to her perch on top of him, so he rolled so that his complete leg could support her sitting up, stretching his other leg lazily across the sheets. "And what do you want to do today, my lady?"

He was thinking about obtaining a marriage license, and arranging a wedding ceremony, and telling Mrs. Peterborough to go about whatever business she might want to go about in regards to acquiring Letty a wedding dress. Unless she wanted to wear the one she had worn last night. Which would be faster.

She said, "I think we should launch a horse-training business."

CHAPTER 23

WHEN LETTY finally crept toward her room, holding around her the remnants of her shift and petticoat, she felt that it was scandalously late in the morning. Hopefully, hopefully, everyone had been awake so late the previous night that Sarah would not be on her usual schedule.

Silently she pushed open the door.

Sarah was already there, laying out items for a bath and looking worried.

When she saw Letty, the two young women both froze. Sarah looked shocked, and Letty wondered what she should say, anything she should say, to make this appallingly inappropriate situation somehow unobjectionable.

But then Sarah shook her head, some of her red hair escaping from her cap, and she just smiled. Nothing knowing, nothing that made Letty feel ashamed. Just a small smile.

"My lady," said Sarah firmly. "I'm so glad you're home."

"Oh Sarah." Letty's legs felt unsteady. "I owe you a description of the party last night."

Sarah grinned so hard her nose wrinkled. "I am dying to hear, my lady. Everything. What did the other ladies wear? How did they dress their hair? What did the vicar serve? I want to know everything."

Letty shut the door and came into the room trailing her petticoat. She perched on the dressing bench, shaking her head with disbelief.

"You have been so kind, ever since I arrived on the doorstep smelling entirely of horse. You never need to address me as my lady. Please, call me Letty."

Sarah sank on to the clothes chest at the foot of the bed and the two girls stared at one another in disbelief. How few days it had been.

"When we're as old as Mrs. Peterborough," nodded Sarah, "I'll sit at the breakfast table with you gumming my scone, and I'll call you Letty."

Their laughter spilled out into the hall and down the stairs.

* * *

MICHAEL HADN'T the time to investigate the laughter upstairs. He rolled into the kitchen at top speed.

"Sir Michael!" Mrs. Dunphy gasped. The baronet did not often breach her citadel here in the kitchen, and she was well aware of all the shortcomings of her environment that Mrs. Peterborough had spotted, and explained in detail, for the last few days. "You're up early."

"Not so very early, Mrs. Dunphy; best get used to it, it seems that Miss Stapleton keeps very early hours. And it appears that you alone in the house managed to get some sleep."

"I slept like a top."

"Your shawl had quite the excursion last night, but I knew it wasn't you."

"I beg your pardon?" The woman checked the buttons and ties on her blouse. She wasn't sure if Sir Michael was accusing her of something, but it certainly sounded as if he might be.

"Nothing. You'll find it's gone; I'll buy you a new one. See here, can you go ... no, Griggs and Jim and Anthony will all be asleep if they're here at all."

"I'm awake, Sir Michael," said Jim from the doorway. He was clutching a basket of roses.

250

The boy saw Michael notice them. He looked down sheepishly. "Miss Stapleton likes them, sir. I've been bringing them up to the house."

Michael's smile spread slowly, nearly startling the boy, who had never seen him smile before that he could recall. "I'm glad you thought of it, lad," he said gently. "Are you too tired to run to the village again with a message?"

"No sir!" Jim was full of the excitement of all the doings at Roseford Manor of the last twenty-four hours, and of being trusted with messages again.

"Take this note to the vicar personally, will you? I'd like to catch him before the morning service, if at all possible."

* * *

THE BREAKFAST ROOM seemed like a repeat of the days before, yet Letty herself as she approached it felt very different.

She didn't care that she probably looked like an iced cake in the pink dress. She didn't care that she couldn't stop smiling. She felt that she was probably still glowing and she couldn't have stopped that either, even if she'd tried.

When she arrived at the table, she found Michael alone.

He stood to welcome her, as if she were a lady, just as he always had. And he held out his hand.

"Come join me, my love. Mrs. Peterborough is not yet arisen, though she has decreed, through the channel of Mrs. Dunphy, that it is time for us to eat the last few jars of preserved pears. Come have a scone with me, though I much prefer your bread."

She stepped forward and took his hand. Letty hadn't realized until he'd spoken how much she wanted him to treat her here the same way he did in the dark on Maggie's back, and in the stable, and in his room.

"Thank you, Michael," she said softly, nodding. "I will."

When Griggs arrived with the preserves, they were sitting side by side at the breakfast table. Michael was shuffling through yesterday's post, and Letty was nibbling on a rasher of bacon. And between them, their hands on the table were clasped.

"We won't be attending services today, Griggs, not that there's anyone in the stable to ready the horses if we were," Michael told him without looking up.

Then he seemed to remember. "Have you caught up on your sleep? Can't have you catching cold or the like."

"Not at all, sir, I'm fit as a fiddle. The evening air rather agrees with me, I think," said the old butler thoughtfully.

"You're welcome to keep sleeping across the dining room entrance if you like." Michael sounded dubious. Letty just raised her eyebrows.

"No sir, if the household is all settled now, I'll return to my usual habit, sir."

Michael just nodded. "All settled now, Griggs."

* * *

THE AFTERNOON SHADOW had caught up with Letty, curled up on the library's sofa and murdering needlepoint, by the time Griggs disturbed them again.

"The Marquess of Faircombe, Sir Michael," Griggs announced.

Michael looked up from his papers. Blake Leighton hadn't shown, damn the boy, as if chasing miscreants around the forest all night were a good reason for sleeping in. Or maybe because it was the day of rest. Michael felt like he was swimming in letters; resting he was not. "You'll take care of this, my lady, won't you? I'm expecting the vicar any moment."

"Of course," said Letty, stabbing her embroidery firmly one more time before setting it down and following Griggs out.

It steadied her steps, knowing Michael was completely confident in leaving it to her. When they'd discussed it this morning, clearing up various misconceptions from the day before, they had both had the same thoughts, and very clearly agreed completely. Now it was her opportunity to make them clear to the marquess waiting in the parlor.

Their parlor.

When the marquess saw her, he stood, and he pointedly looked past her.

"Pleasure and all, but I have actually come to see Grantley, I've got rather a short time for business this morning…"

Letty just smiled and waved him back to his seat.

"Of course! I know just how you feel. Let us be quite quick, then. Is this about the horse training venture you discussed with Sir Michael yesterday?"

"Yes, I—don't like to leave a local lad with a bad taste in his mouth, you understand, and I meant what I told him about housing some of my horses to train if he likes."

The big man was shifting himself back and forth on the settee as if he couldn't quite find the right angle at which to sit.

Letty smiled again. Her small hands rested comfortably on the wings of the Grantley embroidered chair.

She said, "That business venture is mine, so we can discuss it now. We don't wish you to have any hard feelings either, Lord Faircombe. But we are quite united in that we don't wish to house—or train—any of your horses."

Faircombe's high forehead, with its receding dark hairline, wrinkled as if he had not understood. "I came to ask him—"

"Yes, thank you. I don't wish to go into business with you."

"See here, I think you had better let me speak with Sir Michael. I've no wish to have competitors in my neighborhood, what, and this is a generous gesture of friendship."

Letty's eyebrows climbed her forehead. "You and Sir Michael have a friendship?"

"Well." The big man coughed. "We ought to have."

"I understand your wish to be friends, Lord Faircombe, and I am sure that we will all get to know each other better in future days. However, I don't anticipate that it will be a problem at all to have a competitor in my neighborhood. I believe that Roseford's stables will do very well."

"Well, I—" Roseford doing well was not what Faircombe was here to hope for, that was clear enough.

Letty reclined back into her chair. A late sunbeam through the window seemed to light up her hair like a halo, and she looked angelic for a moment. But no angel ever came into Lord Faircombe's dreams and said what Letty said, which was, "I believe that it will probably be attracting a great many of your customers, Lord Faircombe, but do not worry. I am sure that will not stand in the way of our friendship."

He blinked at her. And blinked again.

"In fact Miss de la Peña has sent a card over this morning and would like to discuss what I might be able to do for her before she leaves our mutual neighborhood. She asked me to help her purchase a horse, and train it. Won't that be nice? I so enjoyed meeting her yesterday. What a pleasure that will be."

Faircombe did not look like it would be a pleasure at all.

"As both Sir Michael and I mentioned to you last night, my lord... I am the horse trainer."

* * *

MICHAEL RECEIVED the vicar in his library and saw to it that Griggs plied the man with sufficient sherry to relax two vicars, possibly three.

But the man never blinked when Michael explained his desire for a marriage license.

"Yes of course, Sir Michael, I was expecting it."

Relieved, Michael sat back. "You were?"

"Oh yes. I read the banns just as you asked in your note, since I was indeed expecting it. You know when I talked to Mrs. Peterborough last night and she was telling me what a difference Miss Stapleton had made in your household since she had arrived, so much more order and comfort, she explained to me that a man of your age naturally needs a wife, and especially one who knows how to manage a manor. She confided in me, very confidentially—" here Mr. Herrings leaned close as if telling a secret, and Michael worried about not being able to catch him if he fell—Griggs had really given him enough sherry, "—*very* confidentially, you understand, that she was hoping to see you settle down with Miss Stapleton even if you don't quite get along, because you are so reluctant to go out into society, and she didn't expect you to make a love match before she died, and she *so* wanted to see you settled."

"She did." Michael was no longer relaxed.

"Yes of course. And then when I commented on the lovely jewel Miss Stapleton was wearing last evening—just curious, you understand, as one wants to know the provenance of something so rare—it was Mrs. Peterborough who reminded me that it had been your mother's. And then I recalled, I have seen your mother wear it before. So she didn't tell me anything out of turn, you understand, I know you wouldn't want Mrs. Peterborough to get above herself and she did not, I promise you, but she did let me *understand*, you see, that you had offered the jewel to Miss Stapleton to wear with your permission and that she considered it a great *rapprochement* between the two of you, because you had not been getting along at all and it was quite putting paid to her dream to see you wed to someone who would take care of Roseford well."

"Mm hmm."

Michael just let the vicar ramble on after that, things about writing to Letty's home parish and reading the banns, digesting this unique new picture of his and Letty's relationship, and wondering whether he was angry or delighted with Mrs. Peterborough.

* * *

"I DON'T CARE how you feel about it, Michael, the point is that it worked very well. None of the neighborhood will possibly imagine that you have compromised Miss Stapleton, but neither will they be shocked when you marry."

Michael had rolled himself all the way to the servants' quarters behind the kitchen, and stayed standing there. Mrs. Peterborough was sitting up in bed, her usual day cap on her head and her Chinoise scarf around her shoulders, with a rug over her lap as she tended to her stitching. She wasn't even bothering to look at him.

"Mary."

She looked up.

He rolled closer and bent down so only she could hear.

"Just so we're quite clear, I have *absolutely* compromised Miss Stapleton."

He was standing close enough that he could see the corner of one side of her mouth fighting to turn up in a smile. But she ruthlessly repressed it.

Michael went on. "I hope to continue to compromise Miss Stapleton. In this house. My house. I'm going to marry her, make no mistake. In two weeks, I believe. That's the earliest time the law allows, thanks be to our vicar. But I don't want you to imagine for one second that it is solely because I have compromised her. I love her."

She just rolled her slightly fogged eyes at him. "*That* is no one's business but yours. And hers, I suppose."

She looked a bit more smugly down at the linen she was stitching and Michael felt twelve years old again, and a bit lost, as if she had won some sort of a game.

When he was still standing there a minute later, she gently poked his cart with her toe. "Go on about your business, child, don't be standing there like a statue. I'm sure she loves you too, and that's all I want."

* * *

LETTY SERENELY WALKED Lord Faircombe out to the portico where his carriage awaited him.

The big man did not look back as he climbed inside. Nonetheless, she waved as the carriage rounded the lawn and headed down the drive toward the road. He was a neighbor, and she hoped to keep his good graces.

Down the hill, with the corner of her eye, she saw a dark head sliding closed the door of the stable.

* * *

"ANTHONY?"

He looked up as she slid the door open, smiled at her. He shook his head.

"No bonnet, no gloves, no escort—"

"Anthony, I'm going to be married."

Time stopped for a moment as they looked at each other.

And all she saw in his dark, dark eyes was a fierce joy.

"Ah my princess," sighed Anthony. "What a brilliant lady of the manor you will be."

She ran to him, throwing her arms around him as she had when she was little. "I am nervous!"

"But not frightened," he murmured, stroking her hair.

"Not at all. Isn't that odd?"

"Not at all," he echoed back to her, and set her back on her heels. He seemed to search her face. "You are happy?"

"Ecstatically," she admitted, under her breath, as if saying it too loudly would make something go wrong.

He smiled, his hands dropping from her arms.

"I'm going to stay," she said a little louder.

"I imagine so, princess, if you are to be married to the baronet," he nodded.

"What... I mean, what would you like to do?"

Anthony shrugged. "I have been very happy being your grooms-man, Letty."

"But you... is that all you want to do?"

Huffing out a breath, Anthony sat down, rather suddenly, on a hay bale. "I don't know, actually. I haven't, there hasn't been time to think about what I would like to do, only what I had to do. For a long time."

"I know! You see, it was exactly the same way with me!" Letty tossed herself down in the straw at his feet. "So now you must ask yourself: what would you like to do?"

Anthony just nodded, as though listening to music far away.

"There are some things I would like to do, princess, but I'm not sure what I should do, and I certainly don't know what I *will* do."

"Michael would like you to handle some business for him in London."

He smiled down at her. "Would he."

"Yes, I would," Michael said gruffly from the open door, swinging with his crutches over the threshold, "but not for the reasons you probably imagine."

The tall man swayed over to the hay bales, and sat himself down on a handy one.

"You have a home here for the rest of your life if you like, Anthony," Michael said, his grave expression at odds with something suspicious shining in his eyes. "When I think of everything you have done to take care of Letty for all these years... I owe you everything, everything."

Anthony just blinked, mouth a little open, before he gathered himself. "No more than any man would do for his family, sir," he told Michael, but his smile as he leaned over to grasp the hand of the baronet of Roseford was genuine.

Michael nodded. "This business in London is just to see to some arrangements I would like to make with a man leasing me a warehouse. If it's not to your taste, just say the word."

"Oddly enough, Mr. Leighton also has some business for me in London. He has recommended me to a colleague there who says he would like to take advantage of my particular talents."

Letty's face was shifting from happy to sad so fast that neither man could miss it. "What, princess?" Anthony prompted her.

"I don't want you to live forever so far away in London!" Letty burst out.

"I don't imagine I will live in London forever. I'm not sure I will ever live anywhere forever."

"That's all very fine, as long as your real home is here." Letty's chin was set.

"I understand," Anthony said solemnly.

"Your real home *is* here." Michael sounded just as firm as Letty.

Anthony broke into laughter. "I'm not going to fight you both over it!"

"No need." Letty shifted backward to lean against Michael's shin. In her stall, Maggie shuffled, whoofing out a breath, and Letty smiled at her. "Yes," she said, feeling utterly at peace within herself. "Plans are wonderful."

EPILOGUE

THE WOMAN JUMPED up from her seat when the lady of Roseford Manor made her way into the kitchen.

"Don't get up," said the lady, but her steps were so ponderous that the woman couldn't restrain herself from coming forward to offer a hand.

The woman pulled a chair back from the old smooth heavy wood of the table, making space for both Letitia Grantley and her belly.

Lady Grantley just waved her back to her supper. "Please, sit down. Your hands are like ice. Is the little one warm?"

The little fellow sitting next to his mother nodded vigorously as though he entirely understood the question, hands clasped around the bowl of soup Mrs. Dunphy had provided as soon as the rain-soaked travelers had been shown on to the flagstones of the kitchen.

Letty smiled at the child. "And how old are you?"

Big eyes just stared up at her.

"He isn't yet two, but he's smart so people think he's three," said the woman, looking proudly down at her child and tossing his hair a bit so that it would dry more quickly.

Letty looked at the traveler, at her glossy brown hair also undone to dry the more quickly in the warmth of the stove. "You've traveled a while?"

The woman nodded, but offered no details regarding her home location or how far they had gone.

"And Griggs tells me to call you Mrs. Childs."

Pale blue eyes oughtn't be so piercing, thought the traveler as she shifted in her seat, uncomfortable under Letty's direct, unwavering gaze.

The silence between them stretched, and stretched more, until finally the woman said, "Or my lady is free to call me Abigail."

Letty closed one eye, as if it helped her to see better, peering closely. "No need, Mrs. Childs. I much prefer to give a widow the respect that is due to her."

Abigail just nodded, uncomfortable, and turned her attention to helping her son drink his soup.

"And this is Thomas!"

"Yeh!" piped up Thomas, sitting up straight, clearly excited to be addressed.

"Thank you, Thomas," Letty told him gravely. "I'm delighted to meet you. Well, Mrs. Childs, my understanding is that you are looking for a position as a housekeeper. Tell me about your experience."

"My husband was a soldier lost in battle with his horse," the woman began, as if she'd rehearsed saying it many times.

Letty just nodded. And looked at her.

Till Abigail seemed to see what Letty's eyes were telling her.

"I understand," said Letty softly. "Just tell me about your knowledge of housekeeping."

Sinking slowly into the chair, Abigail began to list the work she had done in taking care of a house before. Managing the food stores and the linen stores, keeping count of the china and silver, and ensuring the maids kept both above and belowstairs clean.

Letty nodded.

"I have only been married for about a year and a half myself, and I can tell you that these are exactly the sort of things Roseford needs. I will soon be required to rest for some undetermined amount of time," here Letty scowled fiercely, putting Abigail in mind of a furious kitten, "and I need to replace our housekeeper, I cannot wait any longer. Your arrival is fortuitous."

"Your housekeeper, your previous housekeeper I mean, has she left the position?"

Letty sighed, and smiled, and her eyes sparkled with something Abigail suspected, with horror, were tears.

"She had been part of this house for a very, very long time. She just left us a couple of months ago." Letty rested her hand on her belly. "She knew the baby was coming, but I am so very sad that Mrs. Peterborough did not get to meet her."

This seemed to Abigail like a very familiar way to speak of a housekeeper. Surprised, she just said, "You seem as though you were very close."

"Yes." Letty nodded firmly. "We expect to name the child after her. Mary."

Abigail chuckled, the first sign of anything other than nervous worry in her face. "What if it is a boy, my lady?"

"Then he will be named Mary," Letty said again just as firmly.

Abigail licked her lips as though she were wanting to ask questions but holding them back.

Letty reached over the table—she could just barely reach—and patted Abigail's hand. "Yes. She was family. But never fear, that's no reflection on what we'd ask of you. All we need is a good housekeeper. I hope the position will suit you. If Thomas were to grow up friends with my Mary, that would delight me. He seems like a wonderful boy."

"Yeh!" said Thomas again, and Letty laughed.

"I hope I won't drive you mad, but I have very particular opinions about the way I want the onions stored, and I'll need you to follow them. My husband assures me that I won't be able to stop commenting on the state of the floors or the cooking. Truly, that is part of the reason why we don't have a housekeeper yet. But Mrs. Childs."

Abigail started, and met Letty's eyes again. Letty's knowing eyes.

Letty said, "A woman ought to be able to keep herself with work that suits her, don't you think? And a woman with a child even more so."

"Yes," sighed Abigail, relaxing minutely into her chair. "Yes. I do think so."

"So do I. And so does Sir Michael. As I started to say. If the position suits you, we hope you will stay. If it doesn't, or if you need to leave us, we expect to be able to give you a sterling reference. But I hope you'll stay."

Abigail's eyes started to fill with tears. "You don't even know me," she whispered.

"I think I know more about you than you think. And a woman who's come all this way with a small child is a woman who is strong. I expect I'll learn a thing or two from you, Mrs. Childs."

"My lady!" a large male voice boomed off the walls and flagstones, followed by a man rolling himself very quickly down the hallway in the most peculiar wheeled cart.

He used his standing leg to stop himself right at Letty's side.

The man was tall, with wild red-brown hair sticking out at every angle, and was in only his shirtsleeves.

Abigail drew back.

"Sir Michael! Now Mrs. Childs will think you are a barbarian or something worse, and we need a housekeeper! Have you not been hounding me day and night to choose a housekeeper? What can I say to her now that will make a good impression on her?"

The tall man looked as abashed as Thomas did when caught doing something naughty.

"My sincere apologies, Mrs. Childs, I do take the most appalling liberties in my house, but only with niceties that bore me. And rugs. We don't have many rugs. My wife has put up with it for more than a year, so I hope you will too? We do need a housekeeper, that is only the plain truth. Perhaps you would consider it for at least six months? Through my wife's confinement? I appeal to your kindness as a mother yourself. I will need your assistance to convince my wife to sleep occasionally once the babe arrives."

"Sir Michael, I can assure you that you won't need to convince her to sleep," Abigail nodded her head, unsure how to address a baronet in his shirtsleeves in his kitchen at night.

"There, you see? I only cannot sleep now because the child is so big."

Michael looked genuinely concerned. "Also likely my fault."

"Undoubtedly." Despite the acid tone to her voice, Lady Grantley extended her hand and allowed her husband to help her up from her seat. "No rush, Mrs. Childs. You two be warm, and Mrs. Dunphy will show you to a room that I hope will be comfortable; if you need anything, just let her or Griggs or Sarah know. Anyone. We'll talk about this again in the morning."

As she made her way toward the door, her husband rolling at her side, Letty looked back again with a sweet smile. "I do hope you will take the position."

Without thinking about it, Abigail said, "I imagine I will."

"Good," Letty nodded to herself in a satisfied way, turning back to let Michael's arm help her toward the door. "I think that would be efficient."

* * *

IT'S NOT OVER - it's just begun! Michael and Letty return in *The Countess Invention*, as Michael's London inventor Mr. Cullen is secretly *Miss* Cullen, who has given up on love, and that's another story...

Dear readers, have you read the story of when Anthony and Letty met?

The Winter's Night Princess *is free and available here (or you can find it at judithlynne.com) exclusively for my readers.*

And Anthony's own love story is

Book 4, *Crown of Hearts*, though Anthony is also in every Lords and Undefeated Ladies book!

IF YOU ENJOYED NOT Like a Lady, *keep these books coming - share a review at Amazon or Goodreads!*

TURN the page for a sneak peak at Cass and Oliver's love story in *The Countess Invention.*

BOOK 2 - A SNEAK PEEK

Read Cass and Oliver's love story in *The Countess Invention*, Book 2

* * *

He held just her fingertips in his hand, and his thumb stroked gently across her knuckles.

It was the most intimate sensation she'd ever felt.

It wasn't just that it sent tiny shocks up her arms into her body, as though she were waking up from a cold dream into a place of heat. It was also that his hand felt warm, and somehow familiar.

Apparently Dr. Burke had *no* interest in behaving appropriately.

Not that dressing in a man's suit and receiving him in her home was behaving appropriately.

Still, Cass felt like this situation was getting away from her.

Cass tugged her hand free from his touch, and pressed both her fists to her forehead as though preventing her head from exploding.

"I am Mr. Cullen," she said.

"I know," Oliver nodded agreeably, resting a hip on the edge of her desk. "We have just been discussing the artificial leg about which we have been corresponding for months. I didn't say you weren't Mr.

Cullen. I said I was confused. I am simply wondering if you truly wish for me to address you as Mister Cullen. Or, perhaps, if you would like some advice on how to make your outfit more convincing."

The worst. Cass had truly hoped that her subterfuge would not be a complete failure. And apparently it was a complete failure.

The man's calm was horrifying.

It was the combination of dressing like this and talking at the same time, she decided. Talking in person with new people was always disastrous. If only they had not had to converse. But then, if they had not had to converse, she could have kept up her convenient charade forever.

Certainly almost forever.

Her heart started pounding. This would require moving to her second most favorable plan, possibly her third.

Meeting in person had been an awful mistake. She couldn't make the same mistake with the Grantleys. Everything, everything could fall apart if her actual customers spread tales that she was not the Mr. Cullen she purported to be. No one would request her services and she would not have the funds to provide for this little household of hers.

But then she realized in the next second, Dr. Burke's knowledge of her secret wasn't the same as him *keeping* her secret.

Perhaps that was the key. Now that this man had her secret, perhaps he could be persuaded to help her keep it.

Just because he'd discovered one of her secrets—or two—didn't mean all was lost.

* * *

Keep reading *The Countess Invention* now!

Find Judith Lynne Books and sign up for updates at judithlynne.com

AFTERWORD

I love romances where the characters who are falling in love are equally interesting. It was important to me to do justice to Michael's amputation and desire to ride again, especially since it was the reason Letty came into his life, and at first, why she stayed.

I learned that there are many ways to ride a horse for people who have had an amputation or are without limbs for some reason. It is very common to ride with a prosthetic leg, for many reasons better understood by horse riders than by me (balance and so forth). It is also not uncommon to ride without a prosthetic leg, for people with very high amputations, or who are uncomfortable with their prostheses, or even for other reasons. There are many resources out there with advice for folks who have had amputations on how to ride, and this book is not among them. A little online research will turn up many examples of different riders and ways to ride for anyone who would like to learn how to ride after a leg amputation.

Sir Michael is living in a small village in Britain in the early years of the 19th century, and Letty is a young woman who has not had wide experience of the world. I've tried to make it clear that Mr. Cullen, who is known for adaptive furniture, had never before made a prosthetic leg or an adaptive saddle, and Mr. Cullen is also in London.

(More about Mr. Cullen in the next book in this series, *The Countess Invention*.) So Michael and Letty are figuring things out as they go.

France was at war for a very long period before and during the British Regency. The French wars of independence bled into each other and into the Napoleonic Wars. Artificial legs had been around for centuries, and had long been available for veterans, and the technology for good artificial legs improved drastically during these long wars. The famous Marquess of Anglesey lost a leg at Waterloo, and later made popular an artificial leg that was shaped a great deal like a flesh and blood leg and had a sophisticated connection system that allowed good movement of the joints.

Apparently it is very common for prosthetic legs to be uncomfortable or just a hassle, even today, and for people with amputations to use many types of mobility devices. Michael can afford to buy himself multiple devices for his mobility, and his personal preference for avoiding the prosthetic leg except when he is most concerned about his appearance is certainly not a statement on anyone else's preferences.

I am also not a trainer of horses. It seemed obvious to me that the best outdoors method of transportation for anyone at that time, much less someone who had survived an amputation, would have been a horse. Despite generous outside help, I am sure I have made mistakes in writing about horses and riding horses. My horse mistakes are all my own, but Maggie forgives me.

Like Letty I admire those who can stack onions and never have any rot. Apparently sand in a cool cellar is an ideal storage medium for carrots and onions over the winter. England isn't particularly sandy, but perhaps sand was Mrs. Peterborough's secret weapon. That and experience. In dabbling with housekeeping techniques, I enjoyed reading *Preserving Food without Freezing or Canning: Traditional Techniques Using Salt, Oil, Sugar, Alcohol, Vinegar, Drying, Cold Storage, and Lactic Fermentation*—a fascinating book by The Gardeners and Farmers of Centre Terre Vivante, collecting old methods of food storage from the French countryside. Mrs. Peterborough would have loved it.

I've read romance novels my entire life. When I was reading books I was probably too young to read, they were often epics, covering years of the heroine's life, and they had the most glorious covers. Later I read category romances for years, and even later I was grateful for the invention of e-books, as I could pursue devouring them without having to find homes for them afterward.

All those years of reading romances and I was never bitten by the Regency bug. Then I remember vividly one day when I, for complicated reasons of the plot, was in a phone call meeting, in a bookstore, and mostly on mute. I idly skimmed the bookshelves in front of me while I was listening. For some reason I found myself looking straight at the spine of a Regency romance, and for some reason, I bought it.

It was marvelous. I started snapping up all the author's books. And I couldn't get enough. I needed more of these charming, witty, sensual romances. It felt like a romance lover's rebirth.

Sometimes you just really want more books but, you know, you want them to be *exactly* the way you want them. That's the sort of thinking that leads to writing books of your own. This one appealed to my own particular tastes, not only in interpreting the characters, but in interpreting the Regency period. I hope you liked it too!

ACKNOWLEDGMENTS

I'm so very fond of the village that helped me launch this book into the world. Thank you always to Holly, sounding board and master enabler. I'm so grateful that you always pick up the phone. Thank you to Anna and Whitney for enjoying first drafts and giving me all-important feedback. And for believing in me, as well as very sharp-eyed line proofing, thank you always to the best husband in the world.

Postscript 2021: I could not have imagined that Letty and Michael's love story would find so many readers around the world. Thank you from the bottom of my heart and the top too. These books are for you.

ABOUT THE AUTHOR

Judith Lynne writes rule-breaking romances with love around every corner. Her characters tend to have deep convictions, electric pleasures, and, sometimes, weaponry.

She loves to write stories where characters are shaken by life, shaken down to their core, put out their hand...and love is there.

A history nerd with too many degrees, Judith Lynne lives in New Jersey with a truly adorable spouse, an apartment-sized domestic jungle, and a misgendered turtle. Also an award-winning science fiction author and screenwriter, she writes passionate Regency romances with a rich sense of place and time.

Please sign up for the first information on new books from Judith Lynne, as well as sneak peeks and exclusive content on your favorite characters, at judithlynne.com!

ALSO BY JUDITH LYNNE

Lords and Undefeated Ladies

Not Like a Lady

The Countess Invention

What a Duchess Does

Crown of Hearts

He Stole the Lady (January 2022)

And stay tuned for *Cloaks and Countesses*!

The Caped Countess

The Clandestine Countess (July 2022)

CPSIA information can be obtained
at www.ICGtesting.com
Printed in the USA
BVHW031300190822
644999BV00014B/843